THE SOLOMON TWIST

Dan Hammond Jr.

ISBN: 0692249052
ISBN 13: 9780692249055
Library of Congress Control Number: 2014919042
Solomon Texas Press, Denton, TX

Dedicated to my wonderful friends:
Tyler Hammond and Travis Hammond.
They also are my wonderful sons.

1965
New Year's Eve

So the king said, "Bring me a sword," and they brought a sword before the king. The king said, "Divide the living boy in two; then give half to the one, and half to the other."
I KINGS, Chapter 3, Verses 24-25

Mothers are fonder of their children. For they have a more painful share in their production and they are more certain that they are their own.
Aristotle, Nicomachean Ethics, IX

BIRTH, n. The first and direst of all disasters.
Ambrose Bierce, The Enlarged Devil's Dictionary

A LONG PULL, A STRONG PULL

Mazel Albright wanted one, just one cigarette. A couple of hard draws off a Lucky. Was that too much to ask? To reacquaint her lungs with their old buddy Smoke, the frequent guest who left abruptly a couple of months ago. Smoke would help calm and cloud Mazel's mind, for a few moments at least, from her impending doomesticity.

She liked that word–*doomesticity*. Created it herself. A special talent of sorts. Doomed to domesticity: doomesticity. Could there be any better way to describe how she felt about the rest of her life?

Making plans to marry in her eighth month of pregnancy held no embarrassment for Mazel. The only people she might humiliate would be her parents in Arizona, and she hadn't even written them about the baby yet, much less the divorce and remarriage.

Johnny Cash's voice crackled through the busted speaker in the front dash. Mazel turned the radio louder and, as always, joined in the chorus somewhere between The Man in Black's growl and the static accompaniment.

> I fell in to a burnin' ring of fire
> I went down, down, down
> And the flames went higher
> And it burned, burned, burned
> The ring of fire, the ring of fire

The song only deepened her longing for one of the interred Luckies. They lay beneath a heap of repair receipts and the tattered owner's manual in the glove compartment.

Mazel survived previous cravings for Smoke with stick after stick after stick of licorice-flavored Black Jack gum. Little blue wrappers littered her house and covered the floorboard of her Ford Falcon. She tried chewing other gums and some tasted better, but none could snap louder than Black Jack. And if she couldn't smoke, by God, she would sure as hell snap.

Chewing and snapping though were poor substitutes for drawing and puffing. What she wanted most right now was one tiny cigarette. Well, not entirely true. What Mazel truly wanted was to be *un-pregnated,* another word she created. She also wanted to be engaged to someone other than Richard McDonald, a man whose only talents consisted of gun spinning or belching a few notes of "Love Me Tender." The cigarette, however, happened to be a want over which she had a greater measure of control.

Then again, maybe not. Reaching the glove compartment was no longer a given. She could barely reach the steering wheel. In her sixth month Mazel had been pleased with the slow, steady stretching of her midsection. Just baby fat, she would laugh. A little here, a pinch there, nothing to set off alarms.

During the seventh month she swelled like the slug Johnny Morris salted and threw down her blouse in second grade. She could only assume the existence of her feet because visual contact with them ceased two weeks ago. In bed one night she bent her knees and as they came into view, she let out an involuntary yelp. Certain moles and childhood scars were scattered in patterns which gave her knees the appearance of two jowly baldheaded men.

Being repulsed by the sight of her own body was one thing, but what, she wondered, must her fiancé be thinking? Richard had promised to take Mazel to see one of her favorites, Rock Hudson, in *The Last Sunset* but backed out just an hour ago. The lousy weather excuse. He owned a wrecker and with the rain possibly changing to ice, he said he would be in for a long night of hauling fools out of culverts, gullies and ditches.

As excuses go, it was a good one and if anyone else had pitched it but Richard, Mazel might have believed him. Truth was Richard would never let a little ice come between him and a little ass. Of course, Mazel's derriere now looked like two sixteen pound bowling balls trapped in her underwear. If she didn't watch out, Richard might abandon her altogether. Where would she be then? A divorced woman with a baby. Good luck snaring a man in Solomon, Texas, lugging around those credentials.

She suddenly regretted having lost her temper with Richard and going alone to the movie on such a dreadful night. With all of his faults, Richard had been the one to step up and say, "I'm the daddy. I'll marry you." Though a noble gesture that temporarily endeared Richard to Mazel, she had thought it only proper to say that she would need time to think about it. After all, they had only been intimate one time.

But Richard didn't contact her again for a week, then two weeks. He took everything so literally. A "no" meant "no" to Richard, not the "maybe" or "probably" or "ask one more time" it generally meant to a budding relationship. Her options came down to either raising her baby with no money, no job, and the stigma of being a divorced, single mother…or marrying Richard. Mazel had called him and accepted his proposal.

"So, the baby is mine," Richard had responded. "You and me made this child and that idiot Virgil can't say any different, right?"

Virgil Albright, her recently exed-out husband, had an entirely different reaction when she told him that he might be the father. He said that the divorce papers would have his name on them before the ink could dry. "You can't pin this little bastard on me," he had said. "You were unfaithful."

Mazel had been faithful throughout most of their marriage. But then she started hearing other women whispering this or that about Virgil and so-and-so while spraying perfume samples at Woolworth's or being combed out at Sue's Styling Senter. Of course, the rumors bothered her, but she would always in the end dismiss such stories. Virgil was all she knew of love. They had been a couple since seventh grade, trudging the narrow hallways of Solomon High with one arm soldered around the other's waist.

Then one day she came home from work early and found Mamie Rausch, her favorite checker at the IGA, bent over their new Zenith console television with Virgil dogging her from behind. Hearing secondhand about Virgil's affairs in no way prepared Mazel for seeing one in living color.

Damn, she thought. The Surgeon General be damned. I have got to have a cigarette.

She pulled to the stop sign at Third and Vine considering her options. She could struggle her way out of the driver's seat, walk or skate to the other side of the car, wrestle with the passenger door, which tended to become stuck in cold weather, and possibly get into the glove compartment that way. Or maybe she could lay her enormous body across the front seat and stretch her arm far enough to reach the entombed Luckies. Outside, the icy rain intensified and decided for her.

After shifting the Ford Falcon into Park, Mazel laid on the seat, popped open the box, and seized the Luckies with surprising ease. The difficult part was getting up.

She tried to leverage herself, wedging her right arm under her ribs, and when that didn't work, grabbing the top of the seat with her left arm and pulling up. That didn't work either. She extended her arm toward the steering wheel, but it lay just beyond her fingertips. Blindly she felt for the passenger door handle. It lifted along with her hopes, but the door would not budge.

What have I gotten myself into, she thought? She squirmed, grunting to maneuver the slightest distance. A drop of perspiration rolled down her forehead and into one eye. Slowly, the realization set in that she indeed was stuck and would not be able to extricate herself without help. The only possibility of deliverance seemed to be that someone might drive by and come to her rescue. Mazel's face reddened, embarrassed at the idea of being discovered in such a position. She hoped her rescuer wouldn't be anyone she knew.

She could reach the lighter, however, and so accomplished her original objective, laying on the front seat sucking hard on a Lucky Strike. Heat from the vent blew ashes, scattering them over her face and into her tangled black hair when she would take a long draw.

The longer she lay there, the more uncomfortable and upset she became. Upset with Richard, of course. Upset with the Surgeon General and his stupid report on tobacco and cancer that caused her to throw the Luckies into the glove box in the first place. Upset with her obstetrician for his new-fangled ideas about natural childbirth. Upset with the university for firing her when they discovered her pregnant and no longer married. Upset with the whole damn town of Solomon, Texas, for not having enough nerve to venture out on a night like this. Where the hell was everyone?

Finishing the Lucky, Mazel figured she might be able to reach the gear shift and pull herself up that way. Extending her arm as far as possible, she seized the knob-end of the stick between two fingers and her thumb. She tugged and tugged again until she felt her right shoulder come off the seat an inch, two inches, then…no more. Mazel let herself back down and gathered her energy. Grabbing the knob, she gave a long pull, a strong pull and thought she had made it when the stick suddenly dropped out of Park, crashing into some unknown forward gear. She slammed hard onto the vinyl seat and could feel the Falcon moving.

"Oh, my God."

She tried to roll right, but her size would not allow such a move. Lifting her left leg over her right, she attempted to cross one jowly knee over the other but couldn't negotiate their girth. As she flailed about, a glint of white on the floorboard reflected from a street light outside–the tip of her umbrella. Seizing the handle she extended her right arm fully. The shiny umbrella tip pressed against the brake bringing the Falcon to a jolting halt.

"Oh, my God."

Pounding hard and fast, the noise from her heart filled her ears. "Please, please, please," she cried. "Someone please help me."

A minute later the situation remained tenuous but unchanged. Mazel attempted a slight adjustment in order to ease the strain on her shoulder. The umbrella began to slip from the brake, however, so she reverted to her original position. Nothing to do, it seemed to her, but wait. If she could just hold out until someone came along. She felt light-headed, her heart continuing to slam out a rock and roll beat, like one of those new British bands, like the song playing on the radio, "Help!" The main thing to do was calm down.

She tried to lay still. She tried small turns and twists, but the stress of her bizarre contortion could not be remedied. Mazel felt a kick or two in her midsection and thought her baby might be uncomfortable, too. She had to calm down.

How? How did she usually relax? She remembered the breathing lessons her obstetrician, Dr. Robbins, taught her. When she first visited his office, there had been doubts. Still were for that matter.

Dr. Robbins was unlike any OB she had ever heard tell, but he had come highly recommended by one of the professors at the university. Only after several visits did she fully comprehend his concept of natural childbirth. He studied under some guy in France named Lamaze and by his own admission was the only OB in all of west Texas who adhered to the idea that a woman should actively participate in the birth of her own child.

Yet, the controlled breathing methods he taught her worked for Mazel and within a minute, her heart rate dropped. She needed something else though. Something to distract her, a focal point Dr. Robbins called it. Something to complete the relaxation process. Something neither her obstetrician nor the Surgeon General would recommend. With her free hand, she tapped the cellophane.

The next half minute dragged at a slug's pace. When it ended she took a long, soothing breath, responding with Pavlovian anticipation to the reassuring click of the hot, primed lighter.

2

LE BON VIVANT

Existentialism was Al Pozzo's bag, not driving. So Enrique, his surly teaching assistant, sat with one hand on the wheel, Pall Mall burning in the other, and a martini in a Mason jar between his legs. No one else from the party would brave the brutal norther just to see a foreign film–with sub-titles, no less. But Al Pozzo could always rely on Enrique to do his bidding even if he did so with an attitude, a certain *bouderie.*

Too much brie and Bordeaux, Beaujolais and escargot. Al's passion for all things French had been indulged tonight and rightfully so. At age thirty-six, after twelve years of teaching philosophy in one crap college after another, a big-time, New York City publisher had finally issued the first copies of Al's book.

He would have been satisfied with an academic treatment of his life's work, a limited run lining the shelves of university libraries: yellow and dusty with unopened pages still stuck together from the printing. However, the publisher believed with the right advertising campaign, maybe more emphasis on the emerging self-help trend, Al's book might have real commercial possibilities. His editor, Quentin Barnstable, restructured entire sections and created new ones. Al barely recognized the finished text and, in fact, felt obliged to offer Mr. Barnstable a listing as co-author–an offer Mr. Barnstable politely, and thankfully, declined.

Weeks were spent deciding the color and design of the book jacket, which ended up looking more like some Jackson Pollock knockoff than the desired Seurat-like quality Al preferred. His bio portrayed Al as a mysterious and fascinating character whose exile from the upper echelons of academia was self-imposed instead of, well, the failure it had been.

And the title change. From the academic *Toward a Theory of Relative Existence* to the more sellable *Is That All There Is? Getting the Most Out of a Meaningless Existence.* Though Al's book gave no remedies or prescriptions of how to cope with anxiety, deal with angst or avoid the absurd, it did leave the reader with the impression that a meaningless life is not such a bad thing if given half a chance.

Meaning in life, argued Al, could no longer be viewed as an arbitrary given if society were to survive. Meaning must be derived from the meaningless, extracted and cultivated from the desolate and arid climate in a desert of nothingness. The cover of his book indicated the hope inherent in Al's philosophy by depicting a flower growing in the wasteland. Unfortunately, most people thought the cover represented a mushroom cloud obliterating an atoll.

It would now be only a matter of time before a major university hired him away from this obscure, oppressive setting. Imagine, an existentialist teaching at Texas State Tech Agricultural and Military College. It could be worse, he thought. It had been worse during that three year stretch at Tennessee Lutheran. But soon he would be somewhere in the northeast, liberated from the constraints of small-town life, free to follow his instincts instead of subduing them. An enlightened campus where his existential philosophy might be praised and embraced instead of ridiculed and shunned, where he could speak his pet French phrases to someone other than the wine steward at *Le Bon Vivant,* a Tex-French restaurant which demeaned itself by serving chicken fried crepes with white lard gravy.

He stubbed a butt into the ashtray and immediately reached inside his jacket for another. Al lit the harsh-tasting, rough-looking European cigarette in his mouth and did not return a hand to it until the ash hung like a crescent moon over his lap. He noted how

Enrique imitated his hands-off method of smoking, but the Pall Mall ash was not as sturdy or rugged as the European variety. Most of Enrique's pants sported at least one burn hole.

At some point during their drive, the heavy mist changed into a steady drizzle, almost icy. Enrique leaned closer to the windshield, turning his head to the left to allow his good eye, the right one, a better view of the road. Al had listened patiently time and again as Enrique obsessed about the retinal detachment during his infancy that went undetected until it was too late for remedy. His eye now turned out and looked off in another direction. At times, Al thought Enrique purposely aimed the dead eye toward him, which he found discomfiting. On other occasions, Enrique would refuse to make visual contact with either eye leaving Al no point of reference and no clue where to focus.

Checking his Timex, Al estimated they would miss at least the first few minutes of *Fellini's 8 ½* It all depended, as usual, on the length of the Roadrunner-Wile E. Coyote cartoon playing beforehand. Even in a rundown, semi-art house such as the Campus Cinema, where the neon 'P' never lit at night, one could expect to see the latest Warner Brothers animation. And though Al would never voice such a thought in public, he was disappointed to be missing it. He could identify with characters such as Wile E. Coyote, Daffy Duck and Sylvester. Silently he rooted for them to vanquish their nemeses–Roadrunner, Bugs Bunny, and that lisping little twit, Tweety.

"Can't you drive any faster?" Al asked.

"It's difficult to see," countered Enrique. "The damn heater blew ash into my eye. I can barely keep it open."

Always whining about the eye, thought Al. "I don't want to miss the beginning of the film."

Enrique turned left onto Vine Street and skidded just a bit as he pressed on the accelerator. "Well, if we had left the party when I suggested…"

Whining, bitchy, brownnose.

Al felt their exit from the party came at an opportune time. The earlier, forced courteousness of his fellow faculty members deteriorated with each mouthful of scotch and gin. Deep-seated jealousies and frustrations were slowly working their way into conversations, and within the hour his colleagues would be trampling on his ego like a herd of stampeding buffaloes. Such being the state of academic criticism.

He shivered and put a hand to the blower. Not as cold, but not warm either. Damn Corvair. Sometimes it took fifteen minutes, maybe twenty, to start blowing hot air. His tweed jacket with suede elbow patches had worn thin from overuse and provided little protection from the bitter chill.

Yet his desire to participate in the greater world of taste and culture would be worth any degree of discomfort. He had waited years to see this film. Stuck in this culturally deprived hellhole, he resented those living in more civilized places, enjoying avant-garde arts and ideas as they happened instead of in retrospect.

His time drew near. Al fantasized about the success of his book. Maybe next year he would be able to walk from a Greenwich Village flat and around the corner to see any foreign film he desired. And afterward, he would frequent his favorite jazz club where the musicians knew him by name or end up drinking espresso with his new dilettante friends discussing the latest *empaquetage* of Christo. Then the ultimate reward of his profession, the *coup de grace*: a grand finale in bed with a luscious student, a fetching secretary, a stacked teaching assistant, or anything else within reach.

Such would be the life of a renowned professor and acclaimed author in the big city lights of his dreams. As he described, or had it been Quentin's idea, in *Is That All There Is?*: there exist degrees of meaninglessness on the grand continuum of the absurd. Living out his days in this rear-guard hovel would rank as the most insignificant of possibilities.

"This is like an episode of *Outer Limits*," said Enrique. "Nobody's out here but us. It's spooky."

Al watched Enrique tilt the Mason jar allowing the fingers of his right hand to more easily slip into the glass and coax olives from the clumpy cubes of ice. A half-burned Pall Mall hung from the side of his mouth. Al could feel the Corvair slowing as Enrique's concentration shifted from the road to the extraction of a particularly plump olive. He slid the swollen morsel between his teeth, but the Pall Mall came unhinged from his lips, falling into his lap, and rolling onto the seat.

"Jesus Christ!"

Al grabbed the cigarette as Enrique frantically dusted burning ash from his pants. "We're late and you're over there doing a goddamn juggling act."

Enrique turned his head facing Al, but where he looked was anyone's guess. He placed the Mason jar once again between his legs, wrapped both hands around the wheel, and punched the accelerator. Al could feel the Corvair fishtailing, but the tires gained some traction straightening the car's path.

"Watch the road, would you, please?" Pale green glowed from the speedometer illuminating Enrique's angry face as he turned slowly back to the road. The Corvair continued to gain speed as street signs counted down their arrival.

Eighth.

Seventh.

"Slow down, Enrique. This is absurd."

Sixth.

Enrique no longer accelerated but kept the speed constant, near fifty as they passed the IGA. "Gee, Professor, I don't want you to miss one or even a half of this movie. What would you tell people then? I only saw seven of *8½?*"

Fifth.

Enrique laughed at his joke and slapped the steering wheel a couple of times. He turned toward Al and repeated the punch line. "Seven out of *8 ½* You'll have to say, 'I went to see *8 ½* but saw 7 instead.'"

Fourth.

"Enough already!" Al barked. "It wasn't funny the first time, the second time or even –"

Third.

"Jesus Christ!" Enrique screamed. The Corvair spun hard to the left, almost completing one full revolution before Al saw the car in their path. And the last thing Al would see before his head slammed into the dash was–nothingness–black-robed darkness where the olive-green car's driver should have been.

3

ONE CLEAR CALL

Richard lay in the dark, hands behind his head, eyes open, fully aware. An intense reevaluation of his upcoming marriage to Mazel churned through his gut. If she hadn't gotten herself knocked up, he would have been out of the relationship months ago.

Still, she was going to have a baby and by marrying her, he could show everyone, the doubters and the finger pointers, that he, Richard McDonald, had live ammunition just like the rest of his brothers. Talk had been that Richard fired blanks, which for many men in Solomon, Texas, equated to having a limp pecker.

Four of his brothers had become notorious for getting teenage girls pregnant, marrying them, then after two or three miserable years, disappearing in the middle of the night, never to be heard from again. Richard, the eldest, turned twenty-seven last week and had not one little bastard to show for it.

Even the deal with Mazel felt a bit iffy. Backing out now would cast doubt on his claim to fatherhood and leave her ex-husband Virgil with the uncontested title. Richard had to consider again the possibility that maybe he was firing blanks. Marrying Mazel could be his only shot of having, or at least appearing to have, a child of his own. That was the appealing side of marriage.

On the negative side of matrimony stood Mazel Albright or, as Richard knew her before she tied the knot with that shithead Virgil, Mazel Banks. Not many women around Solomon looked better than his fiancée. She didn't try to look like the skinny, short haired models that were in fashion. Who could get hard for a girl called Twiggy? Instead Mazel accentuated a short, curvy frame with clothes that held tight to her smaller parts and stretched enticingly over the larger ones. Her deep black hair fell midway down her back and framed her slightly tanned face like that Mona Lisa chick in the painting.

Richard had been eyeballing Mazel since she sprang a nice set of tits back in junior high. But Virgil Albright went all out to capture Mazel Banks' heart and that was something Richard wouldn't do with any woman. Why should he? He did real fine bagging women with very little effort.

But it never hurt to leave your calling card with a female. A compliment here and an admiring look there, even with what looked like the most hopeless of possibilities, could pay off in the long run. It did with Mazel Albright after she got an eyeful of Virgil plowing that checker from the IGA.

No, the problem with Mazel had to do with attitude. She seemed to believe a lot of beatnik bullshit. She liked that new movement with those faggy-looking long hairs–the hippies. Her work at Texas State Tech Agricultural and Military College had probably made her susceptible to those simple-minded degenerates. The college campus is where they seemed to breed. To Richard's mind, Mazel being fired for getting knocked up was absolutely the best thing for her. Staying away from those ivory-tower pinheads would help straighten out her way of thinking.

For now though she still carried some weird ideas. This deal with natural childbirth and having him present in the delivery room set his teeth on edge. Not a single solitary soul he knew in Solomon agreed with the concept. After all, the year was 1965. The U.S. of A. had men flying around in outer space. The science of delivering a baby had been perfected long ago.

The way a child comes into the world was well-known and accepted: the mother receives a shot, conks out, the doctor removes the baby, and later, walks into the waiting room to tell the proud father if it's a boy or a girl. The mother wakes up in a hospital room, a nurse puts the baby in the mother's arms and there you go. No muss, no fuss, just leave everything to the professionals. Allowing amateurs like the mother and father into the act could only serve as a distraction. Can't let too many cooks into the kitchen or you get lumpy gravy.

The bell inside the telephone clanged loudly. Richard immediately rose to his elbows but was restrained from rising further.

"Hey, I got to get the phone," he said.

"Mmmmmm, don't go." Sunny, the freshman TSTA&M College cheerleader, had her arms interlocked around Richard.

"Hey, it might be a job. Let go." He spoke with just a trace of urgency, not wanting to offend Sunny who had been bucking passionately beneath him just a few minutes ago. With the fourth ring, however, Richard grabbed her wrists and ripped apart her embrace.

"Ooowww, that hurt."

Richard jumped from the bed, ran a few steps down the hallway, and picked up the phone during the seventh ring.

"I was about to give up on you," the gravelly but sexy voice griped into his ear.

"What have you got?" Richard asked, in no mood to explain the delay.

"I'm just fine, darlin', thanks for asking," said the dispatcher.

"Is it a wreck or just a tow?"

Richard kept silent, waiting for the voice to continue. Margo Chandler. It was bad enough having an ex-girlfriend call you at home, but it was especially bad when that ex-girlfriend had a legitimate, job-related excuse to call you every night, 365 nights a year.

"It's a wreck," she answered. "Did I catch you at a awkward time, hon'?"

Sunny came out of the bedroom, walking seductively, raising high the cheerleading sweater Richard specifically requested she wear for their secret date.

"I was sleeping, Margo. Now just give me the damn address so I can go about my business."

Sunny pulled the sweater back down, touched her fingertips to Richard's chest, and slowly traced a path downward. When Sunny's fingers hit pay dirt, Richard placed his hand over the phone and whispered forcefully, "Get your clothes on and go. I've got a job to get to."

Sunny's eyes looked downward as she said, "But look."

Sure enough, she had already coaxed him into another erection. "Finish me off," he whispered, "and be quick about it."

"Sleeping with who, Richard?" Margo finally spoke again. "I heard someone there."

"There's nobody, Margo. If anyone was here, it would be my fiancée." Richard felt Sunny release his penis.

"Finish yourself off, asshole!" Sunny yelled and ran down the hallway.

"Well, that nobody don't like you much," Margo said. "Sounded like a teenager. I hope you're staying legal."

"Up yours, Margo."

"Fuck you, Richard."

"I miss that nasty mouth of yours, girl." Richard dragged the telephone into the bathroom and locked the door. "Give it to me like you used to."

"Give you what?"

"Your dirty talk, baby." Richard's voice softened, unlike the rest of him. "Get me off the way you used to."

"I get paid to dispatch this tow job, not listen to you jerk off," Margo said.

"Well, then, I'll pay you for it." Richard knew he sounded a bit desperate. He also knew Margo worked two jobs and was desperate for money. "I'll give you five dollars, I promise. Just get me off with that filthy mouth of yours."

"Won't that make me some kind of prostitute?" she asked.

"Come on, Margo, it's just you and me. Nobody will know."

"Something about it sounds just plain wrong," she said.

"I never heard anyone talk as nasty as you, girl. You have a real gift. Come on, baby, be my phone wrench."

"Ten dollars?" Margo asked. "And you mean *wench,* not wrench."

"Seven-fifty," Richard answered. "After all, I'm doing all the physical wenching here."

For the next couple of minutes Richard listened to Margo rattle off an endless stream of lewd profanity while he groaned, moaned, and cussed back at her. When he finished, Richard slid to the bathroom floor and hung up the telephone.

On the other side of the bathroom door, Sunny yelled, "You're a real pervert, you old fucker." If she had only talked like that in bed, he thought. A few seconds later the back door slammed so hard that Richard could feel the floor vibrate.

Having hours and hours of sex with a nubile nineteen-year old cheerleader was as good as it gets. Or so Richard thought until Margo Chandler started spewing sex talk into his ear. He couldn't remember being so turned on in his life. Richard had never paid for a woman and never would, but an odd thought flashed through his mind. He would pay another seven dollars and fifty cents for Margo to do that again. He closed his eyes and replayed Margo's vulgar litany, repeating in a whisper some of his favorite phrases.

With a shaky finger, he dialed the telephone. After more than the usual number of rings, Margo answered.

"Where's the wreck?" he asked quietly, almost submissively.

"Third and Vine."

4

A LONG TRADITION

"**M**y thinkin is there was sumptin out of the ordinary goin on in this here vehicle," theorized Sheriff Oat Smith to his new deputy, Del Broten.

Oat Smith believed the number one cause of traffic accidents was not drunk driving or excessive speed as the public is so often led to believe. Five years of poking around smashed and mangled cars had brought Sheriff Smith to the conclusion that, both in its natural and perverse forms, the primary origin of every collision and crash was sex.

Oat pushed his mostly bald head through the open space where the driver's door had been. He grabbed the steering wheel and moved it back and forth while his other hand maneuvered carefully among the slivers of broken glass on the vinyl seat.

The Sheriff's theories were never proven right or wrong or made any difference in the least. On occasion, Oat would scare some dim-witted teenager into saying, yes, we were doing it when I misjudged the curve and ran off the road. And by admitting such, Oat might disregard the case of empties in the back seat or the 200-foot skid marks.

The accident reports that Oat filed did not reveal his theories but stayed within normative and acceptable limits of propriety so as not to embarrass the participants. Yet the locals anxiously awaited Oat's gossipy, juicy morsels on the latest sex mishap. Word traveled faster around Solomon, Texas, than a Corvair skidding on ice.

When Oat reemerged from the car, Deputy Del stepped forward with an umbrella to protect the Sheriff from the icy drizzle.

"They was performin some kind of unnatural act in there is my opinion," Oat continued.

"How can you tell, Sheriff?" asked the dutiful deputy.

Oat walked around to the other side of the Corvair. Del, a half-step behind, stretched his arm to ensure Oat would stay dry. The sheriff opened the passenger door and bent to the floorboard picking up a wadded pack of cigarettes. He flattened out the pack with his fingers, looked puzzled for a second, and then smiled.

"Looky here." Oat shoved the empty pack close to Del's face. "What's that say on there?"

Del hesitated, maybe still unsure of what should and shouldn't be handled at the scene of an accident. He leaned near Oat's long fingers and looked confused.

"Well, can you read that, Deputy?"

"No, sir. I never seen letters put together like that. Is it some kind of code or something? Were they…Communists?"

Oat's incredulous look was brief. In three weeks with the new deputy, he was beginning to get used to these types of questions. He drew the pack closer to his own face and began studying it again.

"No, boy, it's French. Makes my theory that much stronger. Cocksuckin' Frogs."

"How's that?" Deputy Del appeared thoroughly perplexed.

Oat moved a step closer to his deputy and said quietly, "They's faggots, Deputy."

"You mean *all* the French, sir?"

Oat took a step back, not believing his ears. Del stepped forward just as quickly, ever mindful of his umbrella duty.

"Well, son." Oat gave a bewildered smile. "I didn't quite mean it that way. But you know, most of 'em is a little limp in the wrist."

"What do you think happened here, sir?"

"Between me and you, Deputy?" Oat whispered.

Del nodded, his eyes wide with anticipation.

"The way I see it, these boys was drunk, pretty tight. Couldn't wait to get where they was goin to do it, so the older one starts doin the younger one while he's drivin. Do you know anything about homos, Deputy?"

Del shook his head from side-to-side with vigor.

"Well, it's pretty damn pathetic, especially the older ones. They'll go to desperate measures to hold onto these younger, good-lookin ones."

"But how did that have anything to do with the wreck?"

"The driver, you see, was so distracted that he didn' notice the Falcon crossin in front of him. He had all kinds of time to react but sumptin kept him from seein it in time. And my theory is: it was a blow job. Plain and simple."

"What makes you think that?"

"Did you see the positions of their bodies when we got here, Deputy?"

"Yes, sir. The driver was seated and the passenger was laid down."

"Where was his head, son?"

"In the driver's lap, sir, but they hit the tree pretty hard. I thought he just got thrown around some and ended up there."

"Listen, Deputy, in all my years of experience, people don' get *throwed* into that position. People put theyselves in that position of their own accord for one reason and one reason alone. Know what I mean?"

"Yes, sir. But how did you figure all this out?"

Oat counted the fingers of his left hand with the index finger of his right as he cited the evidence.

"One, neither one of 'em is married and the older one is thirty-six years old. That ought to tell you sumptin right there. Two, look how they was dressed. Almost matchin outfits. Tweed jackets with elbow patches. Now they ain' Tweedledum and Tweedledee, are they? Three, they's professors, teaching philosophy. Do you have any idea who the first homo was?"

"No, sir."

"Socrates. And he was also the first philosophy teacher. Now that's a long tradition goin on there."

"Yes, sir."

"Four, how many men do you know drink wine or gin martinis?"

"Nobody around here."

"Damn straight! And five, what kind of self-respecting American smokes these sissy-ass cigarettes from France?"

Deputy Del appeared overwhelmed by Oat's conclusive listing of the evidence. He didn't speak as they made their way back to the sheriff's car.

Richard McDonald pulled his wrecker slowly into the intersection next to Sheriff Smith.

"Getting off to a bad start tonight, aren't we, Richard?" said Oat.

"What's bad for your business is good for mine, Sheriff." Richard grinned.

"I been meanin to talk to you about that. You stop by my office next week, you hear?"

"What about?"

"Just a little bidness idea I been kickin around. You ain't opposed to a little bidness between friends, are you?"

"Whatever you say, Oat. What have you got here?"

"Two cars," called out Deputy Del.

Oat quieted the deputy with a shut-your-blamed-mouth look. "Why don' you get that one over yonder out of here first?" He pointed down Third Street.

Richard slid out of the wrecker and took a few steps toward the car. He stopped for a moment and then ran the rest of the way. Darting from one side of the Falcon to the other, Richard yelled, "The woman in the car, is she alright?"

"A lot better than those other two fellas," Oat said. "Only problem was she's real pregnant and breathin funny when the ambulance took her away."

"Like this," said Deputy Del, as he blew breaths out hard and fast like a train barreling down the track.

"Holy shit!" Richard sprinted to his wrecker, jumped in and threw it in reverse.

"What the hell's gotten into you, boy?" Oat called out.

"Sorry, Sheriff, I've got to get to the hospital. That girl in the car, we're supposed to be getting married."

As Richard ground the gears trying to find first, Deputy Del waved goodbye and shouted, "Congratulations!"

5

SUB ROSA

"Mazel?"

Dr. Robbins had been in a couple of times–probing, pressing, preparing Mazel for what she already knew. The baby was coming tonight, six weeks early. But that kind of thing is to be expected when you're lying in your car, smoking a cigarette, minding your own business, and somebody rams you from the side. Okay, maybe the Falcon had moved a little. Mazel's arms had become shaky like Jell-O and the umbrella would sometimes slip off the brake, the car creeping forward an inch or two until she could maneuver the shiny tip back onto the pedal. Still, the other car barreled into her like she wasn't even there. She couldn't remember hearing brakes squeal or the blast of a horn.

"Mazel? Are you alright?"

What surprised Mazel was the long silence after the crash. She had expected voices, a rush of activity, people running, shouting urgent commands. All she heard when she wasn't calling for help was icy rain striking the blacktop outside the shattered driver's side window. When help finally arrived, the voices were hushed and subdued. Not until they placed her inside the ambulance did she feel something trickling through her scalp. A gash ran across the top of her head where it had slammed against the passenger door. Twelve stitches now covered the wound, but nothing covered the stitches. A good chunk of Mazel's hair had been shaved to perform the procedure.

"Mazel? Can you answer me? Remember your breathing exercises?"

She could. She simply chose not to. Experiencing labor gave her the right and privilege to be obstinate, downright nasty if she so decided. The first wave of cramps had come suddenly while she lay in the Falcon crying for help. Pellets of ice blew through the broken window, striking her exposed calves like an unending series of chigger bites. The lower portion of her maternity dress had become soaked and she gritted her teeth to keep them from chattering. By the time help arrived Mazel was scared, angry, and somewhat disoriented from the uteral pain.

Dr. Robbins held her hand. "I can't deliver this baby without your help. Start breathing like we practiced in my office. This isn't a wart we're removing here, Mazel. You're going to be a mother very soon."

Mazel had some vague notion of what life would be like as a mother. She could imagine herself pushing a stroller, warming a bottle, or moving back and forth in a rocking chair with a small bundle wrapped in her arms. But it was like looking through photographs of someone else. She didn't know how to *feel* like a mother.

She hoped something magical would occur, that the mothering instinct would kick in gear allowing her access to some great collective vault of maternal knowledge passed down *sub rosa* through the ages. For now she had nothing to guide her into the mothering mode but a dog-eared copy of Dr. Spock's book that she just remembered was long overdue and racking up nickel-a-day charges from the university library. Of course, what could they do about it? Dock her pay? Ha, too late for that. Bastards. Professors humped anything within reach, including the secretaries. But let a secretary get pregnant under less than perfect circumstances and wham, you're fired.

"Breathe, Mazel. Take it in, take it in. Now hold it. That's it. Exhale. Good, good. Short breaths now. That's it, open your mouth. Breathe out."

Mazel kept her eyes closed along with her mouth. She didn't understand the reason for this desire to remain mute. The condition wouldn't be permanent and might not last another minute but for now it seemed to ease the gnawing sensation below her waist. Yet, something strange was happening this go round. The pain, no longer so much gnawing as…as…as splitting…damn splitting in…two damn pieces. Tearing apart from the inside like a crevice during an earthquake. She clutched the railings of the bed and tried to ride out the spiking torment. Yet, every time she thought the hurt couldn't get any worse, it did.

"Oh, my God!" she screamed. "I'm dying. I'm dying."

"Everything's alright, Mazel." She could hear Robbin's voice, but he sounded distant like an echo. "It's passing. It's passing. You'll be fine. Just hold on. Breathe, breathe."

The heavy-set nurse replaced the washcloth on her forehead with a newly dampened one. Dr. Robbins held her forearm with an almost too-firm grip. The pain dimmed and the doctor's voice returned near her ear.

"A cleansing breath. From way down there. That's it. Now one more time."

She turned her head towards Dr. Robbins and he smiled in return. "It's good to hear your voice again, Mazel," he said.

"Is that going to keep happening?" she asked.

The doctor nodded. "Keep up the breathing. You'll get through it just fine."

"Two things I need," she said, holding up her index finger. "One, my music. I need a transistor radio. One I can hold in my hand." She raised the next finger. "And two, most important, I want the shot."

Dr. Robbins shook his head disapprovingly. "You've made it this far. It won't be much longer. Think about it. A baby so small in your arms. You won't be groggy and out of touch. You'll be glad you didn't have the shot. But the transistor, now that's an excellent idea." He turned in his swivel chair and addressed the nurse. "Miss Thomas, will you ask down at the nurse's station if someone's got a transistor radio we can borrow?"

"Yes sir."

The doctor shifted back toward Mazel. "How's that? We'll get you set up with a radio in no time."

Mazel brought her index finger down, leaving the middle one standing alone. "I don't think you understand. Being groggy, being out of touch, that sounds very good to me right now."

"Mazel, please. I do understand, and I'm here with you all the way. We'll make it through this—together."

"There is no *we*. There's only *me* and I hurt like hell. Go get *me* something. *Now!*"

"Are you certain?" Dr. Robbins leaned near Mazel's sweaty face. "It's going to lessen the whole birthing experience for you."

Mazel yanked the doctor's stethoscope and was disappointed when it came loose from his neck. She wanted his head to come with it. "Nothing means more to me at this point than to *lessen* the whole birthing experience. I don't want to feel this way any-more. I don't want to feel anything anymore."

6

THE GAPING YAWN

Richard hesitated outside the delivery room doors. He had hoped someone would stop him with a "Halt! No men allowed in there," but nobody uttered a word. Two nurses directed him to this spot with a nod and a casual roll of the hand. Still he waited at arm's length from the doors, head bowed like a condemned man desperately praying for a last second reprieve. All he needed was a cigarette and a blindfold. Particularly, the blindfold.

"Hey, what are you doing?" The masked doctor darted quickly from around the corner. "You shouldn't be here."

Richard's relief was immediate. "I didn't think so, either."

"No, no, no," said the doctor as he pulled a surgical mask from the waistband of his scrubs. "You should be in there." He deftly tied the mask around Richard's face and shoved him forward.

Richard sailed through the swinging doors, coming to rest a yard or so inside. Nothing could have prepared him for the sight he faced. Mazel's knees were high and wide. Exposed was what Richard believed to be the most God-awful, gaping yawn of a vagina imaginable.

A nurse, short and stumpy, sat on a stool next to Mazel thumbing through a *Reader's Digest*. Both the nurse and Mazel were humming along with some song from the transistor radio pressed to Mazel's ear. When she got to the chorus, Mazel's voice rang out with slightly slurred words.

Chug-a-Lug, Chug-a-Lug
Makes you want to holler, Hi-De-Ho
Burns your tummy don't you know
Chug-a-Lug, Chug-a-Lug

The doctor sidled up to Richard and attempted to explain the scene. "She's having a little trouble pushing the baby out. A real trooper though. This kind of thing happens sometimes. Nurse Thomas helps with the pushing. We're just taking a little break right now."

Mmmm, mmmm, mmmm, moonshine still
Hmmm, hmmm, hmmm, drink my fill
Mmmm, mmmm, mmmm, mmmm
I run ten miles
Chug-a-Lug, Chug-a Lug

Richard felt like a rubbernecker watching him load another mangled vehicle onto the wrecker. Their timid curiosity bordered on the pathological, unable to disengage their eyes from the wretched remains.

"Back to work," the doctor said, while slipping on his surgical gloves. "Be supportive but don't get too close. Whatever you do, don't let her get hold of your hand. I've seen a husband's fingers snap like chicken bones. Not a pretty sound."

The doctor sat on a swivel stool and placed himself strategically between Mazel's legs. He called out gentle yet firm commands– breathe, push, ease down, harder. He spoke encouragement not only to Mazel but to the baby within. At times the doctor reminded Richard of his high school baseball coach with his *come on, baby; you can do it; keep your head up, kid; bow your neck; atta baby, atta baby*.

Though the doctor mentioned that Richard was with them, Mazel ignored his presence, not even acknowledging his weak, little "Hey, baby." He worried about how she might react to having the baby early and without the benefit of marriage. Yes, he wanted to have a son. Or daughter if things shook out that way. But what a price–marriage.

It was easy to stall the deal for the first month or so. Then, when he would gird himself for the inevitable, his will would cave in and crumble into a pile of rubble. He gave Mazel one excuse after another–tough week at work, low on cash, the wrecker is running rough, I need to get under the hood this weekend, I think I'm coming down with something–anything to give him more time to mull it over.

One weekend he even drove to see his brother, Punches, to ask for advice. He would have asked one of his other brothers, but Punches was the only one whose whereabouts was known, being in the Huntsville State Penitentiary for the next six to ten years.

Punches' advice had been fairly predictable considering his penchant for hit-and-run romance. "I don't understand your thinking here," he had said. "Spent my life trying to deny these little bastards was mine. And now here you are, trying to convince the world that this one *is* yours. And chances is, it ain't, being you only popped her once. With your track record and all… My advice is to do what I done–head west and don't look the fuck back."

Richard watched in horror as the doctor worked his hands between Mazel's thighs. He understood clearly that his previous conception of gynecology as the premier job around was way off base. The poor bastards didn't get paid enough to face this hideousness day in and day out. Richard covered his face momentarily as a shudder of nausea rose from his gut.

A squishy sound like shoes or boots stepping in and out of some muddy slop caused him to view the scene again. A head emerged from the pit. A child entered the world and Richard gagged, the stale aroma of pork rinds and Sunny's perfume barely retained within his body.

"It's a boy," announced the doctor. Richard moved another step closer and studied the child's face. This baby doesn't look like me, he thought. Then again, it didn't even look human. But, by God, this baby would show everyone in Solomon that he fired live bullets and even better, he fired boy bullets.

Mazel finally turned her partially shaved and sweaty head toward Richard. "No more babies, Richard. No more kids. This is it. No more babies."

Back in his swivel seat and between Mazel's legs, the doctor cleared his throat. "I wouldn't bet on it," he said.

"What?"

"We've come upon...an unexpected complication. Well, not exactly a complication as much as a pleasant surprise."

"Why is it still hurting so bad?" Mazel asked. "What surprise? What are you talking about?"

"Mazel," the doctor started, "it's only hurting because you're not finished yet. There's another little rascal inside there, and he's not as ready to face the world as the first one."

She wailed, a cat-like howl, the kind that sends chills down your back in the middle of the night as it did with Richard now. And from the other side of the room, Richard heard an "Oh, my God!" and the sound of boots racing out of the delivery room and down the hallway.

7

A CAUTIONARY TALE

L ifting Deputy Del Broten to his feet took less of an effort than it had been to keep his limp head from dipping below the rim of the toilet. Oat Smith still held the deputy's shirt collar in his right hand, which only moments ago had enabled his left hand to continuously flush the remains of Del's dinner away. Quite a strain, yes, but necessary to ensure that Deputy Del not plunge to the bottom. A couple of years ago, Oat almost lost another deputy to a toilet drowning: two good old boys giving the kid swirlies until they noticed the deputy turning blue. At least justice had been served when one of the dunkers was forced to resuscitate the deputy with mouth-to-mouth to avoid a murder charge.

Oat steadied Deputy Del and walked him to a wash basin where he splashed Del's face repeatedly with cold water. He felt partially responsible for Del's condition, having pulled the deputy through the delivery room doors against his will. But Oat thought the kid was up for it. After all, they had just come from a gruesome accident with one man pronounced dead at the scene and the other, a bloody mess who stopped breathing for several minutes before being revived. Oat wagered a fiver with the ambulance driver that the poor son of a bitch wouldn't last until daylight.

Del handled the gory details alright, not once having to avert his eyes or take a break for some air. Oat naturally assumed that anyone who could handle the aftermath of such slaughter would have little problem with afterbirth. Of course, upon further reflection Oat recalled the flips his stomach turned during the first of three birthings of which he had, by duty and necessity, participated. And the scene in this delivery room was particularly disconcerting. The woman, a Mazel Albright, the lower part of her body totally misshapen, frighteningly large and unrecognizable.

Well, not totally unrecognizable. Oat had been having dreams. Nightmares actually. Of being wet and cold. Lured to a warm and comforting cave but, once inside, being devoured by the mouth of the cave which exposed its secret teeth and clamped down hard on him. Oat had interpreted the dream as a cautionary tale, a warning to take more preventative measures during deer season.

"You okay, boy?"

Del's elbows rested heavily on the sink, his shoulders pinched inward, his head sagged toward the faucet. Sweat appeared in patches on the back of his deputy shirt, but Oat could see bumps rise on Del's arm as he shuddered with a chill.

"I'm sorry you had to see that, son," Oat said. "I forget sometimes what it's like for the uninitiated. Why, I been sheriffing so long that seeing a baby pop out the chute ain't no big deal. You'll be the same way in a year or two. One day you'll be able to reach into some ol' heifer, yank out a kid, and be in Sorrento's thirty minutes later munching down on one of them greasy old burritos. It'll happen."

The force of Del's sudden convulsion caused Oat to jump back into the towel dispenser, knocking it to the floor. Del kept opening his mouth into the wash basin but nothing came out, not even a retching noise. When his dry heaves ended, Del turned toward Oat. The deputy stood hunched, a pale, ghostly figure with an oval mouth. It appeared Del wanted to speak, yell, or scream, but his open mouth remained silent.

"Del, I can't wait on you all night. I got to go back in there and see what she can tell me 'bout the accident. Do you *comprende?*"

Del wiped a corner of his mouth with a shirt sleeve and braced the other arm against the mirror. "No, sir. I don't understand.

Why can't you just wait a bit til she's all through and cleaned up? Or come back in the morning?"

Oat leaned down, palmed the towel dispenser, and lifted it with ease. He took the roll of towels from inside and tore off a long section. "Here, boy, take this. You need to dry off. Especially behind them ears."

Del nodded in agreement and accepted the wad of paper towels.

"Every fifteen minutes," Oat continued, "a person forgets one important fact about their life. Eva second I waste getting in there is another opportunity for somethin' to slip right on out of her memory. And if for some reason she was to see a lawyer between now and tomorrow, hell, she'd probably get amnesia 'bout the whole thing. Are you followin' me on this?"

Del rubbed the back of his neck with the paper towels. "Yes, sir. That cut on top of her head looked pretty bad. Head injuries can make you forget who you are."

"Good Lord, son, so can Mescal. That's not exactly what I was drivin' at." Oat sank down to the wash basin and ran cold water over his hands for a while before splashing himself in the face several times.

"You comin back in there with me, Del? You ready to get back on that horse that slung ya?"

"No, sir," Del said, taking a step back. "No, sir. I'll stay right here till you're ready to go."

"Here? You gonna stay here? In the bathroom?"

"It's a mighty nice bathroom, sir."

Oat looked around the restroom as if seeing it for the first time. "This is a mighty nice pisser they have here."

"Yes, sir," answered Deputy Del, "the hospital is a good place to get sick."

***

The worst aspect of law enforcement for Oat Smith had to be refereeing domestic disputes. For that reason, he crouched outside the double doors, staking out the delivery room: his moves slight, his breathing shallow. A gap, maybe up to two inches, existed between the doors as the base of one had warped. This defect allowed Oat an unobstructed view when he would close one eye and focus with the other.

Things had changed from when he and Deputy Del first barged into the delivery room. The woman, Mazel Albright, and her doctor remained in place. Richard now stood on one side of the bed as a new player stood on the other side, his face red as he yammered away at Richard.

"I was married to her when she got pregnant. That gives me the right to be here. You're the one who doesn't belong."

"To hell with you, Virgil," said Richard. "The mother says who the daddy is, and Mazel says it's me."

"Who you trying to fool?" called out Virgil. "Everybody in this town knows you can't make a baby, you im-*poe*-tent son of a bitch."

"That's not impotent," answered Richard, "It's sterility. There's a difference."

"Stop it," interrupted Doctor Robbins. "Both of you stop it and clear out of here right now before I call the sheriff."

Oat cringed and inched away from the opening. He'd been in the middle of nearly every kind of family squabble, but this one ranked as unique. However, the issue involved didn't rate as so terribly unusual. Lord knows there were enough kids in Solomon, Texas, of questionable lineage. Possibly it was the setting, yes, the setting which unsettled Oat. Lots of sharp surgical instruments lay on trays around the room, easily accessible. As much as he wanted to interrogate Mazel Albright, he didn't want to find himself on the wrong end of a scalpel.

Something else bothered him, too. What the hell was everybody still doing in there? Oat had seen the baby. What was left to do? Surely, they could argue paternity in some other location— like a courtroom. And that woman, splayed out there for God and everyone to see it all.

For a short time no one moved. Only an occasional squeak from the doctor's chair would break the silence within the room. Oat considered going through the double doors, taking advantage of the temporary truce and possibly asking the woman a few questions in order to help verify his theory about the accident.

His sheriffing instincts though told him the silence was like the lull before the storm, an unnatural, stagnant stillness that would surround him when he watched a norther whip dust into a frenzy miles away. Within minutes, Solomon would be buried under a rolling cloud of dirt. And if this was the lull, he'd be receiving a call soon to come and babysit these two daddy-wannabes. Oat decided to make his presence known, but as he placed his hand on the unwarped door, Mazel Albright spoke. Her words were thick and slightly askew.

"You didn't want any part of this baby," she said to Virgil. "You said you wouldn't help raise him, you wouldn't help out with the money. Why are you doing this, Virgil? Why?"

"Just claiming what's due me," Virgil answered. "Put up with your shit for half my life. Figured I should get something out of it."

"But what? Are you going to help me raise him?"

"No."

"Are you going to pay child support?"

Virgil answered with an irritating cackle. "Hell no."

"Well, then, what are you doing this for?"

"Real simple. I don't want my son to be a bastard. It's not right."

Damn honorable, Oat thought.

"It's my son," Richard barked from the other side of the room. "We're getting married. He won't be a bastard."

"That's an open question," answered Virgil, "which it wouldn't be if I was listed as the father. We were married at the moment of conception no matter who else she might have been screwing around with. So, the boy is mine–biologically, legally, morally, and any other-*ly* you can think of."

"The kid is mine," Richard said.

"Nurse Thomas," Doctor Robbins called out, "please, go get the sheriff."

"The kid is mine," Virgil yelled.

"He's mine, you weaselly piece of grit," Richard said, taking a step forward.

"He's mine, you limp dick fairy," Virgil responded, taking a small step of his own.

"Mine!"

"Mine!"

"Mine!"

As they stood nose-to-nose, Mazel Albright intervened. "The boy isn't yours, Richard."

Virgil began his cackle again, but Mazel interrupted. "Don't be so damn smug, Virgil. The boy isn't yours, either."

Oat opened the door just a bit wider allowing both eyes to take in the scene as Mazel Albright strained to raise her sweaty and partially bald head from the pillow.

"*The boy is mine.*"

8

THE FAULTY HORIZONTAL HOLD

The melee continued but Mazel, with neither the energy nor inclination to focus on their insults, lapsed into something of a trance. All of her efforts had gone into that one line–the boy is mine–and now she felt spent. She stared at the ceiling, allowing its pure white to blank out the nastiness going on around her. At some point a line appeared in the ceiling and it began to move, rolling like the faulty horizontal hold of the Zenith console. She tried to adjust herself and reset the ceiling to its original stable position, but it didn't hold long. She was reminded of the times when too much drink had set the room spinning.

Mazel did hear the sheriff come into the delivery room, lots of voices speaking at once, then suddenly silence. Just Doctor Robbins remained. Nurse Thomas returned. Everything seemed right again in this little world except Mazel couldn't remember why she remained there. Her mind moved back and forth between clarity and fantasy like a ping pong ball.

"You're wearing me out, Mazel," Doctor Robbins said.

Control of the horizontal could not be completely reestablished, but she did manage a few accommodations to keep its effects to a minimum. Her pain became muted and modified into a manageable level of discomfort. Whatever medications the doctor had given Mazel were kicking in big time.

The boy is mine.

Yes, the boy was hers. Mazel remembered why she remained here. The other one still clinging inside her belly. In her mind she could see the baby clutching, tiny fists holding tight to whatever might keep him from leaving her body. Two babies for her to care and protect as best she could. But what was her best?

She didn't have a job. She had nothing to fall back on—no savings, no parents who would help, no Virgil. How could she care for her kids without a paycheck? To be honest, if Richard proved to be nothing else, he was a steady source of income.

Maybe love would come later. She wasn't averse to being in love with Richard. In fact, ever since high school Mazel had allowed her eyes to linger an extra beat or two whenever she turned his way. His look appealed to her: his dark, slicked-back hair, the long-sleeved shirts he always wore rolled to the elbows or higher, the pegged pants or jeans, the easy way he would lean against a wall or post when talking to a girl, and there always seemed to be a girl around. For now though, the basic attraction mattered little.

She needed a father for her babies. She needed money for their food, money for the next rent payment, money for their diapers, money for a crib—two cribs. Good God, there was so much that she hadn't yet considered.

Thankfully her mind slipped at once from stark and brutal reality into a fanciful flight where children were laughing. She could hear a band, a marching band. There were fireworks and a parade of lights. Everyone was happy. Not a cigarette butt in sight. The towers of a castle rose into view. Everything so clean, so spit-and-polish. This place existed. Yes, yes, it was…it was… Disneyland. *The Wonderful World of Disney.* Just like she had seen on TV. A little fairy dust to erase the mistakes. A wave of the wand to undo the accident.

"But I need to talk with her now," a man's voice intruded into her fantasy.

"You can't," answered Doctor Robbins. "She's had a tremendous trauma, and I've given her scopolamine. She can't think clearly now so come back tomorrow."

"But this is some serious bidness," said the man. Mazel opened her eyes to a tall, handsome man wearing a police uniform and a cowboy hat. He looked like a slightly diluted Rock Hudson.

The trip from Disneyland to Solomon ended abruptly for Mazel. What had occurred to her earlier came into the open now. "Are they dead?" she asked.

"Out, Sheriff." Doctor Robbins raised his voice. "Now. We are about to have another baby here, and we don't need any more distractions. Go."

The sheriff edged toward the door as Mazel asked again, "Are they dead?"

"Mazel," Doctor Robbins said, "don't do this. Not now. Nothing matters but getting your baby out safe and healthy. You've got to stay focused to do that. Do you understand?"

"They're dead," Mazel stated flatly.

"Not both of 'em," the sheriff said from across the room. "Not yet anyways."

Mazel's need to cry was stifled by Doctor Robbins as he placed his latex gloved hands around her forearms and spoke softly. "Alright then. From what I know, they were going way too fast and with the ice, just couldn't stop in time." He filled his cheeks with air before expelling it and continuing. "One man is dead. The other man is alive."

"They'd been drinking, too," noted the sheriff. "They were drinking wine and martinis right in the car. If you ask me, they was some perversion goin on -"

"Sheriff, do as I said and leave. Or I will call the state police."

"Oh, yeah, sure." Sheriff Smith looked to Mazel one more time. "You remember anything 'bout the wreck?"

"Sheriff," Mazel called out.

"Yes, ma'am."

"I want Richard back in here. I can't remember anything right now."

"Doc?"

"Whatever she wants. Just don't let the other guy back in."

"Don't know where he is," Oat Smith said. "He kind of high-tailed it when I came in before."

"Good. Now, if you would kindly bring Richard back for her, it would be appreciated."

"Sure thing." A few seconds later Mazel heard the sheriff in the hallway whistling through his teeth.

Within a minute, she heard, "Hey, baby."

"She knows about the accident," said Doctor Robbins. "She needs you. Don't be afraid."

Richard moved hesitantly toward Mazel. When she could reach his hand, Mazel stroked it lightly with her fingernails. He flinched at first when she held his wrists and pulled him to her. But her eyes were filled with tears and, seeing that, Richard's gaze turned soft, comforting.

"Forget everything else. We'll get married as soon as you get out of here. You're the mother of my child and I love you."

She squeezed his hand. "Don't say that. It's not true and we both know it." She watched his head move from side to side. "Look at me, Richard." She searched his eyes and imagined a trace of what she was hoping to find. "That's not to say we can't love each other someday. I think it's possible."

Mazel had maintained a presence in the real world for too long. The drugs within demanded she return to a better place. She drifted into her house with Richard, with the baby whose face she had seen earlier, and the other child whose grip was loosening inside her belly. *The Wonderful World of Disney* played on the Zenith console. Food sat in abundance on dinner trays. Richard - loving, attentive and true.

Yet, something lingered in the corner, a dark figure with slight but rapid hand movements. Sitting in a rocking chair, drool from his lips, he looked out a window. She felt repulsed, yet drawn to the man. The face seemed almost recognizable though it was contorted and stared blankly outside. She wasn't surprised the man sat in their living room, but having him there brought great sadness.

"Who are you?" she asked.

The dark man did not reply nor did he change in any way his small movements. His eyes never ventured from the tree outside as if the answer to life would occur in that very place. The only question in doubt was when the answer would be revealed.

"Who are you?"

9

THAT LAUNCH WINDOW

Richard continued to hold her hand even though Mazel's grip loosened as she stared vacantly toward the ceiling. He did not become offended when she mumbled over and over again, "who are you?" Maybe the first couple of times she asked, he thought the query was aimed at him. Quickly though he understood the "who" in question resided in Mazel's mind alone. Yet, the inquiry–who are you?–reverberated through him like a tuning fork struck gently on its side. Not normally an introspective man, the circumstances of this night caused Richard to examine his motives for being there, which in turn led him to survey his past.

"Who are you?"

I'm the older brother, he thought, the surrogate father, the responsible one. Richard's father, Hank, had died in a refinery explosion when Richard was eleven. The oil company not only refused to acknowledge their culpability in the incident but turned the tables and made Hank McDonald the culprit. The *Solomon Chronicle* ran stories of the investigation on the front page and when Pinnacle Oil pointed the finger at his dad, so did the rest of Solomon.

Five men dead and everyone blamed Hank McDonald, but because his dad was no longer around to take the abuse, Richard, his mom and his brothers bore the burden. The only people who didn't blame his father were a handful of workers at the refinery. Some of them believed that the safety engineers doctored the final report. In fact, rumor had it that another, more factual report had been rejected by the powers-that-be. They sent it back with explicit instructions as to how to place fault with one of the workers. Just the breaks, just a one-in-five shot, but Hank McDonald got saddled with the accusations of negligence and possibly even drinking on the job.

"Who are you?"

In time, the people of Solomon forgot. The sons of Hank McDonald, however, would never forgive the condemning leers of their neighbors or the savage insults of their aping children. His brothers wreaked their revenge by knocking up the daughters of Solomon, marrying them, making them miserable, and finally, deserting them. Punches McDonald did even more. Not only did he impregnate several women, but he stole their jewelry.

Only Richard remained somewhat above the fray. His brothers had been so profligate and prolific, word reached the streets that poor Richard couldn't make a baby. That his semen were DOA and these stories evolved into the most hurtful of all--Richard couldn't get it up. Of course, the issue became gender-specific because many women in Solomon knew this not to be the case at all. Sunny, the TSTA&M cheerleader, being the latest recipient of his seemingly infertile loins.

"Who are you?"

He was here tonight because the opportunity finally presented itself to rectify this mistaken image. Though he resented Solomon for treating his family with such disrepute, on another level Richard deeply craved the town's acceptance. That's why he stayed. By marrying Mazel and claiming a son, he would no longer be guilty by association with either his father or his brothers. Once and for all, he would be considered a bona fide family man who could sire a son with the best of them.

"Ain't this a cozy sight?"

One problem remained and it had returned–Virgil Albright.

"People, please," Doctor Robbins stated, "a simple blood test would clear this up."

"Give me some credit, Doc," Virgil sniffed. "We're both something negative. Anyway, it could be either of us."

"Mazel said that was all settled," Richard said with disgust. "I don't get it."

"I told you before. No son of mine is going to be a bastard."

Richard resorted to his argument one more time before he would leap onto Virgil's neck and choke him senseless. "I'm going to marry her as soon as we get out of the hospital. They'll be my sons."

"Yeah, well, it'll be mighty awkward with them having the last name Albright," Virgil snickered.

"Don't be so dull, Virgil. We can change their name–legally."

"Not if I contest it. Not if the courts count your bullets and you come up short."

"Do what?"

"They can count how many little soldiers you got in a battalion. Then they'll know if you've got enough to plant your flag up Mount Fallopian there."

"Semen count," interpreted Doctor Robbins. "If you come up with too few, it's virtually impossible to father a child."

"And if you come up with too many," Virgil said, "Katie, bar the door."

Richard's stomach lurched at the idea. Suspecting his condition was one thing, but having scientific substantiation of his sterility would be quite another. No, this opportunity with Mazel and the baby, the twins, well, this kind of chance didn't come along every day. And she had given him "an out" for the rest of their marriage. *No more babies.* There were witnesses. Those had been her exact words. Such circumstances would never open up to him again. He had to act now and the only solution was to pound Virgil into submission.

Of course, the flip side could be that Virgil might pummel him. Richard held a distinct height advantage, but Virgil was built like a fire plug and made rapid, jerky motions which always caused Richard problems in the clinch. Richard had scaled his barroom fights down to three or so a year and always made a good account of himself, but it was the short, stocky, and swift ones who could smack him silly.

Yet, how else might the matter be resolved? Paternity was all or nothing–there was no middle ground. How could there be compromise?

"Too bad we can't split the little boogers up," Virgil said.

"Do what?"

"Split them up. Didn't somebody do that in the Bible? Some king or something?"

"Solomon," said Doctor Robbins. "It was a ruse to find out the true identity of the child's mother."

"You wouldn't think that would be such a problem," said Virgil, pointing to Mazel. "I mean, it's self-evident. Not anything like trying to figure out a kid's father."

"King Solomon threatened to split the baby with a sword," Doctor Robbins said, "giving half of the baby to each woman. The actual mother was willing to let the other woman have her child in order that it might live. Quite a successful strategy to flush out the imposter."

"Well, hell, Doc," said Virgil, "we've got two kids. We don't need no sword. He can have one and I'll take the other. Maybe we each sired one anyways."

"You are such an idiot," said Richard. "That kind of thing isn't even possible. Tell him, Doctor Robbins."

The doctor gathered air in his cheeks once again before blowing out and speaking. "Truth is, there have been a handful of cases where twins have had different fathers. It's extremely rare, but the possibility exists."

"You know, Doc," said Virgil, "you look kind of like that trumpet player, that Dizzy Gillespie fellow, when you do that with your cheeks except for that vein in his neck makes me nervous. Like he's going to explode."

"How is that possible?" Richard asked.

"Quite simple, actually. I read a journal article on it while I was in Paris with Lamaze. All that's necessary for a double insemination to occur is two men, one woman and a quick turn-around time. You ever watch them launch a rocket from Cape Canaveral?"

Richard nodded and Virgil went into a Jose Jiminez imitation with a thick Mexican inflection like he had seen on *The Ed Sullivan Show*. "My name…Jose Jimenez and I aaaaaaammmm-mmm an astronaut."

The doctor ignored Virgil and continued. "Have you ever seen when they had to scratch a flight? There's that launch window. If they can't get the capsule up within that limited time span, they won't send it. The same thing with double insemination."

"What kind of time span are we talking here?" asked Richard.

"The sooner, the better the chances. But the actual window has been documented up to twenty-four hours."

Virgil smiled at Richard. "She had a busy day before getting to you."

Doctor Robbins said, "No, no, no. People, we're talking a handful of cases in all of recorded history. The chances are… astronomical."

"But can you say it definitely didn't happen here?" Richard asked.

"I can if they're identical or the blood type…oh, yeah, you're the same. Something negative, right?"

"And if they're not identical, can you say there's no chance each of us didn't father one?" asked Richard.

"An infinitesimal possibility might exist, that's all. I wouldn't bet a penny against a thousand dollars on the chance."

"You're not a very sporting man, Doc," said Virgil. "I'd bet on a poodle against a pit bull if you gave me those kind of odds. God loves a longshot. If there's one thing I've learned, it's that anything can happen. And I'll keep betting that way until it does."

Richard pressed the doctor further. "If Mazel says it's so and we say it's so, who's to say it isn't so?"

"The entire scientific community for one," answered the doctor.

"Who cares what they say," said Virgil. "All that matters is, is it binding and legal?"

"I guess that's what I'm asking," said Richard. "If we decide to split the twins up, paternity-wise, is there anyone to say we can't do that?"

"Not to raise them," inserted Virgil. "Just siring rights."

"Yeah," said Richard, "if it's done all legal and stuff, you or anyone else can't come back and say it's not so. Can you?"

Doctor Robbins pushed and pulled the skin of his face before speaking. "Why would I dispute it? I don't think it's possible and if they're identical, there's no way you can pull this off. But if you want to claim fraternal twins as the products of a double insemination, it's yours and Mazel's choice. She'll be the judge of the way it goes."

Right you are, thought Richard. How could he persuade Mazel to take part in such a scenario?

"It would be a might easier," said Virgil, "if each of them had a different last name."

"I told you we can do that later. We can change one to my name..." It wouldn't be the same, he suddenly thought. Virgil could still go around saying he fathered both twins and that Richard just changed the name legally in order to claim one as his own. The whole situation would be so much simpler if he had already married Mazel. The twins would be McDonald, no legal ifs, ands, or buts about it. But it was too late. He kicked himself for being so damn stupid and not realizing the potential problem before now. One baby was already out, an Albright. The other would be born any time and be...

...why not a McDonald? If time permitted, why not?

Richard leaned to Mazel's ear and whispered, "Hey, baby. Let's get married."

She nodded slightly and said, "Okay. Who are you?"

"It's Richard, baby. Let's get married right now."

"But my hair–"

"It's fine."

"I need my purse, my lipstick, my eyeliner, my radio."

"We'll get them for you, Mazel. You've got to do one thing though." Richard whispered even quieter so Doctor Robbins wouldn't be able to hear. "You've got to hold the baby till we get back with the preacher. Can you do that?"

"What baby?"

"That a girl. I'll be right back. Whatever you do, don't push."

He pulled away and released her hand. "Hey," she called out, "who are you?"

"The father of one of your children."

"Oh, good," Mazel replied.

Richard huddled with Virgil quickly and relayed his simple plan. He asked Virgil to phone Reverend Yates and tell him to get ready for Richard's impending arrival.

"Why the hell would I help you? Virgil said. "I don't give a damn if you get married now or not."

Richard retrieved his wallet from the back pocket of his jeans. "I'll give you some money."

"I want it all. Give me everything you got in your wallet."

Richard counted out a small wad of bills, a couple of fives and the rest were ones. "There, eighteen dollars."

"Change?"

Digging into each of his front pockets simultaneously, Richard emerged with about ten coins and handed them to Virgil.

"Alright then," Virgil said. "I'll call Reverend Yates."

"You're a real piece of work," Richard said, as he ran down the hallway.

"And you're a real piece of shit," Virgil called out after him.

Richard could drive to Reverend Yates' home and be back at the hospital in a matter of minutes. Mazel and Richard would be married in the delivery room and the next baby to pop out would be a McDonald. Details or unforeseen circumstances could be negotiated later.

Time was the foe. Richard burst through the double doors like a rocket loosed from its moorings. That launch window remained open.

10

MOTHER AND FATHER...AND FATHER

Mazel gently maneuvered a brush around the stitches and through her sweaty, matted hair. Observing the dismal results in her compact mirror, she moaned and wondered why she cared. The swirling, dense clouds in her mind had, if not cleared, at least settled, smoothed over, stabilized. No illusions of a fantasy life at home or within the enchanted gates of Disneyland remained. The drooling man lingered, keeping watch at the window, but Mazel no longer seemed concerned with his identity. She would deal with him later.

For now she dealt with a knot of hair near her bald spot which refused to be tamed. Nurse Thomas had clumsily helped with the eyeliner and mascara, several times uttering an "oops" or "sorry", but all-in-all, considering the circumstances, Mazel found her face presentable in a bride-of-Dracula-like-way. Pale face, obscure shadows surrounding vacant eyes, lips puffy and unevenly drawn with a new color stick, terra rosa. Her hair on the other hand appeared to be styled by the bride of Frankenstein.

In a matter of minutes, Mazel Albright would be transformed into Mazel McDonald, bride of Richard. That is, if Richard and Virgil were swift enough to catch up with the Reverend Ezzie Yates. A couple of minutes earlier the good Reverend had entered the delivery room and began crossing himself in a most un-Protestant manner. Reverend Yates was fifty-two years old but seemed to age in dog years. This night he appeared particularly old, grizzled, and unkempt. His eyes, covered by thick wire-rim

glasses, were always wide and tonight, somewhat wild. After uttering a couple of Hail Mary's, Ezzie Yates had bolted through the
double doors as if just encountering the anti-Christ. Odd behavior for a Free Will Baptist.

Not that Mazel had been keeping up with Baptist theol-
ogy in recent years. Maybe an alliance between the Catholics
and Free Will Baptists had taken place without her hearing
about it. She remembered the Catholic president from a
couple of years ago, but he got shot in Dallas. Maybe it was
a conspiracy of Free Will Baptists. The absurdity of such a
notion caused Mazel to think that she might be lapsing again
into fantasyland. A growing commotion outside the delivery
room brought her back to reality. Richard's voice strained to
be heard above the other.

"Look, preacher," Richard said forcefully, "you're going in
there one way or the other."

"No," called out Reverend Yates. "I'm not going in there
again. God never intended for man to see these things."

"The doctor's a man," said Virgil.

"He's not a normal man," Reverend Yates responded.
"Gynecologists are chosen for this kind of work. God gives them
the strength to face such abominations. It's God's will that we
stay out of that room."

Virgil spoke again. "If God chooses your work, then what the
hell is 'free will'?"

"Not now, dammit," Richard said. "Hold him!"

"Wait a minute," pleaded Reverend Yates. "What are you
doing? What is that?"

"You're bound to have this wedding stuff memorized," said
Richard. "You don't need to be reading from that book. I'm
going to tie this here surgical mask around your eyes so you
won't have to see a thing."

Mazel couldn't make out Ezzie Yates' response. She was dazzled by Richard's diligence in pushing the wedding ceremony
forward even at the risk of a kidnapping charge. *Why* was too

weighty a question in her exhausted and pained condition. For the moment, however, she enjoyed the feeling of being…prized.

Mazel's approach to the impromptu marriage had thus far been fairly noncommittal, somewhat like her approach to Saturday afternoon chores. At least she would be married by a preacher this time. And in the United States.

Her wedding to Virgil had been a botched elopement to Mexico. They limped into Juarez with a busted radiator, a blown tire, and a shock so worn that Mazel had been car sick the entire trip. The repairs took most of their money. A wizened, foul-breathed JP officiated the ceremony, taking most of the rest. The few dollars that remained were just enough for an hour's worth of a room at a Juarez brothel. She had hoped for better this time around. And now this.

The double doors banged open. Virgil and Richard marched inside with Ezzie Yates between them, each holding the Reverend's arm near his elbow. With the surgical mask over his eyes, the Reverend appeared to Mazel like a condemned man facing a firing squad.

"Hurry up," Mazel wheezed. "This baby is wanting out."

"My God," said Nurse Thomas. "You've kidnapped the preacher. Have you no shame?"

"This is the only way we could get him in here," hissed Virgil.

"Do the shotgun version, Reverend," said Doctor Robbins. "We're running out of time."

"OK, OK…uh, uh…uh, uh…uh, uh–" The uhs came in rapid-fire pairs, a most annoying rhythm to Mazel.

"Get on with it."

"…uh, uh…uh, uh…dearly beloved, yes, dearly beloved. We are gathered here today in the sight of God…"

"Go on, Reverend," Richard urged.

"We are gathered here in the sight of God to join together this man and this woman in the bonds of holy matrimony." Reverend Yates paused, fingering the book in his hands. "Uh, uh…uh, uh …"

"What the hell's wrong?"

"I...I...I...I can't remember the rest."

"You've done this a thousand times. What do you mean you don't remember?"

"I memorized the first line. I look out at the crowd, the bride and groom. Then I read the rest."

"Take the blindfold off," said Virgil.

"No, no, no, no. No, no, no, no. Don't touch it. I'll try again."

"Here comes the head," announced Doctor Robbins.

Reverend Yates crossed himself and started again.

"Uh, uh...on this solemn occasion, we reaffirm our belief in the Almighty. No, no, wrong ceremony. OK, OK, here we go. Lord, bless these young men as they take the field tonight."

Everyone in the delivery room seemed to stop breathing at once.

"Try it again, Reverend," said Nurse Thomas. "The wedding vows, remember?"

"OK, OK. Uh, uh...uh, uh... His ways cannot be known to us. His will be done. Ashes to -"

"This ain't no fucking funeral," yelled Richard.

Virgil snickered. "The hell it ain't."

"You've got about thirty seconds," Doctor Robbins said. "Push, Mazel."

"Please, preacher," Nurse Thomas said.

"Belly to belly, skin to skin–"

"Hey," Richard screamed. "That's it. Off with the blindfold."

"No time," said Doctor Robbins. "Just get to the 'I do's'. Mazel, push hard on the count of three."

"OK, uh, uh...do you...who are you?"

"Richard."

"Do you take...her..."

"Richard said, "I do," before the Reverend could get the rest out.

"One," counted Doctor Robbins.

"And do you..."

"Mazel," Nurse Thomas inserted.

"Two."

"Do you take…him…"

"Three."

Mazel tried to push hard, her entire body rigid with this one final effort that tapped all of what little reserves she had left.

"Oh, my God," she cried.

"I'll take that as a yes," said the Reverend. "I now pronounce you…"

Mazel could hear the squishy sound just as the Reverend made his dramatic pause.

"It's another boy," announced Doctor Robbins.

"I now pronounce you mother and father…"

"…and father."

1991
Early September

The child whom many fathers share
Hath seldom known a father's care
                John Gay, Fables, Part I

There are no illegitimate children – only illegitimate parents.
     Leon R. Yankwich, Decision, Zipkin v. Mozon (1928)

Always go to other people's funerals, otherwise they won't come
to yours.
                Yogi Berra

11

WHICH ONE?

When the phone rang at 11:27 p.m., Clovis McDonald knew that something was wrong. The scenarios varied. Someone in his carrier crew might be coming down with the flu. Another could have symptoms replicating the latest contagion-like virus they had seen on television. One guy, unaware that the appendix only came one to a body, had his removed repeatedly. Not until his fourth appendix exploded did Clovis fire him.

The prospect of bad news kept Clovis from answering for a couple of rings. Sometimes they couldn't throw their *Fort Worth Daily News* due to a broken down car. A flat tire and no spare, he had heard that on more than one occasion. Not enough money for gas. Some nights one would call and just say, "I can't take it anymore."

What it meant for Clovis were long hours of gut-wrenching work to get the papers out. The residents of east Fort Worth felt entitled to have a newspaper at their home by six a.m. If it wasn't there, they felt entitled to yell at Clovis.

He rolled onto his side and let the phone ring one more time. His voice croaked out an I-just-woke-up, "Hello."

"Hi, Clovis. I'm sorry to bother you so late, but something's happened here."

Clovis kicked the sheets away and stood next to the bed before his mother finished speaking. "Are you alright, Momma?"

"I'm fine," Mazel McDonald answered. "I'm over at Elsa's right now."

"Why aren't you at home?"

"He shot himself, Clovis," Mazel said. "Your father killed himself."

"Which one?"

Clovis regretted saying it as soon as the words came out of his mouth, but he didn't apologize. He let the words lay there, the air on the phone line as heavy as a September afternoon before a storm.

After an uncomfortable silence Mazel said, "That's something I'd expect from your brother, not you. Is Bubba there?"

"No, he's got a new girlfriend or something. I haven't seen him for a couple of days."

"Richard provided for us," Mazel said. "That's more than a lot of fathers do. It wasn't in his make up to do much more than that, you know?"

Clovis knew well. He had thought about it often. His conclusions were simple. There are fathers who beat on their kids. There are fathers who scream and yell at their kids. There are fathers who never allow their kids to feel safe in their own homes. His father wasn't any of these.

His father just never seemed to care.

"What happened?" he asked.

"I came home from the movies like usual, and Oat stopped me down the street before I got to the house. He said Richard shot himself. That's pretty much it. He didn't have any details."

"I'm sorry to hear that, Momma. What do you want us to do?"

"I just want you boys to drive home tomorrow, okay? We'll have the funeral as soon as we can and put this all behind us."

Clovis knew he had acted like a jerk, a normal reaction when the subject of his father arose in any context. For his mother's sake, he attempted to recover.

"How are you doing with it?"

Mazel expelled a lot of air into the phone before Clovis overheard her ask Elsa, "Could you close that door? We need some privacy for a minute."

Clovis lay back in his bed, covered himself, and began shivering.

"Of course, I'm in shock," Mazel spoke in a quieter voice than before. "He never seemed the type to do anything like this. Although, he's been more down-in-the-mouth since the cancer."

"I thought that was all taken care of," Clovis replied. "Had it come back already?"

Clovis recognized the sounds of his mother lighting a cigarette. "Not that I know of."

"Did you tell him about the divorce yet?" he asked, tightening his grip on the sheets and pulling them over the chill on his neck.

"No, thank God. But I don't think that would have made a difference anyway. There wasn't much communication going on between us."

"Did Oat say if he left a note or anything?"

Mazel hesitated before speaking. "You know, that old fool looked pretty torn up about it. Oat only told me the basics. I can ask him tomorrow."

"So, you're doing alright?"

Mazel spoke in even more hushed tones. "Clovis, I feel like a giant weight has been lifted off my back. Going through with this divorce scared me half to death. He would have made it as ugly as sin. Truth is, I feel relieved."

Clovis had known of his mother's divorce plans for a long time. After working up the courage to finally go through with it a couple of years back, she had been halted by the discovery of his prostate cancer and its treatment. "You have to be a total shitheel to divorce someone when they get cancer," she had told Clovis. Mazel hung with her husband through the hard times, the radiation and the chemo, out of a sense of duty. She even mentioned to Clovis that it might be a penance for some of her past mistakes.

Clovis had urged her to leave despite the cancer, but she never considered doing so. His mother took care of business and bided her time until she could be free. In actuality, he knew that she had been doing so since Bubba and he were little kids. Biding her time, waiting for them to get through school, putting as pretty a face on their life with Richard as possible before experiencing a different life. Relief? He could understand the feeling.

He didn't want to talk about Richard any longer but struggled with how to proceed further with their conversation. So he fell back on routine and repeated the same question he asked his mother every week when they spoke on the phone.

"What movie did you see?"

She blew out smoke and said, "*The Prince of Tides.* Do you know the story?"

"Yeah, momma, I read the book. He paints a pretty picture, but it's a sad one."

She inhaled a puff and Clovis could visualize the smoke escaping her lips as she spoke. "Burying the past made them all miserable," she said, "but they come to terms with it in the end. A redemption story is good for the soul."

"Yeah, at least Daddy Two didn't knock us around like in that book. He just never seemed to notice we were there."

"He's gone now, Clovis. Do you think you could stop calling him Daddy Two?"

"It's how Bubba and me kept them straight. It was confusing when we were little."

"We'll talk about it when you boys get here, alright?"

Clovis left the conversation at that. He stared into the dark and planned out how the *Fort Worth Daily News* could do without him for the rest of the week. The death of Daddy Two was as good an excuse as there is to be out for a few days. Most people could only use the death of their father one time to get out of work, kind of like the appendectomy. But Clovis still had a Daddy One, a Virgil Albright, out there somewhere. Daddy One could be both their biological fathers. Who knew? But legally, Bubba

Albright was Daddy One's son; Daddy Two belonged to Clovis McDonald.

After a couple of sleepless hours, the front door of the apartment opened, and Clovis recognized his brother's sounds–the keys clanging into the empty pineapple ashtray, the refrigerator door opening, a bag of chips being ripped into, the television clicking on, and the boots thudding onto the coffee table. Clovis slipped on a pair of jeans and walked into the living room. It was time to go to work anyway.

"Momma called."

"Something wrong?" Bubba asked.

"Yeah, our father killed himself."

Bubba put a couple of potato chips into his mouth and as he chewed asked, "Which one?"

12

THE TUMBLEWEED REST HOME

Though Mazel McDonald could appear to others as unpredictable, impetuous perhaps, the fact remained that habit and routine served to maintain her shaky emotional equilibrium. Monday nights, for example, were given over to the cinema. That's where she had been last night when Richard shot himself.

In solitude with a large bucket of butter popcorn, Mazel experienced release from her worries by watching the neat, clear-cut problems of those on screen. Fictional life pushed characters inexorably toward *the* right answer as if other possibilities did not exist. Complexity and paradox were lost in the rapid, one-way movement of celluloid frames. No matter the issue presented, life looked to be manageable in the end.

The cinematic experience worked well for Mazel, but its effects never lasted more than a few days. Chaos and the absence of order had a knack of bullying their way past the elegant solutions of screen life.

Over the years, what succeeded best in soothing her wounded spirit had been, in fact, a heavy dose of a sobering reality. Every week Mazel would make the thirty minute drive on a monotonous, unbending stretch of Ranch Road 537 to the Tumbleweed Rest Home.

Sitting atop a stunning, red-tinged mesa, the nursing home had become a mecca for the followers of Professor Al Pozzo. Though the ones responsible for the professor's care would not permit the masses to actually visit him, they did allow the congregations to gather just east of the facility.

Mazel pulled her Honda Accord between two dumpsters and walked into the Tumbleweed. Administrators, nurses, orderlies, food service and maintenance workers greeted her warmly. She always brought them treats and this time was no different–candy bars, exotic flavored jellies, and white-worm mescal for her friend, Manuel Daza.

Though the staff groomed Professor Pozzo especially for her visits, the sight of Al in his rocking chair, staring out the window, the perpetual drool leaking from his lip, and in recent years, the hand twitching in his lap startled Mazel to the point where she would let out a long, aching moan. Tears sometimes followed, as they did today, and for the only time during her stay, she allowed herself to feel the burden, the guilt that remained airtight and deeply hidden to those on the outside. Almost twenty-six years later and she still felt nauseous remembering that icy night and the wreck that brought Al Pozzo to this place.

Within minutes Mazel pulled herself together and pulled a chair next to Al. She spent the next hour discussing a wide range of subjects.

"*Newsweek* says that more people came to The Tumbleweed last year than went to Paris to visit Jim Morrison's grave."

"You probably don't remember Jim Morrison, do you?"

"You probably never even heard The Doors."

"TSTA&M is naming a chair in your honor, whatever that means."

"Your book is going into its eleventh printing."

Al Pozzo's book, *Is That All There Is? Making the Most Out of a Meaningless Existence*, hadn't attained immediate success in the sixties, but by the early seventies had developed a sizeable cult following that continued to grow over the years. Followers, the true-believer types, flocked to the Tumbleweed and sat around one of several growths of cacti, reading passages from his work or writing his words in the ever-shifting sands. As the professor sat helpless in room 1010, the disciples discussed how his book changed their lives.

In rather opaque terms, Al Pozzo forecast the final paradigm plunge of the millennium: the subjugation of mankind to binary thought processes. The prospect of this occurrence alarmed the author only insomuch as to how it would sharply alter mankind's ability to think and, therefore, feel as human beings. He saw people losing the ability to struggle against hopelessness, the one human quality that could ultimately define the difference between man and machine.

The more serious and dedicated disciples organized themselves into a group known as Al's Agnostic Angels, a designation rife with negative capability. Since 1975, one or more members of the Angels remained outside the Tumbleweed twenty-four hours a day, in what they promised would be an everlasting vigil to honor their leader.

In 1983, several of the Angels recognized Mazel from a photograph in one of the half dozen or so biographies on Professor Pozzo. Some blamed her directly for the accident that left Al incapacitated for life. Others blamed Enrique, his driver, but somehow still believed Mazel to be indirectly responsible.

As she had approached the front entrance of the Tumbleweed that day eight years ago, the Angels swarmed over her, screaming crude epithets and beating her to the ground using both hardback and paperback copies of Al's book. Some orderlies and nurses intervened, holding off the Angels while carrying her bruised body inside the rest home. Ever since then, she had been allowed access to the loading dock where she could enter unnoticed through the delivery door in the back.

"Richard is dead."

She hesitated as if anticipating a reaction.

"Shot in the back of the head."

Mazel lit the last Lucky Strike Light in her pack and inhaled before continuing.

"You just don't say this to anybody, but I am so relieved he's gone. You probably wonder how I could have stayed with him all these years."

Mazel drew on the Lucky a couple of times before rising and flipping the remains into the toilet. Instead of returning to her seat beside the professor, she stood behind the rocking chair and stroked his thin, white hair with her fingertips.

"I don't have a good answer, Al. I mean, once Richard committed me to this fine establishment, I didn't have a lot of options. Not to say that I didn't deserve to be watched for a while. I still don't remember climbing up on our roof, and I sure as hell don't remember taking my clothes off.

"I do remember coming home from the hospital. The sun was shining so bright, and I had a baby in each arm. Richard drove the wrecker real slow through the middle of town like we were in a parade or something.

"Then, I see your face in the window of Jenkins Bookstore. The goatee and beret. There's a couple of dozen books propped up around this big picture of you. And your eyes ... your eyes are following me. I ask Richard to speed up, but he's got the window down, waving at people. It's freezing outside, but to him, it's 'show-and-crow' time. *Show-and-crow*, that's not half bad. Anyway, he stops right there in front of Jenkins and starts jawing with someone.

"I don't know how much time we're there, but it was too long. Long enough that to this day, I can still feel your eyes on me. By the time we got home, I was a wreck. A complete and total wreck.

"Oh, God, I'm sorry, Al. Poor choice of words. You know what I mean."

Mazel walked to the window and crouched so Al's gaze fell directly on hers. For the briefest of moments she detected a light from his eyes, but just as quickly, it was replaced by a desolate blankness that cut through Mazel and beyond to the lone mesquite outside. This wasn't the first time she had noticed a second or two when Al appeared something other than what Richard called "the old drooler." Then the moment of recognition would pass and leave Mazel wondering whether the event had been real or imagined.

The orderly, Manuel Daza, said these brief happenings were common with long-term patients. Family members and friends would often comment that "so-and-so gave me a look today, like he might have known I was there." Or "she made a sound like she was trying to say something to me." And Manuel didn't deny these events were real.

"When someone is taken from us suddenly," Manuel had told her with his thick, Mexican inflection, "we carry around a pocketful of things left unsaid. Our hopes maybe help determine what we see. But then, sometimes I feel their eyes on me, too, and they look different for a time. Fermina, my wife, she say they are ghosts. She say they have things left unsaid, too. All I know is that when I'm in bed at night, I can sometimes feel their eyes on me still and my heart, it aches along with the ghosts."

And so too, Mazel's heart grieved for years. A short time after the boys birth, Mazel had been committed to the Tumbleweed for a six month stay. Upon her return home, she was at least able to function again. She washed clothes, cleaned up after dinner, and bathed the boys. She had sex with Richard, watched *Petticoat Junction*, and played solitaire in hours-long binges. By all appearances, the psychiatrists had succeeded in returning Mazel to a normal life as a wife and mother. Still, she had been a wreck.

"Everything seemed to be happening at a distance."

Mazel moved again to the chair next to Al's rocker. "I would pick up Clovis or Bubba and I could see myself doing it, but I couldn't *feel* them in my hands. I cared for them, tended to their needs. I loved them. I really did. I just couldn't connect to that love and know they felt it. I was like a Stepford wife. All's well on the outside but inside, things were just a shitty mess.

"Richard said if I ever tried to get a divorce, he'd take the boys. Like he said, I was not only a nut job but certifiable. Certifiable."

Mazel continued to scour the depths of her past for the remainder of the hour, rubbing old wounds to make them bleed anew, ransacking the neatly packed chests of memories within and exposing them, one-by-one, to the light. This trip to the Tumbleweed served as a psychological housecleaning, and at its conclusion, the wounds would be dressed and the past scrubbed, polished, and put away until next time.

Al Pozzo sat without expression–the perfect therapist. He never tried to interpret or evaluate what she said, never imposed his world view or values into her life. He didn't nod his head or utter an appropriately placed "Uh-huh" here and there. Mazel determined the ebb and flow of her dialogue, not he. Al did not facilitate nor attempt to direct the content of her consciousness. The only microcounseling techniques he employed involved a steady, consistent stream of saliva and a 120-count per minute twitch of his left hand.

When her voice became hoarse, her soul emptied and dry, her body crying out for more nicotine, Mazel rose to say good-bye. She touched his cheek softly and brushed his hair with her fingertips as she had done so often throughout the hour.

"You weren't a bad man, Al. A little cocky and full of yourself maybe, but you weren't a bad man at all."

Once more she placed her face directly in front of Al's, her eyes searching for another moment of light.

There was none.

13

OU F O DER

"**H**ungry?" Bubba asked.

Clovis glanced at his brother guiding the truck with the thumb and index finger of his left hand, his right being occupied with a Shiner Bock. "Not really. There'll be a load of food when we get there."

"No doubt."

Before a body could go cold in Solomon, ovens were heating up. Most women prepared the same thing death after death. Mrs. Comstock baked a spiced ham. Mrs. Trujillo prepared chile rellenos in nogada sauce. Nellie Robin made a cinnamon-apple-pecan cake, the aroma alone enough to curl your toes. More solace came from walking the streets, inhaling the customary funeral dishes than listening to the feeble-minded Reverend Yates mumble how God works in mysterious ways or it was his time to go.

Clovis had trouble believing it was Daddy Two's time to go. Especially during *Monday Night Football*. If Daddy Two intended to shoot himself, he would have at least waited until after the game to see if he won or lost his bet. Something felt off.

Monday nights had always been eventful around the McDonald household. Their mother would go see a movie by herself or with Elsa. Daddy Two would then call Vic Tannyhill to place a couple of bets, fill his Coleman cooler with ice and Budweiser, and plop himself in the La-Z-Boy for the next several hours of *Monday Night Football.* If Bubba or Clovis passed through the room, Daddy Two's menacing glare worked better than a "Do Not Disturb" sign.

"I can't wait," Bubba said. "I've got to have me a fish sandwich to tide me over."

Bubba exited the highway and found the drive-thru behind a Dairy Queen. For a minute or more they waited for someone to ask for his order.

Finally, Clovis leaned across the seat and pointed to a wrinkled piece of lined paper taped next to the picture of Dennis the Menace holding a Blizzard. "What's that say?" Clovis asked.

Ink had smeared and run, but Bubba still tried to sound out the letters: "OufOder, OufOder. Out of fucking order?"

Bubba popped the clutch too quickly which sent the Dodge Ram lurching toward the drive-thru window. Not being able to reach the glass, he gave the hollow counter ledge several raps with his fist.

"You could honk," Clovis offered.

"You could shut the fuck up."

A pimply, stringy-haired, multi-pierced girl arrived, slid open the glass with a thud and said, "He'p yew?"

"Yeah, a fish sandwich with mustard only. No tartar sauce. You want anything, Clovis?"

"No."

"Come on. You haven't eaten anything all day. How about a Dilly Bar? You like them."

"I said no."

"Anything else?" asked the teenager, rubbing the rugged terrain around her cheekbone with the eraser of a pencil.

"Yeah, a Dilly Bar," Bubba answered. "That'll be it."

They sat in silence while the DQ hummed with activity. The sun would be completely gone in a few minutes, and Clovis eased the sudden tension around his nose and ears by removing his sunglasses. A loose string on his sleeve near the wrist drew his attention. Round, round, and round his index finger–tightening the thread and letting it go, tightening the thread and letting it go.

"Pull that damn string off or leave it alone," Bubba said.

Clovis yanked the thread with such force that the button popped off and onto the floor.

"Crap!"

"What the hell's eating you?" Bubba asked.

Clovis felt around on the floor and under the seat for the button but came up with only two sticky pennies, a grimy pencil, and the smooth surface of Bubba's Smith & Wesson .38 caliber lemon squeezer. He started to ask Bubba what it was doing there, but his brother's attitude already sounded confrontational.

"I said, what the hell is your problem?"

Clovis found the button and sat back in his seat. "Something doesn't sound right about Daddy Two shooting himself."

"And why should I give a damn?"

Clovis said, "Cause he was the father we ended up with. I'm still thinking we should get a DNA test."

"Like here," called the voice from the window. The DQ girl held the bag of food as if she didn't really want to be touching it. "Here yew go."

As they returned to I-20, Clovis watched Bubba pull the Dilly Bar from the bag. Clovis accepted the nippled ice cream treat without comment. He stared out the passenger window and took a bite.

The road from Fort Worth to Solomon looked less familiar and less welcoming with each trip home. Stretches of highway once surrounded by low brush expanding and dissolving into distant tableland had been replaced by Wal-Mart and Petsmart and Kwikee Mart. If the ritual sprawl of corporate commerce wasn't enough to ruin the view, then all the enormous billboards blotted out the rest. Who wanted to see a European-looking model with no shirt, shaved pecs, and the top button of his jeans undone staring down at you from one hundred feet? Was he selling jeans, cologne, or waxing?

The fish sandwich sat untouched between them. Clovis looked for Bubba's rakish grin to return but it didn't. The rest of Bubba's good-old boy look though was in high gear today: the lizard skin boots, a turquoise Bolo tie, pressed Levi's, and his latest gimme cap, this one promoting some gambling service called *West Tex.* In appearance, Bubba seemed unencumbered by worry, disengaged from their past. Clovis knew better.

Blood is truth and nobody could deny Bubba and Clovis were brothers. Not close to identical but they shared enough features–their mother's olive skin, her hard-edged facial structure, the head of thick, coal black hair–to provide a physical link. But not even a hint of a resemblance to Daddy One or Daddy Two.

He watched Bubba unwrap the thin, oily paper from the fish sandwich and scoop some of the greasy mess into his mouth with one fluid motion while steering the truck with his knees.

Though the lining of their relationship had frayed in places, unraveled and worn thin over the years, the bond remained strong. Yeah, thought Clovis, an occasional button might pop off, but they still looked out for one another. From all the years of living with Daddy Two, they had learned to protect an exposed flank or guard a flaw in the other's stitching, covering a hole in their brother's coat.

Bubba chewed for a moment, then rolled down the window and spit the bite out.

"Shit!" He flung the food back onto the seat.

"What the..." Clovis started.

"This is a goddamn Hunger Buster."

Clovis lifted the sandwich and took a bite.

"No (he chewed)...no (he swallowed)...it's a Dude."

"Like I *care* which one it is?" Bubba yelled. "Like I really *care?*"

14

TO THE LIVING

Though Mazel had never attended the reading of a will, she watched enough TV series like *Murder, She Wrote, Matlock,* and reruns of *Perry Mason* to know what to expect. She sat quietly next to Clovis, reading the degrees and awards filling the wall behind Darval Rash's desk. Flicking a Bic and firing up a Lucky Strike Light, she read the plaques and certificates that encircled them–the attorney's life defined through each plastic frame.

Many items had nothing to do with law whatsoever. Plaques for third place finishes in the Texas State Open Softball tournament hung next to certificates acknowledging completion of cheesy-sounding seminars such as:

Acquiring Legal Clients: Beyond Ambulance Chasing
Who to Sue: Extraneous Sources of Liability and
Creative Techniques to Tap Them.

Mazel could not find an ashtray so she tapped the ashes into her hand and nonchalantly scattered the remains onto the shag carpet at her feet.

"Clovis, are you doing alright?"

"Yeah."

Mazel's attempts to communicate with her son since yesterday's funeral continued to be met with monosyllabic, perfunctory responses.

"You act like your dog ran away or something," she said. "What's bothering you?"

"If I knew that, then nothing would be wrong."

"What?"

"I'm not feeling anything, Momma."

Mazel's gaze fell to an ashtray on a bookshelf behind Darval Rash's desk. She rose to get it and said, "It's been a busy couple of days with the funeral and all. There's nothing unusual with feeling kind of blank right now. Don't make yourself miserable about it."

"But a son should feel something when his father dies, don't you think?"

Mazel touched the hair hanging over his collar. "Listen, we were like Muzak to him–always there but never noticed much. He wanted his life to look like a Norman Rockwell picture, but he didn't really want to live that life. I don't know why. I don't think he ever wanted to know either."

"Sorry to be whining, Momma. Shoot, if anybody's got a right to complain, it's Bubba. It's just like Daddy Two to leave him out of the will."

Mazel hesitated to respond. Richard had given his attention, as weak as it was, to Clovis. Sometimes she would watch Richard yell at him for some little thing and notice Bubba peeking around the corner with almost a look of envy, maybe wishing it was he receiving the tongue-lashing instead of his brother. Then when she reached out for Bubba, he would flip on his protective shield and who she hugged was not the hurting boy but the hard little man.

Darval Rash burst through the door at full gallop.

"Clovis! How the hell are you, son? Long time, no see."

Clovis rose slowly and took Darval's outstretched hand. To Mazel, it appeared they didn't shake so much as squeeze.

"Hey," Darval said to Clovis. "Before I forget it, Oat said to stop by his office before you head out."

"Did he say why?" Mazel asked.

"Who knows? Oat's getting so senile, he's probably forgot by now." Darval looked from one to the other and back again. "Sorry to be running so late. I got litigation coming out of my ears."

And bullshit running out of your mouth, Mazel thought.

"I'm so sorry for your loss," Darval said, changing his tone in an instant from down-home-good-old-boy to a cross between preacher and funeral director. "I'm sorry," he continued, "would you mind putting out your cigarette? They just changed this place to a no smoke facility."

You little dick, she thought. Why, I remember when you used to dunk doughnuts in sewer water and eat them. She held her tongue, though, not being certain what legal problems he could throw between her and whatever was coming to her.

She stubbed the Lucky out between the "P" and "J" of the "PJ's Gentleman's Club" on the ashtray and placed it on the desk.

Darval Rash addressed Mazel directly. "We'll roll the money you owe me on those divorce consultations into this final will and testimony visit. No rush but Clarissa will have the total on your way out."

Clarissa Weatherby's skinny frame filled a good portion of the tiny waiting area outside. She acted as Darval Rash's collector and was impossible to dodge in the cramped office.

"It must be difficult to suddenly be alone, without a husband, without a father, after all these years." Darval cocked his head, striking what looked like a much-practiced sincerity pose.

"Anyway," he continued, "life goes on. And to the living go the spoils."

He opened the folder on the middle of his desk and read silently for a minute.

Mazel meanwhile read the BA degree above Darval's head. Texas State Tech Agricultural & Military College. It was the all-purpose degree in Texas. Speaking with a Longhorn alum? Tell him, "I went to Texas." In the presence of some fanatical Lubbock native? You could say, "Tech's my school, too." Business meeting with an Aggie fan? Tell them, "I went to A&M the year they got off probation and went to the Cotton Bowl. Right before they went back on probation again." For many TSTA&M students the truth was more like, "I went to this crap college in my hometown, because no other school would have me."

"Well, I can either read all these 'wherefore's' and 'as to's" or tell you straight what's coming to you."

"Shoot," Mazel replied. The inadvertent reference to the way in which Richard died escaped her recognition until she noticed the odd looks from Clovis and Darval Rash. She felt her face redden.

"Mrs. McDonald, what you saw with Richard is what you got. No surprises here. No stash of cash hidden anywhere. No legal debts that you are unaware of. You'll keep your house, of course, and the car, and that's pretty much it. Except for the insurance money because I heard tell that Richard bought a butt-ton of it. Now that's something between you and the insurance company. But if you need some assistance, I'm sure we can work something out. Any questions so far?"

"Life insurance?"

"Yeah, evidently Richard was something of an insuraholic. I bowl with Horace Pettigrew on Thursday nights, and he said he bought him a big old hot tub with all those commissions."

"Horace Pettigrew?"

"Yes, ma'am, just go see Horace and get the ball rolling on this. It's the Pettigrew Agency down on the square. Now, any policy he bought in the past two years won't pay because of the suicide and all. But anything older than two years, they've got to pay out."

Mazel remembered a small life insurance policy they bought together when the boys were in diapers, but that was it. Nothing else and the amount of that policy was only about three thousand dollars. This news went against everything she understood about Richard McDonald. Why would he be so generous after death when he had been so stingy with her when he breathed?

"Clovis." Darval turned to him with a wicked grin. "I envy you, son. Your daddy left you the wrecker business."

This pronouncement caught Mazel by surprise.

"Richard said he was going to turn it over to his brother," Mazel said.

"Well, he and Punches had this big to-do a few months back. Richard marched right over here and took Punches out of the will–just like that."

"But Punches is still over there," Mazel said. "He went back to work right after the funeral."

"Yes, ma'am, he is. To be honest with you though, I'm surprised he didn't quit. Richard cut his pay when all the fit-hit-the-shan. I hear he got awfully irate about the situation."

Clovis leaned forward and folded his hands on Darval Rash's desk. "Can you handle the sale for me?"

"The sale?" Darval asked. "Richard said you knew the business, said you used to work for him."

"Yeah," Clovis said, "Bubba and me worked there for next to nothing. Since high school and through college. He didn't even pay us minimum wage. Said we'd been living off his sweat since we were born."

"Why don't you take a look at it first?" Mazel asked. "You know the work. You know the business."

"I heard it's a real cash cow," Darval added. "But if you want to sell it, I'll sure enough handle it for you."

"We'll get back with you on that," Mazel said.

"I'm going to sell it," Clovis answered.

Mazel turned to Darval. "Is this it? No complications or anything? Nothing you or any other lawyer can do to deny what's coming to us?"

Darval shook his head from side-to-side. "Well, ma'am, I guess anything's possible, but I'd say that you're on solid ground here. I don't think Punches will try anything, not with his felony record. Don't know of anyone else who would contest anything. He didn't have any other children, did he?"

"I'm pretty sure he didn't."

"Then, I think you two are good to go. Now you'll need some advice on handling that insurance money. My brother and I run a very successful money management company. Unbelievable returns on your money. Here's a brochure."

"Good," she said, reaching into her purse for a cigarette. "I'll take a look at it." Lighting it, she inhaled deeply and blew a lifetime of frustration across the desk as the smoke dispersed around Darval Rash's face.

"What are you going to do with all that insurance money, Momma?" asked Clovis.

Mazel took Clovis' hand as he helped her to her feet. She remembered a family life that she dreamed of but that never came to be. She remembered her hallucination in the delivery room so long ago and the perfect place that they never got to visit. The smile on her face felt good for a change.

"I'm going to Disneyland."

ABSENCE OF MOTIF

"**T**hey's an absence of motif," said Sheriff Oat Smith, speaking from the side of his mouth opposite the chewed and deteriorating stogie. "Tha's the first thing alerted me it wasn't no suicide."

Clovis attempted to follow Oat's thinking but was having a difficult time relating Daddy Two's death to some ungratified desire to find a recurring, salient thematic structure.

"What?"

"Absence of *motif*," Oat responded impatiently. "Of all people, your daddy had no reason to splatta his brains all ova the TV set. He had eva thing goin for him."

Clovis began to follow the Sheriff's rhythm of speech and comprehend his convoluted thought processes. "So, based on this absence of motive theory, you're ruling this a homicide?"

"Yep, among otha things."

Oat suddenly appeared distracted. He took the raggedy remains of the cigar from his mouth and placed it in an ashtray that Clovis noticed displayed the emblem from PJ's Gentleman's Club.

Clovis attempted to get the conversation back on track. "What do you mean, other things?"

Oat turned his back to Clovis and walked to the file cabinet beside his desk. He opened the top drawer and pulled out a fresh pack of Roi-Tans. After a couple of failed attempts, he finally unwrapped the box and then, one of the cigars. Looking away from Clovis, he said, "As I said before, they's otha things to consida."

"Like what?"

"You know, some of them things is police bidness, on-going investigation, confidential and all."

Clovis grew weary of Oat. "Look, as his son I have a right to know. Just tell me why you think he didn't kill himself. What makes you think somebody might have shot him?"

Oat bit off the end of the Roi-Tan, spit it in the trash can, stuck the rest in the center of his mouth, lit it, and rolled it to the side of his mouth. Blowing out the first plume of smoke, he looked to the floor and mumbled, "Absence of weapon."

"Say what?"

"They's an absence of weapon. No gun by his chair or in the room, not nothing no wheres."

Clovis took a step closer to Oat. "Are you telling me that you thought it was a suicide, even though there wasn't a gun lying around?"

"We ova looked that detail, that's all. When I had a chance to sleep on it, well, we figured it all out. That and the bullet direction."

"What do you mean, bullet direction?"

"Well, to splatta like he did all ova the TV set..." Oat parted his hands in an expansive motion, "...he woulda had to twist his arm all the way to the back of his head. Like this." Oat could get his arm to move only so far. "You know what I mean?"

Clovis nodded to keep Oat talking.

"Anyways, I neva seen nobody shoot theyselves like that befo. Now some folks take great pains with how they put a bullet through their skin. Some a them is creative about it. But yo daddy wasn' like that. I mean, he wouldn' go to all that trouble, you know?"

"Any idea who might have killed him?"

"Nothin yet, but we ah workin on it. We surveyed the funeral yesterday. Got some leads to work on there."

"Sheriff, other than you, nobody attended but family and not even a good percentage of them were there."

"Well, family usually done it is my experience. Money, un-conjugal humpin, or just livin with somebody you can't stand fo too many years. Hell, Amy Talbott blew George's nose away just cause of his snorin. Family is dangerous stuff."

Clovis discounted Oat's family theory and instead tried to gather a list of suspects in his mind, but realized he'd been away from Solomon too long. He didn't know the day-to-day life here anymore. Didn't know who pissed off who last Friday night at the football game, or who ran away with Mrs. Armstrong, the IGA manager's wife, or even who hated Daddy Two enough to blow his brains out.

"But if I was puttin a list of suspects together, I'd start off with that piece a shit brotha of his."

"Why?"

"Cause Punches is a piece a shit, that's why."

Seeing that line of questioning reaching a rapid dead end, Clovis tried another tactic. "Who else?"

"Vic Tannyhill, maybe," Oat answered. "Ya daddy owed that man a pile a money."

Clovis nodded his recognition of the name. A Tannyhill had made book in west Texas ever since the days of The Four Horsemen and The Galloping Ghost.

"I don't think a day went by," Oat continued, "Richard didn't have a coupla bills riding on a game. He was a addict, but he couldn't win a two-headed coin flip. He owed Mr. Tannyhill fo' years, but the man let him keep playin. Maybe Mr. Tannyhill had enough. I don' know."

"So, Punches and Vic Tannyhill. Anybody else?"

Oat tongue-flipped his Roi-Tan from one side of his mouth to the other a couple of times. "Well, this is kind of a touchy subject." He took the cigar out of his mouth and looked at it as he spoke. "Yo' momma is said to be comin into a lot of insurance money. And then there's you inheritin the wrecker bidness. And

I can't rule out ya brother since I heard tell he was seen around these parts the day Richard got shot."

That last bit of news jarred Clovis. He stood and then sat back down.

"Of course, ya daddy was partial to some strange eva once in a while. He liked them young girls in their twenties. Did ya notice that girl about your age at the grave site? She was hangin' back aways like she didn' wanna be seen."

"No." Clovis shook his head. "No, I didn't see anyone like that. Look Sheriff, I need to get going." He took a couple of steps toward the door.

"Wait, hold on there just a minute, son." Oat followed Clovis and spoke in a different voice, quiet, almost conspiratorial. "I was needin to talk with ya bout our relationship." Oat whispered though nobody else was around. "A big part of ya wrecker bidness come from the county contract, you know. Me and Richard had this little, uh, this little deal worked out. What they call a gentleman's agreement. Benefits us both real good and all."

"Can't you work with Punches on that? I'm leaving the day-to-day work in his hands for now. I'll probably end up selling it."

Oat's eyes widened and a look, fear combined with rage, came through his glare. "You don' want to do that, boy." Oat switched the cigar to the other side of his mouth. "This is a real little money maka. You don' wanna throw away something as sweet as this, do ya?"

"Why can't you just talk to Punches about whatever it is you need?"

"I can't talk to that pig-headed piece a shit!" Oat was no longer whispering. "You and me, we need a couple of hours, face-to-face, before ya go deciding to sell."

Clovis saw no reason to agitate Oat any further. "Alright, Oat. I'll be back here next week to check on Momma. We can sit down then."

Oat stepped back from the door and smiled. "There you go. Don' go jumpin to get out of somethin' before you know if ya gonna like the water or not. This might just be the opportunity ya been lookin' to find. Richard said you ain't settled into no kind a real job. He said you was throwin' a paper route or some such."

"I manage newspaper carriers," Clovis corrected.

"Whateva," continued Oat. "Solomon ain't so bad, son, especially if you got the right friends. And havin the Sheriff as your friend is a real good thing. I still remember the night you boys came out the chute. Neva seen nothing like it befo' or since. Shoooweee."

The last thing Clovis wanted to hear was another rendition of his and Bubba's birth. He interrupted Oat with a good bye and a wave.

Oat Smith might appear to be a good old boy and somewhat addled, but Clovis sensed some danger about the man. So, he and Daddy Two had been doing some kind of business together, something that sounded more than a little shady. And Oat just exhibited a flash of a flame-on temper. Clovis added one more murder suspect to Oat's list–Sheriff Oat Smith.

1991
Mid-September

The rest of the world is sweeping past us. The oil and gas of the Texas future is the well-educated mind. But we are still worried about whether Midland can beat Odessa at football.
                    Former Texas Governor Mark White

16

MY DEFENSE IS SWIFT AND SURE

Vic Tannyhill's eyes remained closed as his hand explored the nightstand. First, he searched for the remote which was found next to his laptop. Pressing 'disc select' twice, he paused, hand in the air, anticipating the opening line from Puccini's *O mio babbino caro*. As the voice of Kiri Te Kanawa rose, lovesick and plaintive, Tannyhill again rummaged along the top of the mahogany table.

When he came into contact with the weekly schedule of football games, he lifted it and brought the well-worn pages to his chest like a child hugging a teddy bear. Insights came more naturally to Tannyhill during the first hour of wakefulness even if it was already past noon. He would need all the inspiration and knowledge he could muster to pick some of the matchups this coming weekend.

Te Kanawa became Tosca and as she quibbled with God, Tannyhill recalled the tragic news of last evening. The 76ers were considering a move from Philadelphia to Mexico City. How dismal the state of sports and, in particular, the shifting of teams from one location to another. The only allegiance owners felt compelled to maintain was an illogical attachment to the team name.

So appropriately named teams such as the New Orleans Jazz were moved to Salt Lake City and became the Utah Jazz. It made no sense. Syncopation and dissonance were nonexistent in Utah. In fact, they were probably against the law. Most people got over the incongruity, grew accustomed to the name and never gave it another thought. Tannyhill though could not abide the situation. He was a purist.

Enough already, he thought. Time to get to work.

Minnesota +7 ½ at Syracuse. As long as the spread didn't go to 9, this was a no-brainer. Syracuse minus the points.

Virginia –10 ½ at Navy. Navy would certainly lose, but the spread was too close to call. Besides, who cared? Tannyhill didn't care much for these ill-conceived, non-conference games.

When you got into the meat of the season, trends had time to develop and decades-old rivalries came into play. Dartmouth, his own alma mater, versus Princeton. Texas-Oklahoma, Georgia-Florida, Ohio State-Michigan: these were games of tradition. Players harbored grudges and retribution carried from year to year, from class to class, from generation to generation. In some manner, a late hit by Oklahoma in the 1964 game was still being avenged by the Longhorn class of '91.

Who cared about Southern Mississippi at Indiana? But there would still be idiots out there betting hundreds and thousands of dollars on the outcome.

Gamblers were such degenerates. He had known guys who pawned their wedding ring, hell, pawned their wife's engagement ring to keep playing. Some embezzled from their work. Others hit on family and friends for loans that were never repaid. They would offer Tannyhill bizarre collateral: a prize hog named Boy Buford who blue-ribboned at the Texas State Fair, a lifetime of free chair massages from Harolyn's House of Nails, a Remington sculpture, a Remington 12 gauge, stock options, insurance policies, baseball card collections and a fully-functional, operating chinchilla ranch.

The phone rang, disturbing his concentration on the 52-point spread between Nebraska and Pacific. Did Pacific even have a football program? He lowered the volume of…it was now Verdi.

"Tannyhill," he answered.

"I'm getting complaints already," said Margo Chandler. "Are you going to pick tonight's game or not?"

"Oh, Christ. I can't get used to these Thursday night games." He looked to the schedule and read: Colorado State –17 ½ at TCU. How sad the state of Texas football. "I'm sorry, Margo."

"This is a business like any other," she said. "You're making a pretty penny off my 900-lines, but I won't hesitate for a minute to cancel the lease if you keep screwing up."

"Why Margo, that's not a threat, is it?"

"Just a fact, Vic. Your call volumes are down lately."

Tannyhill didn't believe Margo Chandler would actually pull the plug on his 900-line. Above all, she was a businesswoman, a millionaire, an entrepreneur, a visionary who had foreseen how men would pay for their vices over the phone. Sex came first, then gambling. Now she was tapping into the female market with psychics and personal advice consultants. He admired how Margo had built her empire.

"As soon as we hang up, I'll make the call. I am truly sorry for any inconvenience this may have caused you."

"Forget about it. Just circle Thursday on your calendar from now on. Who are you picking tonight, anyhow?"

"Bartering services, are we? I'll give you my pick if you give me a few minutes of your orgasmic sex talk."

"You couldn't handle a few minutes." Margo hesitated a few moments before emitting a sultry, yet emphatic, "Fuck you, Vic."

The line went dead in Tannyhill's ear. He liked Margo, always had. An undefined attraction flickered below their telephone exchanges like a malfunctioning pilot light. Problem was neither made any effort to crank up the flame.

Restoring the volume of Verdi, Tannyhill looked again to Colorado State at TCU and shook his head. He didn't like the game, but it was the only game in town, so to speak. He had no choice but to choose. Te Kanawa became Leonora from *Il Trovatore* singing, "Timor di me?"

Why fear for me? My defense is swift and pure!

He raised the phone from the nightstand, dialed his 900-service, and took a couple of deep breaths before recording. No longer did he carry the calm, reserved air of an Ivy Leaguer. Tannyhill assumed the persona for which he had become known by gamblers from coast-to-coast: West Tex.

"Hiddy hi there, friends and neighbors. This is your old buddy, West Tex. Listen up close now 'cause we're going to win us some cash tonight."

His voice rose in volume and pitch. The cadence of his speech was reminiscent of a strip joint hawker on Bourbon Street.

"I've started this season *on fire*, folks. My solid gold picks are 5-and-1 over the first three weeks of the season and my Bust Your Bookie Extravaganza is coming up this weekend. So call 1-900-WIN-SOME. Only twenty-five bucks for some surefire winners. Call it now and I do mean now. You've got to take advantage of the early lines 'cause believe you me, if word gets out on what I know already, the line is going to move. *And move big*!

"TCU's defense has been up and down so far. But I've just gotten word from a very high, in fact the highest source, and the word is not to worry. I'm quoting now:

My defense is swift and sure!

"So, bet on TCU and WIN-SOME. That's 1-900-WIN-SOME. *"Go Horny Toads!"*

As Tannyhill clicked off the line, the energy drained from his body. He looked at the schedule again but could not focus his attention on Air Force at Northwestern. Sinking lower and lower into the bed, he slid the extra pillow from under his head and closed his eyes.

Parts of the work he found distasteful. The shilling tout for his phone lines, collecting for his own bookie business. Especially the collecting. Listening to the phony excuses, trying to project a "pay-me-or-else" attitude, threatening to phone their wives or hinting at something worse, something dark and sinister.

His father had maintained a powerful countenance, an imposing presence that combined with a natural orneriness to make the gamblers quake in his path and drop their wallets at his feet. Tannyhill inherited the business from the old man as well as his father's imposing physique. His cultured and reserved manner, however, were passed down from his mother.

Collections were not going well. His latest method of intimidation, unlocking his briefcase in the presence of a debtor to reveal a long, shiny pistol, had backfired. Instead of becoming frightened by the implied threat, the degenerates wanted to touch the gun, pass it from one hand to another like a football, look down the barrel, and point at objects.

Richard McDonald had twirled the gun from one hand to the other, behind his back and around his neck before finishing with a flourish and pointing it directly between Tannyhill's eyes. "I forgot to ask," Richard had said. "Is this *thang* loaded?" Then he laughed. Whenever Tannyhill felt a wave of guilt about his actions toward Richard, he would reflect on that derisive, disparaging laugh.

Other facets of his work compensated for these drawbacks. Like sleeping until noon or beyond. Like listening to *Tosca* any time of day or night.

Love and music, these have I lived for,
Nor ever have harmed a living being.

These ideals he strove to find and to live by. Music, yes, he had always lived with a Mozartian melody in his heart. And the idea of love had been there, was there still, but his life was devoid of a human object for his desire.

Nor ever have harmed a living being.

Drifting back into sleep, he could envision Richard walking up his caliche drive. Tannyhill's attempts to run away became increasingly futile as his feet sank deeper and deeper into the mushy rock and gravel around him. Richard stood now, set to strike a crushing blow. Then Tannyhill saw something behind Richard and suddenly froze in place. A statue, a baritone from Hell. He turned away in fear from the statue and faced his savior, an enormous statue-like figure himself, arms raised to the heavens in praise. In praise of another touchdown. The iconic mural overlooking Notre Dame Stadium.

"Thank God," he spoke in his dream, "it's Touchdown Jesus."

17

AN IMPRIMATUR OF SORTS

Somehow the crackle and pop reached Punches' ear before he experienced the pain. Kneeling had become a noisy exercise in misery over the past twenty years, so he practiced the move only when necessary. He rested his bad knee in the pea gravel and tested the bumper sticker in different locations, searching for the ideal spot. When satisfied, he peeled the back of the sign from its sticky adhesive and pressed it gently and evenly across the shiny bumper. Repeating the process three more times, once on each corner, he stepped back several yards now and then to admire his work.

Punches had previously placed stickers on the wrecker, but Richard forced their removal, yelled and screamed about defacing his property, ordered him to take a razor blade and scrape away the gluey mess left behind. But now, he no longer answered to his brother. The idea of putting his own signature, his stamp, what his ex-cellmate called an imprimatur of sorts, on Richard's prize possession filled Punches with a sense of justice, a symbolic righting of a lifetime of wrongs.

Richard said some folks around Solomon might take offense, maybe complain about what they called "sexist" bumper stickers. He said it might even jeopardize their exclusive contract with the county.

"You got to be careful how you express yourself nowadays," Richard had told him. "You can't say what you think or feel.

You've got to say what other people *believe* you should think or feel."

Maybe in other places, Punches argued, but not in the Solomon, Texas, he knew. Womens libbers didn't exist here. Maybe a few babes over at the college might get upset, but the chances were no one would call to bitch about it. Even if they did, who took those skanks seriously anyway? With Richard out of the picture and his nephew Clovis back in Fort Worth, Punches could be himself and express his vision of the world in a bold and brash manner that until last week had not been an option.

He limped thirty to forty yards from the wrecker and was pleased to be able to read the two front bumper stickers, which were the same as the two in the rear. The silver background highlighted the red lettering trimmed in blue that read:

SHOW ME YOUR HOOTERS

Punches couldn't resist a smile as he entered the office. If only one woman exiting the Piggly Wiggly or IGA would raise her blouse, then the cost of the bumper stickers was well worth it. And if he planned on staying in Solomon, he would buy some of those sexy, silver silhouettes to put on his mud flaps–all tits and ass and hair. The ideal woman.

The phone rang as if on cue the moment he closed the front door. Instead of answering his phone in the outer room, he pushed open the door to Richard's office and settled into the plush executive chair behind the cherry desk. He hit the speaker button. "Rebel Wrecker."

"You're not supposed to answer like that," spoke the prim and proper voice of Wilma Shenkman. "The name is McDonald's Wrecker Service. That's the name of your business and that's the name on our contract with you."

"What do you care what I call it?" asked Punches.

"What? You sound like you're in a well. Are you using that speaker phone on me again? I don't talk to people who don't have the common decency to pick up the telephone."

Punches lifted the receiver. "I said, what do you care what I call it?"

"At least show some respect for your brother. From what I understand, he didn't leave it to you to decide things around there, did he?"

No, he didn't, thought Punches. That lousy scrap of worm food. Just because Richard stumbled onto part of Punches' stash–a couple of high-end boom boxes and a nice collection of emerald and diamond jewelry–he had disinherited his brother. But not before sucker punching Punches with a kick to his right knee, the one that had been torn up during his stint in Huntsville, the one no prison doctor saw fit to repair. With that advantage, Richard beat him up one side and down the other like a rag doll.

Maybe Punches had gone too far in taking a couple of items from Mazel's jewelry box, but they were family. And family forgives. Family gives you another chance. As if Richard was some straight arrow. Not with the gambling. Not with the dirty sex talk Punches overheard through the office wall. Not with the county contract. Now there was some real theft.

So what if he liked to keep his hand in the game. Punches had acquired a great number of skills over the years in prison, especially from his cellmate, Judas Conroe. Not to put his knowledge and ability to use would be the greatest sin in the world. That's what Judas taught him. It wasn't as if he led a life of crime. He had a steady job. He just stole from time to time when the opportunity arose. Crime had become more of a hobby than a lifestyle.

"I'll call it what I want to call it, Wilma. Now, do you have some work for me or did you just call to give me a hard on?"

"You are a disgusting creature. There's a car burned up out on Highway 52 between Mac Bailey's place and the Grab 'n Go."

Punches didn't have time to respond as the receiver clicked in his ear. Though Wilma disturbed him with her objection to the name change, it excited him to be able to drive through

Solomon showing off his new additions to the wrecker. He turned on the answering machine, which continued to carry Richard's voice though he had been dead for more than a week. He started to clip a beeper to the top of his jeans but decided against it. What the hell did he care? If anybody wanted him, they could wait until he got back.

His mood remained high as he bounded across the lot and into the wrecker. Three gimme caps were lined in a row on the seat and though the white one showed grimy fingerprints, Punches thought it would only be appropriate to don the Hooters cap with the owl unraveling from the top.

From behind he heard gravel churning and bouncing around wheel wells. In the rear view mirror, he saw the sheriff's white Explorer. Oat's door swung open and closed just as quickly. The Explorer kicked up more rock and dust, circled the lot, and came to rest facing the opposite direction right next to Punches. This time Sheriff Oat Smith's window eased down.

"Too damn hot to leave this air conditionin'," Oat said.

Punches' stomach knotted at the sight of Oat. He said nothing.

"You know what I been thinkin?"

Punches saw no reason to let this opportunity pass. "I wasn't sure you could think there, hoss."

Oat's cigar rose as he smiled at Punches. "You an awful lot like ya brotha. He was a wise-ass, too. Only difference was, he's a lot smarter than you."

"He's a lot deader than me, too."

"Well, I'll be." Oat removed the Roi-Tan from his mouth and said, "You must be psychic or something. Maybe you should have ya own 900-number. Tha's exactly the reason I come by to see you. We need to talk some more 'bout your brotha's killin."

"You know, hoss, I don't really give a rat's ass. I got a burned up car to tow so if you'll excuse me."

"Well, I won't hold you up none. I jus' wanna let you know I'm figurin' it all out."

"Figuring what out?"

"I had me a emergency run that Monday night when ya brotha was shot. Gerald Smiley popped a few rounds at Miss Nedemeyer's Chow again. She thought one might a winged her ugly mutt so I had to get over there."

"So?"

"So, I had to pass right by your apartment on my way there. Guess whose vehicle wasn't at your apartment?"

"That's some amazing police work there, hoss. Guess whose vehicle wasn't at his home at the same time?"

"Whose?"

"Yours. So I guess we're both suspects then."

"I'm gonna nail ya, boy. Sooner or later, ya gonna screw up and I'm gonna nail ya ass to the wall. Nobody else had the motif."

"Jesus Christ, Oat. Half this town wanted Richard dead. The other half wouldn't piss on him if he was dying of thirst. Look out that window. Point to anyone. They'll have as good a reason for killing him as I did. Go jerk someone else around for a while and leave me the fuck alone."

Punches left the Explorer in the gravel dust and when the dust cleared in his rearview mirror, Oat was gone. But he would be back again and again and that made Punches nervous. Too many hidden things around. Even a fool like Oat might stumble over some of his stash.

According to Punches' revised schedule, he would be seeing Judas Conroe again much sooner than expected. His original plan to cut out of Solomon around the first of the year would no longer work. Oat might throw his ass in jail just for the hell of it. What Punches needed was to buy a little more time. If he could hold Oat at bay for a while, he could get out of Solomon and not empty-handed this time. Some big paydays were coming, but he couldn't get to them just yet.

As he reworked and edited the particulars of his getaway, a car horn sounded. From the opposite direction, a Subaru full of college girls leaned out their window shouting obscenities and giving him the finger. Punches shook his head and wondered what the hell the world was coming to. In a few weeks it wouldn't matter. Girls in Las Vegas would show him their hooters whether he asked them to or not.

18

PUMP FAKE

Mazel left more than ten messages with Horace Pettigrew's secretary before she began phoning his home. When his wife Jane finally answered one day, she treated Mazel worse than a telemarketer.

"I don't take kindly to some strange woman calling here," Jane said on the last call. "Only tramps call after men. Now don't you call here again. Do you hear me?"

What I hear is one crazy bitch is the first thing that Mazel wanted to say. Being desperate to find Horace, however, she answered, "As you wish, Mrs. Pettigrew. Have a nice life."

The trips to his insurance office became increasingly frustrating as Lorene, his secretary-slash-guard-dog could never give Mazel a time when her boss would be back or even there at all. "He's at a life insurance conference," was Lorene's first explanation for Horace's absence. The next time her excuse was a meeting with an out-of-town client, followed by a property and casualty insurance convention, and then a death in the family.

So, Mazel checked some sources, did a little snooping around, and as a last resort, started hunting Horace Pettigrew down. On Thursday night two weeks after Richard's funeral, she staked out the Spare Time Bowling Lanes, but Horace didn't show for his team's match with the Rolling Pins. On Friday she drove to his office again, his home, his mother's house, Sorrento's Bar and Grill, but no Horace. She wondered how an insurance agent could be so ubiquitous when trying to sell you a policy but so evasive when you attempt to cash that policy in?

On Saturday night Mazel drove to San Angelo. Texas State Tech Agricultural & Military College was going up against Angelo State, and she counted on Horace to not miss his son's game. As a freshman, Lance Pettigrew won the TSTA&M quarterback job and already in their first four games had led his team to two touchdowns, one more than they scored the entire 1990 season. Another White Buffalo winless campaign no longer seemed such a sure bet.

Arriving late, she paid five dollars for a general admission ticket and went to the concession stand where she spent another dollar-fifty for a long bag of popcorn.

"Do you have any butter?" she asked the blonde Angelo State student with the Chi Omega sweatshirt.

"It's butter *flavored*, ma'am," the girl answered with a tone of indifference.

"But that's not the same," Mazel said, looking into her bag. "Don't you have any real butter that you can melt..." When Mazel raised her head, the girl was several yards away talking to a boy in a Kappa Alpha t-shirt.

At the bottom of the visiting team bleachers, Mazel munched the semi-stale popcorn and searched for Horace Pettigrew. Not that she had ever seen him in person. Mazel thought that she could recognize him from the Yellow Pages ad. If that failed, she would ask around.

On the field, Mazel watched quarterback Lance Pettigrew throw a prayer with seconds remaining in the first half, and it was answered. Three defenders tipped the football, but it came to rest in the arms of the wide receiver who nonchalantly trotted into the end zone. With the extra point, Angelo State's lead had been cut to 33-7.

Accepting handshakes and slaps on the back about fifteen rows up stood someone who resembled the Yellow Pages ad that

Mazel held in her hand. Only this man looked older, heavier, and had much less hair.

Mazel slipped up the steps as the rush of fans headed out for halftime. She sat two rows behind the suspected Horace and stretched her legs on the empty bench in front of her.

The Angelo State Ram Band formed a rough approximation of the state of Oklahoma and began a salute to show tunes. The fans booed loudly not for the performance, which was actually quite good, but because it dealt with the hated state to the north. Midway through "Oklahoma!" the band director waved them to a halt and the crowd cheered. The band members quickly scattered along a single line stretching from one end zone to the other. Mazel recognized the tune right away as "One" from *A Chorus Line*. She enjoyed the band members high-kicking somewhat in unison. She listened wistfully to "Camelot" and "I Feel Pretty."

Since learning of the insurance money, Mazel dreamed of doing things that had been impossible while married to Richard. Indulgences and secret desires came to the fore – a trip to New York City, definitely Disneyland with the boys, dining at Le Bon Vivant, meeting a dark, brooding man who could dance the *fandango* as well as the *bourree*. To buy things for the boys, to bring them closer, to bring them home, to have the family she used to dream of, but Richard made impossible. Only one thing stood in the way–the missing life insurance check.

When the tubas opened "If I Were a Rich Man," she watched Horace engulf half a hot dog and thought it an opportune time to speak.

"Your son has one hell of an arm," she said.

"Why, thank you," Horace said, turning around with a proud, relish-rimmed smile.

"Hi. I'm Mazel McDonald."

The smile vanished when he looked into Mazel's eyes. He stopped chewing, coughed, coughed again, and his face contorted into a life-and-death panic.

After his wife, Jane, pounded Horace on the back several times, the hot dog dislodged, and he breathed again.

"Sorry about that," Mazel said. "I meant to shake you up but not to kill you."

Horace took a shiny silver flask from inside his corduroy jacket and poured a couple of jiggers into his Pepsi cup. His hand shook as he brought the cup to his lips and drank.

"Not your fault, Mrs. McDonald," he said, lowering the cup and then pouring in more of what smelled to Mazel like bourbon.

"So, you know who I am and why I'm here?"

"Well, I don't," Jane said. "What's the meaning of this Horace?"

"I can handle this," Horace replied. "It's business."

Jane addressed Mazel. "Are you the woman who's been calling the house? You better have a good explanation or I'll–"

"I said I've got this, Jane. Now let me and Mrs. McDonald hash this out in private."

Mazel scooted down a row and now sat directly behind Horace and Jane. "Why haven't you answered my calls? Is there a problem?"

Horace handed the flask to Mazel. "I think you best have a couple of swallows before I explain."

"Put that down before someone sees it," scolded Jane.

Horace took his wife by the arm and whispered into her ear. She glared at Mazel a couple of times as Horace spoke. But then there was one last glance before Jane rose from her seat and left. A look of pity that scared Mazel much more than the bitchy Jane.

Mazel put the tiny flask opening to her lips and allowed a trickle of bourbon through until it burned in her chest. She offered Horace the flask back, but he raised his hand in denial.

"You probably ought to hold onto that," he said.

"What's going on?" she asked. "Did Richard let the policies lapse or cash them out?"

"I do have a check for you back at the office, but it's not what you're probably expecting. I can give it to you tomorrow."

"Well, why did I have to drive all the way to San Angelo to find that out?"

Horace bloodshot eyes eventually rose to meet Mazel's eyes. "Because I'm a chicken shit. I would have eventually told you but…look, I'm really good at comforting people. I'm no good though at giving people bad news."

"But you have the check. Everything's alright?"

Horace grimaced. "Here's the thing. It's only for three thousand."

"When do I get the rest of it?"

"Mrs. McDonald, I'm sorry but that's…that's all of it."

Mazel did not respond. Her heart pounded louder than the incessant bass drum on the field. She felt nauseous, her stomach knotting in rage and loss. Her legs went numb, and she began to tumble sideways. Horace leaped for her before she fell and held onto her shoulders.

"Here," he said, one hand keeping her in place while he yanked the flask from her grip with the other. He eased her down onto the bleacher seat while at the same time stepping up to sit next to Mazel.

The Angelo State Ram Band strutted off the field playing their school song that sounded suspiciously like "Boomer Sooner." Mazel heard some fans start booing again. She finally blinked and Horace continued.

"You weren't the beneficiary."

"Say what?"

"Your name wasn't on any of the policies except that first one."

This time Mazel took the flask from Horace's hand and sipped quietly. She considered what woman in Solomon would be so conniving, so scheming as to convince Richard to do such a thing.

"Don't you have to inform me if I'm not on the policy? That doesn't seem right. I'm his wife. Don't I get legal notice or something?"

"I'm afraid not. Legally, it's his policy. He paid the premiums so he could do with the policy whatever he wanted. And that includes not naming you as the beneficiary."

"That stinks," she said, sounding more hurt than indignant.

Horace nodded.

"Who's getting the money?"

"It's not another woman, Mrs. McDonald, if that's any consolation."

Mazel could not be any more confused or tormented.

"Well…then…who?"

Horace leaned near her face, his breath surprisingly sweet. He took the flask from her and slipped it into the interior pocket of his jacket. His sigh sounded to Mazel as if filled with sorrow and regret. Though upset at Horace, her hands willingly slipped into his when they were offered. She welcomed the comfort of someone's touch. Someone who failed her but at least seemed to care that he had.

"Mrs. McDonald—"

"What on earth is going on here?" One hand on her hip, the other holding a half-eaten corny dog, Jane Pettigrew wore the look of a woman wronged.

"For pity's sake!" Horace hissed. "I thought I told you to leave us alone. This is business."

"It doesn't look like business." Jane stared at the place where their hands had, until seconds ago, been entwined.

"Jane, I told you what this is about. Now leave us alone while I do my job."

"But I—"

"Please don't embarrass Mrs. McDonald any more. This is a difficult situation."

Jane turned on her short pumps and descended fifteen rows in a matter of seconds.

As if nothing happened, Horace again took Mazel's hands into his and said, "If there was any way possible, I would tell you. I feel terrible about all of this. You deserve better. But I can't tell you the name. I could lose my license and my business if I did that."

There was little fight left in Mazel. Her voice carried no conviction when she said, "I could take it to court."

"It would be a waste of money."

"That's something I don't have. Three thousand doesn't even cover the funeral."

A shudder and accompanying chill ran through Mazel's body from top to bottom. She inched closer to Horace and rested her head against his shoulder. Through the opening minutes of the third quarter, Horace rocked back and forth comforting Mazel in a one arm embrace. The winds picked up and dried the tears hard onto her face.

Lance Pettigrew led his team to another score covering the last twelve yards himself on a pump fake and quarterback draw. Yet Horace Pettigrew did not cheer.

"I'm sorry to have interrupted your son's game for you," she said.

"Shhh, it's alright. I'm the one who's sorry."

Mazel saw the touchdown but didn't move. She just wanted to be held for a while longer. And who better to cling to than a man who hugged away tears as part of his job? She was in the embrace of a real pro.

19

WIN-WIN, LOSE-LOSE

From his prone position on the saggy apartment sofa, Clovis watched as a cocktail peanut arced midway between Bubba and the TV across the room. It held its trajectory, and the goober struck the television just above the bridge of a football player's nose. The thwack of salted nut striking the glass screen was not unlike a chunk of wayward gravel cracking the windshield on the Dodge Ram.

"Bingo! You stupid son-of-a-bitch!" Bubba yelled at the helmeted image.

Clovis closed the paperback he had been thumbing through for the past hour, *The 7 Habits of Highly Effective People*. He watched the University of Louisville quarterback with head down as the coach put on a show of histrionics for the ESPN audience. "What happened?"

"Give it to him, coach, give him hell," Bubba encouraged the vein-bulging, red-faced coach who looked to be well into his fifties. "Stupid moron. Can you believe that shit?"

"Believe what?" Clovis asked.

"Stupid son-of-a-bitch runs out of bounds on fourth and two. Game on the line, last chance, and he prances out of bounds so he won't get hit. What a chicken shit!"

A group of North Carolina players performed a strutting shuffle along the sidelines, filling their space with twists and turns and pelvic thrusts. In the animal kingdom, Clovis considered, gyrations such as these could be interpreted as mating rituals. He turned to Bubba who had shoveled a handful of pea-nuts into his mouth and was spitting them, rapid-fire, toward the television.

"Bingo, you puke," Bubba said between shots, his words gar-bled from the bulge of ammunition crammed into his cheek. "That's nasty. Look at that shit."

Clovis glanced again at the TV and then back to Bubba.

"I've seen you dance ugly when you're on the right side of a game. How much did you lose on this one?"

"None of your fucking business." Bubba threw a couple of goobers at the television.

Clovis placed a folded piece of paper inside the book to mark his spot and set it on the coffee table. "Well, it's my business if you break the TV. Stop chunking peanuts at it." He rose to a sit-ting position. "I don't want to see you end up like Daddy Two."

Bubba settled into his tattered recliner. "You mean dead?"

"I mean hooked on these stupid games. Do you ever wonder how much money he lost?"

"No, that was his business." Bubba aimed the remote at the television and changed sports. David Justice stepped into the batter's box for the Atlanta Braves. "Besides, Momma wouldn't have let it get out of hand. She knew how much money was com-ing in and going out."

Clovis went to the refrigerator and returned with a Pearl. He recalled what their mother had said, We *didn't do without.* Would she have noticed any irregularities? After all, she paid the bills and bal-anced the checkbook at home. She and Daddy Two kept the books for McDonald Wrecker. Clovis didn't know exactly how, but he knew some inspired accounting had to have been going on there.

"Oat said he couldn't win jack," Clovis said, "that he always owed Tannyhill money. That's why Oat listed him as a suspect."

Bubba kept his gaze on the game while laughing. "Tannyhill, a suspect? That's rich."

"Why's that?"

"He's all hat and no cattle," Bubba said. "He tries to come off like a hard ass, but it doesn't work. Not that he won't threaten you if you're late paying or whatever. But you can usually get him to come to some kind of arrangement. Pay him off over time, you know, or some other creative financing."

Clovis had been reticent to bring up the subject since Oat first mentioned it, but the timing seemed right now. "So, is that why you were back in Solomon last week? To set up a payment schedule with Tannyhill?"

Bubba looked away from the television and toward Clovis for the first time during their conversation. "We were both back there. For the funeral. What are you talking about?"

"You're on Oat's suspect list is what I mean. He says you were in town the night Daddy Two got shot."

Bubba bolted out of his recliner and returned soon with a cheap bottle of McCormick from the freezer. After downing a shot of the rotgut vodka, he said, "You'd think as big a place as Solomon is now, you could sneak around and get away with it. But no, it's like when we were growing up. Still that shitty small-town gossip and everybody knows your business."

"What were you doing there?"

Bubba poured another shot. "Well, I was up to no good, for sure. Remember Nancy Lee Graves?"

"She baby sat us a few times. Three grades ahead of us. Spanked our butts when we acted up. Way out of our league."

"Yeah, well, guess who got called up to the majors? And guess who's still into spanking?"

"Didn't she marry that quarterback, the one that took us to State?" Clovis reached for the shot of vodka that Bubba had poured and took a sip.

"Scott Austin," answered Bubba. "They've been married long enough now to be unhappy. I saw her in Sorrento's last Christmas. You and Momma were home trimming the tree while I was out working on some trim."

"You're going to get your ass shot one of these days," Clovis said.

"Don't worry. I'm careful about it." Bubba looked to the television screen and pumped his fists a couple of times. "Yes, yes, yes."

Clovis watched as two Atlanta Braves crossed home plate giving them a 10-3 lead. "I take it you're on the Braves?"

"When they win the Series, I'll get back what I lost tonight plus ten times more."

Clovis sipped at the vodka again. "You obviously weren't careful enough in Solomon. Somebody saw you."

Whenever Bubba concentrated his thoughts, Clovis noticed that he looked up and to the left, which he did now. "I just went to Dillard's Motel and never left the room for two days. Nancy Lee met me out there on Saturday. She'd go into town and get us food every once in a while, but I never even looked out the curtains."

"Did you check in as yourself?"

"Do I look stupid?" Bubba said with a grin. "I checked in as Peter Hardin, same as I always do. Get it?"

"What I get, Bubba, is that Oat Smith knows you were in town the night Daddy Two was killed. When did you leave the motel?"

"Nancy Lee was picking Scott up at the airport that night," Bubba answered.

"Do you remember the time?"

Bubba looked up and to the left again. Then he slapped his thigh and said, "I remember. It was exactly eight thirty-five."

"How do you know that?"

"Yes!" Bubba said, as Clovis saw another Brave cross the plate. "You know that neon wall clock at Sorrento's? The Lone Star Beer one?"

"Don't tell me you went in Sorrento's?"

"Jesus Christ, I'm not an idiot," Bubba said. "I went through the drive-thru."

***

During the next hour, Clovis returned his attention to the self-help book. He would glance at his brother occasionally, but Bubba never looked away from the Braves game, though his mind seemed elsewhere. When it ended and Atlanta's three-to-two lead in the Series was official, Bubba switched off the television.

"What are you still doing up?" Bubba asked.

Clovis stuck a finger in the book once again. "I told you yesterday that I'm taking some time off. Going back to check on Momma. You sure you don't want to come back with me?"

"Being that I'm on Oat's suspect list, no thanks. Then there's the chance I could run into Tannyhill. He'd be dogging me for what I owe him. Maybe Scott Austin is looking for me, too, for all I know. It's probably best that I keep my distance from Solomon for a while."

"I'll tell Momma that you couldn't get off of work," Clovis said.

"Yeah, what would fucking Arby's do without me?" Bubba pushed forward from the recliner and took the book from Clovis' grasp. "So, how do we stack up to these highly effective people?" Bubba asked.

"Not well."

Bubba thumbed through the book and stopped about midway through. "What's this win-win thing?"

"You try to find ways that both people in a relationship, whether it's business or personal, come out feeling like winners. Like if you're negotiating a deal, both sides should come out feeling as if they got something special out of the bargain. Nobody loses."

The only "harrumph" Clovis could remember hearing was in the classic "harrumph" scene from *Blazing Saddles*, but he believed Bubba uttered one now.

"That's the biggest crock of shit I ever heard," Bubba said. "You win or you lose. I bet on Louisville and I lose. Tannyhill wins." He moved back to the edge of the recliner and reached for more peanuts but knocked the jar onto its side. Goobers scattered across the coffee table. "I guaran-goddamn-tee you that if two people in a deal feel like they won, then someone *outside* the deal is getting fucked."

"Like what?"

"Like when we were born." The volume of Bubba's voice rose and his face reddened. "Like when Daddy One and Daddy Two each got a son. Win-Win, right? Who do you think got the short stick on that deal? How did you like being on the ass-end of every joke when we were growing up? How did you like hearing Momma called a slut? Two men in one day, huh?"

Bubba scooped a handful of peanuts off the coffee table, stood up, and threw them all at once toward the blackened TV glass. "How did you like being a freak? Ladies and gentlemen, step right in and see the twin sons of different fathers. Impossible, you say? Well, you're goddamn right. But they struck a deal, a Win-Win.

"Only no one thought what it would be like for us. For the circus-freak kids." Bubba tossed *The 7 Habits of Highly Effective People* across the coffee table and onto the floor. "When does one plus one equal zero? When you have two fathers, of course. It's never win-win. Winning always has to balance out with losing. If there's a win-win, there's got to be a lose-lose to make it work."

Clovis tensed as Bubba's tirade continued with one more scoop of peanuts fired at the blank screen.

"Daddy Two cuts me out of the will," Bubba yelled. "You inherit the wrecker business. I get a big bag of nothing. You win, I lose."

"I told you we would split the money if I sell it," Clovis said.

"*If* you sell it? Don't you mean *when* you sell it?"

Now was not the time to get into this, thought Clovis. Now was not the time to tell Bubba how much Clovis hated his job at the newspaper. Now was not the time to tell Bubba that he had been thinking more and more about going back to Solomon to run the wrecker business. Now was not the time to tell Bubba that he wanted them to move back home and run it together.

"Yeah," Clovis said, "I meant, when I sell it. I told you from the start that we were in this business fifty-fifty."

"I don't need your fucking charity," Bubba said, walking toward his bedroom. "I'll see you when I see you." With that, Bubba slammed his bedroom door behind him.

Clovis never knew what would set his brother off. He only knew that Bubba's anger lay so near the surface that on most days anything, large or small, could pull his trigger. The rage might fire in any direction or at any number of subjects. Rarely did Bubba express, as he did tonight, what Clovis contended was the source of all his anger. He understood the frustration, because it manifested itself within Clovis as emptiness. A hole, a feeling of nothing where a father should be. Because when all was said and done, Daddy Two never felt like a real father. He was like an actor with a role that he never really wanted to perform. He played the part but not well.

The door to Bubba's bedroom opened a couple of inches.

"You know," Bubba said through the crack, "I didn't mean anything against you."

"I know."

"That book reminds me of Al Pozzo and his bullshit book," Bubba continued. "If it wasn't for him, we wouldn't be…do you ever think how things might be different if he hadn't slammed into Momma?"

"Pretty much every day," Clovis said. Pretty much non-stop.

1991
Late September

I prefer a pleasant vice to an annoying virtue.
Moliere

20

AN AUTONEMIC REACTION

"You don't mind if I smoke, do you?"

Mazel drew hard from the Lucky Strike Light while a harsh countermeasure simultaneously rose from her lungs. The resulting cough expelled what smoke she had just pulled into her throat. It filled the space between her and Al Pozzo like a steamy morning fog settling along the highway.

"I'm going back to work at the university, full-time. Going to be a data entry specialist, class II. It's about the same work I did for you guys. Only this time I don't have to fetch coffee or put up with the fanny pats."

Al Pozzo's right hand continuously twitched. Slumped in his chair, he stared out the window at the lone mesquite.

"Remember Terwilliger? English Department? He pinched my ass every chance he could get. I smacked him back once, and that idiot thought I was coming on to him. For a bunch of smarty-pants professors, you acted like cavemen around us.

"No offense, Al. You weren't an obvious letch like the rest of them. But I could feel your eyes on me sometimes. And when you caught me looking back, you always had that *come hither* look. You weren't ever going to settle for one woman though, were you? Especially with a secretary who didn't know shit from Spinoza."

Mazel drew another puff from her Lucky but not as deep and not as long as the first. Smoke ambled to and fro between her lips like a confused tourist before she exhaled forcefully.

"Now why do you do that, Al? That's the strangest thing, that little sucking sound. I wonder what causes it."

Mazel turned her chair slightly in order to stare at the same scene Al looked upon. Her spine grew slack, her shoulders rounded. She assumed Al's posture, however unintentionally.

"I get pregnant twenty-some years ago, and they run me out of that school like I was nothing. And the law was on their side. When I say *their side*, I don't just mean the university. I mean the men that ran everything."

Mazel moved to the window, leaning against the wall next to it, and staring into the distance.

"You kind of went out on top, Al. Men were men and women were, well, less."

Mazel broke into the jingle from the old Virginia Slims cigarette commercial.

> We've come a long way, baby
> To get where we've got to today

"I say 'we' like I did something to contribute. I've just been standing on the sidelines watching things happen."

Mazel placed her hands on the window sill, closed her eyes, and felt the sunlight through the glass warm her face.

"I couldn't even get birth control pills back then. And when they finally made it legal, for the longest time only married women could get them. Barefoot and pregnant isn't how it is anymore Al. We even have a woman governor in Texas."

Turning around with her arms crossed, Mazel crouched slightly to look directly into Al Pozzo's eyes.

"Back then, they could fire a stewardess if she wasn't pretty enough any longer. That's what happened to Elsa when she turned thirty.

"You paid us like migrant workers, too. Terwilliger told me that the only reason women were in the workplace was to find a husband. So you paid us less, because that's the way you saw us. As less.

"It's better now than it was. But I'll still be making about seventy cents for the same work that you'd get paid a dollar for. Life is still a lot more fair for a man than a woman."

Mazel tapped another Lucky Strike Light from her pack and shook her head. "Oh, God, look who I'm talking to. Present company excepted, of course."

Mazel lit the cigarette with the burning remains of the previous one and returned to the chair next to Al Pozzo.

"There you go again. It's like you're trying to suck something inside you."

She smoked the rest of the cigarette in silence, staring out the same window as Al. Her thoughts slowed, and her eyes grew heavy.

"You weren't as enlightened a man as you thought. But you weren't a bad man either. You definitely had some charm." Mazel leaned to one side of the chair and closed her eyes, feeling sleep near.

"And you were at least decent enough to wear a rubber."

She yawned and sighed.

"Although the last time, I didn't much care for that French thing."

***

"Mizz McDonald?"

Mazel released Al Pozzo's hand and twisted around in her chair. "Manuel, come on in." Seeing Manuel Daza immediately lifted Mazel's spirits. The stout orderly had seen to Al's needs for the better part of his stay at the Tumbleweed. In recent years he would sit sometimes for extended talks with Mazel during her visits. Al Pozzo might be regaled as a genius by those locked into their lotus positions in the desert, but Manuel's mind often revealed a truer, poetic gift of insight and a heart-of-the-matter wisdom.

"*Gracias.* I'm disturbing nothing, am I not?" Manuel's English could at times betray him with some minor mispronunciations or syntax flaws, but the overall effect of his speech pleased Mazel.

"Well, Al here was just dictating his new book to me, but I guess we can take a break."

Manuel grinned and leaned against the wall near the door.

"Come on over and pull up a chair," Mazel said. "How's everyone at the Daza *casa*?"

"*Bueno. Muy bueno.*" Manuel spoke in a quiet, forced rasp like Clint Eastwood in a gaucho with a hangover. "I wanted to thank you for the bottle. Fermina and me always have a good time when we drink the mescal."

"Fermina," said Mazel. "What a beautiful name. And the way you say it. With such love, such affection. How long have you been married now?"

"Twenty-three years in November."

"Twenty-three years?"

"*Sí.* And I love her now just like I love her when we first, first meet."

"You are a special man, Manuel."

"She's a special lady, my Fermina."

"So, do each of you swallow a worm? There's still two at the bottom of the mescal, aren't there?"

"Not me. Fermina say she swallow them but she kind of *loca* sometimes."

"How so?"

"A couple of months ago, she fix the popcorn shrimp. The kids, she make them something else. I tell her that this the best batch of shrimp she ever make. She don't use the frozen kind. She do them herself. Anyway, she start to laugh when we finish eating. She have tears rolling down her face and for no reason. So, at last, she say, why don't you eat the worms? I say, what worms? She say, in the mescal, those worms. I say, I don't eat worms and maybe it's time we take you out to the Tumbleweed for a little rest. She gets up and go to the freezer and brings back a baggie. She say, that lady who gives you those bottles of Mescal, it would disappoint her that you don't eat the worms. She put the bag in front of me and say, I've been saving them. For what,

I say. And she say, for your popcorn shrimp. You just ate them. The best batch I ever make."

Mazel rocked back and forth, laughing in loud bursts until she had a couple of tears making their way from her eyes.

"Manuel, you are a lucky man."

"I don't know about that, Miss McDonald."

"You know exactly how good you have it. All these wonderful stories you tell me about your family. What I wouldn't give to have just one story like that."

Manuel stirred in his chair and crossed his legs. "Maybe your stories are just beginning."

"You're too kind, Manuel. With the boys in Fort Worth, what are the odds? I always wished we could go to Disneyland, you know?"

"Maybe you have stories that have already started," Manuel said. "You just don't see it yet. But the boys and you had some good memories. Like what you told me about New Year's Day and counting the pennies. Or the one who buys the trophies at yard sales. They have good memories of their *madre*."

"Being married to you must really be a trip," Mazel said. "Are you the all-knowing Oz at home, too?"

"No," he laughed. "No, Fermina sees me like any woman sees her husband. I can't do nothing right."

"I really would like to meet your Fermina."

"Maybe you come for dinner sometime," Manuel said, a wide smile spreading across his face. "Maybe shrimp night."

"Maybe not." Mazel picked up her purse and dug around for the pack of Luckies. "You don't mind if I smoke, do you?"

"It's against regulations, you know."

"I wasn't asking you, Manuel. It's just something between Al and me."

Mazel took a couple of heavy drags and the smoke came billowing from her lips. "Look at this," she said, pointing to Al's mouth. "Every once in a while, he starts with that little sucking sound. I just noticed it today. Never know when he's going to do it. Isn't that the strangest thing?"

Manuel rose slowly from his chair and then crouched directly in front of Al. He observed him in silence for almost a minute.

"Miss McDonald, would you blow some smoke straight into Dr. Al's face, *por favor*?"

"That's patient abuse, isn't it?"

"Just lean over and blow the smoke right in his face."

"Whatever you say. You're about as *loco* as your wife."

Mazel blew smoke from her Lucky Light into the silent face of Al Pozzo. Almost immediately the sucking sound started.

"Well, I'll be damned," she said.

"Is probably what they call a autonemic reaction."

"Autonomic?"

"*Sí*, that sounds like it."

"On some level, you think he wants the smoke?"

"Yes ma'am, I'd say so. His brain is no good but something in him still have the craving for smoke."

"Isn't that amazing? You know, I remember he used to like those European cigarettes, the harsh smelling ones that look like they're hand-rolled. Maybe I should buy some the next time I come."

Manuel sat back without a response. He looked out the same window and onto the same landscape that Al Pozzo had faced every day.

"What are you doing?" she asked.

"Just thinking."

"About what?"

"There's this boy in the other wing. He never speaks or show no feelings, you know? He's in his own world like Dr. Al."

Mazel blew another blast into Al's face and the sucking started again.

Manuel scooted his chair slightly and cleared his throat. "Well, they bring a man in last year with all these machines, fanciest computer I ever seen. He work with the boy, help him move his hands along the keys. The boy start to type words. He never say a thing before, but now he type a few words on the computer.

I was just wondering if maybe they could do something like that with Dr. Al."

"Doubtful. He didn't get any blood to his brain for quite a while after the accident. The doctors always said even if he had anything left up there, it couldn't be much."

"It just hit me, that's all. Must still be having visions from all the worms I've been eating."

Mazel placed her left foot over her right knee and stubbed out her cigarette with the bottom of her shoe. "Well, I guess it wouldn't hurt to check it out. Do you know what it's called or anything?"

"No, ma'am, but I can find out for you." Manuel moved slowly toward the door. "I better get back before someone misses me."

Mazel walked into the hallway with Manuel. She hugged him and started saying goodbye, but Manuel interrupted.

"It's good. All these years you visit Dr. Al, it's good. But it's not good, too."

Mazel took a step back and leaned against the wall. "How so?"

"You still feel the guilt. About many things. I think time has come to put this behind you. Or at least, put it more to the side."

"Why haven't you said this before? I mean, we've been friends for years. You could have said something a long time ago."

"Maybe you weren't ready before now. You are changing, Miss McDonald."

"Funny thing. I don't see any difference."

"But you are wrong there. You did see a difference–in Dr. Al. You been smoking around him for years, but today you notice the sucking sound. You have to pay special attention to see that. For years you never see it. But today, you do. Why is that?"

"Who knows? A fluke or something. Maybe he just started doing it."

"And maybe you've been blind to him do that all these years. Now that your husband is gone, maybe your eyes open up more."

"You've got a poetic mind, Manuel. Unfortunately, I don't. It doesn't work that way for me. Life just happens, one thing after another. Some good, most not so good. There's no great meaning to it all. It's not like a movie where you can skip past the boring parts. There's no music playing in the background to let you know what's coming or how to feel."

"The music *is* there," said Manuel. "Maybe yours is filled with static, but you got to try to tune it in better. It would be a shame to live the rest of your days with eyes closed, with your signal jammed. You are too fine a lady for this to happen."

"I'm the reason Al is in that room. The reason Enrique is dead. I married a bona fide jerk. My boys never had a father to look up to. Or a decent enough mother for that matter. Most everything I ever touched turned to crap."

Manuel inched closer to Mazel and bore his eyes into hers. "You have this." Manuel thumped his chest with a fist. "It beats so loud I can hear it." Twice more he pounded his rib cage. "You have a big heart if you would only listen. You bury it in guilt and regret, but I still hear it beating. Don't let your past ruin today. Listen to your heart. There is great music there."

Mazel shook her head, dashed away a tear and smiled. "That's funny. I'm trying to hear my music. And all I hear is…the 'Chicken Dance.'"

Manuel walked down the hallway, raising both arms slowly into the air. "That is a start." He flapped his fingers up and down and proceeded to sing the chicken dance while going through all its silly machinations. Mazel followed Manuel and watched as one and then another orderly joined in the dance. An elderly patient wiggled around her wheelchair, arms flailing about, screeching off key. Finally, Manuel took Mazel's arms and moved them around until she, too, repeated the increasingly rapid movements. She even began to hum along.

21

MEN CONFESS WITH EASE/TELL ME MORE

"**O**at?"

"Yes sir, Mr. Tannyhill."

"Oat, I need a favor from you."

Vic Tannyhill had figured all the angles, considered the risks, and calculated the odds for a couple of days before phoning Oat. What he intended to do would draw attention to himself and cause a great deal of discomfort. He no longer cared for leaving the house, period, much less having the entire population of Solomon watching his every move.

Still, last week's collections hit an all-time low and motivated Tannyhill toward a dramatic, almost operatic, moment. Maybe a second act aria of irony and twisted fate. Or maybe an ominous baritone.

What had come to trouble Tannyhill most was the lack of respect shown by his clientele. One gambler, down four hundred forty dollars, simply said, "Vic, I don't have the money, and I don't know when I can get it." The nerve. The unmitigated gall. Not even coming up with an excuse. The audacity to face him, tell him the truth, and not fear the consequences. Something had to be done.

"Word on the street has it that you're investigating Punches for the death of his brother."

"Yes, sir, Mr. Tannyhill. He had the motif and the opportunity. They's a couple a things I need to nail down before I arrest him, but he's the man."

"Good work, Oat," said the sole proprietor of the largest bookie operation in seven counties. "We sleep easy with you in charge."

Though Oat was almost fifteen years older than Vic, he always referred to him as Mister Tannyhill. Sheriff Smith and the Tannyhill family had a long and prosperous relationship though Oat had never been invited to their home. Unless he counted the time that Vic's daddy, Art, got upside down on Super Bowl III and told Oat to come to the house and arrest him.

For the most part, Art Tannyhill had stuck to the rules of the bookie business. When the gamblers would go heavy on one team or the other, Art laid off the excess money with one of his bookmaking friends in Lubbock or Fort Worth or Hobbs, New Mexico. The goal was to balance both sides of the ledger. If three thousand was bet on one team, he balanced the books so three thousand was on the other team, also. Bookmaking is a business that has little to do with gambling. The profit is the ten percent vig commission on the losing bets. The vig. The juice from the losers.

Yet, one time, because of his passionate dislike for Joe Willie Namath and the American Football League, Art Tannyhill let the scales tilt and tilt heavily against the New York Jets. So certain was he that the Baltimore Colts would demolish the upstart Jets, Art handled the risk and didn't lay off one dime of the $87,000 wagered on the long-haired, beak-nosed, know-it-all. The arrogance of the kid to actually guarantee he would win the Super Bowl. Art Tannyhill even took side bets as to how long Namath would survive before one of the old-guard Colts would lay him out on a stretcher.

By the time Joe Willie ran off the field waving his index finger in victory, the sixteen-year old Vic overheard his father on the telephone to Oat.

"Oat," he had said. "Come out here and arrest me."

"Do what, Mr. Tannyhill?"

"Come out here and arrest me tomorrow morning about ten. No, make that about noon."

"But why?"

"Because I screwed up, that's why. I can't pay my losses on the damn Super Bowl. The only honorable way out is for you to put me on ice for a while. I can't pay anybody off if I'm in jail, now can I?"

"No, sir. Goddamn Namath. They need to ship his kind to Vietnam."

"I'll have some evidence for you to pick up when you get here."

"But what do I arrest you for, Mr. Tannyhill?"

"What the hell do you think, Oat? Illegal bookmaking."

Judge Mickey Hargrove had sentenced Art Tannyhill to seven months, which would get him back in action for the 1970 football season. In return, Art wrote off the judge's debt while they commiserated in chambers about the buzz cut they both took on the Colts. Oat set up a fake transfer to a prison facility over in Lamesa. Art gave his wife and Vic explicit instructions that he not be disturbed during his stint in jail. No visits, no phone calls, no letters.

What Vic learned many years later was that Oat drove his daddy to Muleshoe, Texas, and into the waiting arms of a former Miss Muleshoe, Jenny Jo Tolliver. On his deathbed, Art came clean with his son about the "prison" experience, describing it as "the best seven months of my life."

Though Vic Tannyhill had been a perpetually stoned teenager at the time of his father's incarceration, he learned a valuable lesson about using the authorities to good advantage. Now, all these years later, he would ask Oat to use the power of the Sheriff's position to help him out of his own crisis.

"Oat, I would consider it a big favor if you would back off of Punches for a while."

"I don' understand, Mr. Tannyhill."

"I want you to consider me a serious suspect in the murder of Richard McDonald."

Tannyhill knew it would take Oat a minute or so for his request to register so he took the remote from the nightstand and punched "Play." In the two minutes and thirteen seconds of *Les Toreadors*, Oat said nothing. Finally, Tannyhill asked, "Oat, are you still there?"

"Yes, sir."

"Can you handle this?

"Are ya saying ya shot him, Mr. Tannyhill?"

"I'm not saying anything of the kind."

"Well, then, I don' get it. Why do you want me to investigate ya?"

"It's PR, sheriff. My image needs a boost around here and being the subject of a murder investigation would look mighty good right now. I want people looking at me like I'm…like I'm… this isn't easy for me to say."

"Spit it out, Mr. Tannyhill."

"Well, I want people to look at me like I am the…baddest motherfucker around."

"Well, if that's what ya want, I guess…"

"Look, I can provide you with some evidence. Circumstantial to be sure, but something to make people think I could have done it."

"Mmmmmmmmmmm."

"Oat, are you alright?"

"Yes, sir. I think I'm just having me one of them flashbacks. Like I lived all this befo'."

"Déjà vu?"

"No, thank you. What kind of evidence ya got, Mr. Tannyhill?

"What kind of evidence do you need?"

"Well, I guess, did you have some kind of motif?"

Tannyhill knew what Oat meant by motif. "Richard owed me more than anybody's ever owed me. It is almost embarrassing how far down I let him get."

"Ya got something on paper to show that?"

"Of course, if you think that will convince people I could have done it. I'll give you my tally sheets."

"Tha's mighty considerate of ya, Mr. Tannyhill."

"My pleasure. Anything else that would make me look guilty?"

"Maybe something like, uh, where were ya at that night?"

"Now you're thinking, Oat. Good question."

"Thank you, sir."

"I have a client who lives on Oak. That runs right behind Richard's house. I'll knock a hundred off his tab, and he can tell people he saw my car parked there that night. How's that?"

"Ya parked where?"

"On Oak, Oat. Oak."

"Oh, Oak. OK. Why did ya park there?"

"I didn't. But if someone places my car within a block of his house around the time of the murder, that sounds pretty suspicious, don't you think?"

"Well, yes sir, it does at that."

"Good, now we're getting somewhere."

"Yes, sir, we are. Uh, what kind of guns do ya own?"

"My father left me about every kind of weapon known to man. What do you need?"

"A .38?"

"Any particular variety?"

"A Smith & Wesson Lemon Squeezer."

"Got it."

"Been fired recently?"

"Does it need to be, Oat?"

"It would help."

"Consider it done. Is that about it, Sheriff?"

"Well, for now, that's plenty. Do ya want me to come out there and arrest ya now?"

"No, no, no. Whatever gave you that idea? I just want you to throw my name out there. Maybe set it up where I can come in for questioning. Something like that."

"Sure thing, Mr. Tannyhill. Would ya like to set up an appointment to come in?"

"What day do the Kiwanis meet at The Iron Skillet?"

"They moved it to Wednesday instead of Thursday on account of the chicken fried steak special runs on Wednesday. It's liver and onions on Thursday."

"Alright, Wednesday it is. We'll park down the street and wait for them to let out. Then, you'll drive me up in your Explorer with the lights flashing and me handcuffed in the back."

"But ya said ya didn' wanna to be arrested."

"I don't, Oat. This is all for show."

"Oh, right. Drive for show, putt for dough."

Tannyhill shook his head, closed his eyes, and questioned again the wisdom of entrusting Oat Smith to handle this delicate situation. "Can I quote you on that one?"

"Uh…"

"Now start dropping hints about me around town. Turn your entire focus on me, right?"

"Yes, sir."

"I'll see you Wednesday then."

"Mr. Tannyhill, beggin your pardon, sir, but can I ask ya one more question?"

"Sure, go ahead."

"Is it something in your blood or what makes your family confess to a crime every once in a blue moon?"

Tannyhill could almost hear the music swelling from the orchestra pit. *Alea iacta est.* The die has been cast. The aria would end with an open major.

"Oat, some things men confess with ease, others with difficulty. A work of art is a confession. And a confession can be a work of art."

"Alright then. Wednesday it is. So long, Mr. Tannyhill."

***

Tannyhill tightened the cinch of his bathrobe before lowering himself into the leather chair facing his expansive living room window. An ever-so-slight chill had nipped his calves when he ventured outside just after noon to retrieve the *Solomon Chronicle*. The lightweight seersucker robe with the slipping cinch would soon need to be replaced by the full-length terrycloth, which actually dragged the floor when he walked.

Only the weekly round of collections and payoffs could get Tannyhill out of his robe and out of the house anymore. Even if the gambit with Oat worked and the gamblers began to perceive him as one bad mother... Even if their attitudes toward him changed, Tannyhill entertained the idea of hiring someone to work the collections. He had brought up the subject to Richard's brother, Punches, a few weeks ago. If anyone knew the type of person who handled that kind of work, it would be Punches.

Though he loathed the thought of entering into a business relationship with a former criminal, the notion of leaving the comfort of his home week after week bothered him more. In the past couple of years with middle age staring him squarely in the face every afternoon, Tannyhill had come to a better understanding of himself. He now could better accept his own personality quirks and desires, which a short time ago might have seemed decadent or abnormal.

For example, if he were suddenly condemned to live the rest of his days within the walls of this house, the judgment would be a blessing. If he never set foot out of his home again, he would die a happy and contented man. True, this type of behavior is listed as aberrant in the DSM III and any right-thinking therapist would attempt a cure. But for Tannyhill, it looked, tasted, and smelled like Nirvana.

Only two things stood in his way. One, the damnable settling of accounts–collections and payoffs. The other, a bit more idealistic, dealt with his operatic yearning for love. He wished to maintain his separateness, his world apart, yet couldn't deny the want, the need perhaps, for someone to share his heart.

The telephone rang and he lowered the volume on Cassenelli singing "Tarantella" from *La Danza.*

"Tannyhill."

"I'm going to ask you straight up and I want a straight answer."

"Margo?"

"Don't try to sweet talk me, Vic. Just give me a yes or no, understand?"

Oh, no, he thought. Understanding just dawned on him. Christ, Oat had spread the word too quickly. Within the past hour. Tannyhill meant to phone Margo and tell her of his ruse, but Oat had jumped the gun.

"Margo, let me explain–"

"No explanation necessary. Just answer the question. And remember, I can tell if you're lying. The phone is a lie detector for me. I can read men like a book through this damn thing."

Why had he not called her right away? He didn't care that anybody else knew the truth but Margo, well, Margo...he was growing quite fond of her. They were talking on the telephone daily for longer and longer stretches, sharing increasingly personal details of their lives.

"Did you or did you not kill Richard?"

"Where did you hear that?"

"From a couple of clients who heard it directly from Oat Smith. They say he's got all kinds of evidence, even the gun you used. Richard owed you more money than he could ever pay back. But then, why would you kill him? He can't pay you anything now."

Tannyhill rubbed his forehead. If she knew the whole truth, he would have an even more difficult time explaining his way out of this mess.

"Listen, Margo. I didn't kill Richard. I swear to you."

The seconds of silence seemed like minutes to Tannyhill.

"Tell me again, Vic. I think my bullshit detector must have a glitch in it."

"I didn't kill Richard McDonald."

Tannyhill went on to explain how he had set himself up as a suspect, how Oat was a more than willing dupe, and how the entire story was a public relations move, nothing more. He apologized and said, "If I had known this might cause a problem between you and me, I wouldn't have done it."

"Maybe you're just saying all this because I might yank your lease. You're getting awfully rich on my 900-lines."

"No, honest to God. Margo, I think the world of you and not just because we're making a fortune together. It's more than that. Don't you feel it sometimes?"

Margo did not answer.

"I did not kill Richard. I thought you could tell if I was being truthful."

"Normally, yes, I can," Margo answered. "Maybe I'm wishing so hard for…you're telling me exactly what I want to hear, Vic. If you killed Richard, it would devastate me."

"What if I had Oat call and tell you what's really going on?"

"Does Oat even understand what's going on?"

"I'm so sorry, Margo. Please, please, forgive me."

"Ah, Vic, don't be so hard on yourself. We all do things like this. If we knew all the fallout to come, we wouldn't do half the shit we do. And believe me, I understand PR. Did I ever tell you how I got my business up and running?"

Margo reflected on her early years, how she created an entire paradigm, step-by-step, urging men to do more than breathe heavily into the phone. How she taught an entire generation of men to speak the unspeakable during sex, to say things to her they wanted to say to their wives but couldn't. How men paid more for her services, for phone sex, than they would pay for a prostitute. How it all began with one phone call to Richard McDonald.

"You do what you have to do for your business," she concluded. "I understand that. Believe me, I didn't want to think that you killed Richard."

The level of intimacy between Margo and him had seemingly reached a new plateau. In fact, he began to consider that she might be the one person in the world who could possibly understand his seemingly odd turns. His physical relationships had dwindled over the years due primarily to a lack of interest on his part. He preferred his own company to that of others and discovered over the years that he preferred his sex the same way.

An element proved to be missing, however. Connection. Connection with another human being. Emotional, maybe spiritual attunement with a woman. Yet, the price of connection would be the loss of another component of his life that he had come to value above all others–control. Once connected with another, then their actions would effect him and thus, the life that Tannyhill was now striving to attain, a self-controlled existence with minimal links to the one outside his expansive living room window, could no longer work. You couldn't control someone physically unless you strapped them down on the bed, which he had tried once but found totally unsatisfying.

"Margo, would you like to get together sometime? For dinner, maybe?"

"Oh, that's really sweet. But you'd be so disappointed. You haven't seen me for a long time, have you?"

"So? What does that have to do with anything? We get along great over the phone. Does it really matter what we look like?"

"Believe me, Vic, if you saw me now, it would make a difference in our conversation. I don't even like to go out to get the mail anymore."

"Me either."

A long pause ensued before Margo spoke hesitantly and haltingly.

"Vic, does it have to be in person? Couldn't we just…can't we have…maybe even a better relationship…if we allow ourselves…

you know, the freedom…being more true to ourselves…on the phone?"

An elegant solution, he thought. Unconventional, simple and true to each of their sensibilities. "Sure, we could do that. It's a logical step. I'm in the process of limiting my out-in-the-world exposure anyway. The phone, er, uh, situation sounds ideal."

"We think a lot alike."

"Yes, I think we do."

Yet, a longer, more awkward silence filled the line between them. Vic did not know how to proceed.

"What do we do now?" he asked.

"Vic, I haven't seen you in a long time. Tell me what you look like."

He started to answer truthfully, but then decided that Margo didn't need to know about the expanding bald spot on top of his head or the mushy softness around his middle or the liver spots mushrooming on his face and hands. All she needed to know was how he pictured himself, not the mirror-image. Yes, the idealized, operatic, on-stage version.

"That sounds good," Margo said, when he finished the description. "Now think about this carefully. How do you see me?"

Again, he took the reality-based image of Margo from his memory and combined it with fantasy – the lovely Violetta from *La Traviata* or Greta Garbo's *Camille*.

"You're good at this," she breathed seductively. "You're a natural."

"Thank you."

"Now, tell me what you're wearing."

Tannyhill could feel his face flush and the goose bumps rise on the backs of his arms. "What I'm wearing?"

"Let me help you get started. I imagine you're in a silk robe. Maybe you're sitting across from me and you know how silk is. It slides open just a bit when you uncross your legs. You're not wearing anything underneath, are you?"

He unhinged the sash of his seersucker robe and let it slide open.

"No, nothing."

"You naughty boy. You act like you don't know it's open, but you know. Don't you, Vic? You know, don't you?"

"Yes, I am being somewhat the libertine, aren't I?"

"Oh, yeah, baby. Somewhat. And something is going on under that silk robe. Something's moving in there. It's getting so…oh, myyyyy."

Tannyhill opened his robe completely and removed his arms from the sleeves. He yanked the Dartmouth t-shirt over his head and flung it onto the sofa. Standing without a stitch by the expansive living room window, he said, "Actually, it's a full-length silk robe I bought in Chinatown. Would you like to…would you like to touch it?"

"Oh, yes, baby. Yes, yes."

"Can you feel it? It's got fire-breathing dragons embroidered all over the place. And the big one so strategically located."

"Ooohhh, I love details, Vic. Details get me so…moist and runny."

"The belt is a yellow sash with royal blue lotus all around."

"Oh, yes, baby. Will you be my sho-gun?"

"Sho-guns were actually Japanese, you know." Tannyhill felt self-conscious but tried to say the word anyway, "Ba–by?"

"Ooohhh, tell me more, baby. Tell me more."

22

MOON GRAMMAR

On this night, Punches final one in Solomon, power surged through his body like the one thousand volts frying his cousin Ray a long time ago in Huntsville. Actually, the first thousand volts didn't kill him, so they had to ramp it up to thirteen hundred volts for seventy seconds, you know, enough so you can smell the skin burning. He tried to shake the last image from his mind as best he could. After all, Punches had killed two people himself along the way and could easily end up following in Cousin Ray's leg straps. Except that now the state of Texas was more humane and killed people by *legal injection* or something like that. Watching prisoners nod off couldn't be anywhere near as exciting as seeing someone stiffen and boil from the inside out. There's no accounting for taste, he thought.

A half-moon provided enough illumination for Punches to move boxes and bags out of his apartment, even when the occasional cloud would block and ration the light. He removed the interior bulb in his old VW van that he proudly called "The Shaggin Wagen," the name stenciled on the front and back of the rust and white vehicle. Only a single candle burned inside his efficiency apartment. Never in his life had Punches moved when the sun was shining. Only in the middle of the night with no one watching.

How different the night. It flowed smooth and clear like beer from a tap. There existed a nocturnal language with layer upon layer of meaning that only people attuned to the pitch of night sounds could comprehend. His partner, Judas Conroe, former cellmate and teacher, called it *moon grammar.*

Punches understood little about his nature, the whys and hows of the inner circuitry that caused him to act and react the way he did. "Reflection" was what he saw in the mirror when he shaved on Wednesday and Saturday. Even then, he concentrated his attention on the clumps of follicle growth to the exclusion of the face behind it. So inured was Punches to his own image, he would have a difficult time picking himself out of a crowd.

Still, one thing he knew with certainty. He loved the night: the darker, the better. During the day, Punches moved with an arthritic stiffness, unable to fall in step with the rest of the world. Daylight constrained Punches. His words disassociated from his voice. He suffered and endured through the hours of light before the real show began. Like refried beans, days were cooked and cooked again until all life seeped out of them, congealing into a mass of vegetated sludge.

Punches' knee throbbed on his final trip into the apartment, but the pain didn't hobble him as it did under the sun. He unzipped his pants, aimed at the candle in the middle of the floor, and extinguished it with a strong stream of urine that smelled of tequila and beer. He picked up two duffle bags against the wall–one filled with jewelry, the other with money–and closed the door without a sound. The tank was full and besides an occasional pullover for a piss, his next stop would be around daylight in Hobbs, New Mexico. He had alerted Judas Conroe of his arrival the night before.

"What one once did for God's sake," Judas had said, "one now does for the sake of money. The highest power now issues forth from the flow of green. Bring it on, Punches. Let's party."

Punches didn't pretend to follow half of what Judas Conroe said. Moon grammar, the will to power, beyond good and evil. Judas had a term for everything.

Instead of pumping iron like most other inmates, Judas had spent his days reading. And not law books. A con here and there would find *the law* in the same way others found *Jesus*. They both were obsessions for which that Punches and Judas had little use unless, of course, they were before the parole board. At that time, they invoked the Lord's name time and again without shame.

What Judas studied were the Germans and related Aryans. Schiller and Goethe, Heidegger and Nietzsche, Mann and Kafka. In two years of being cellmates, Punches had been subjected to an education in German arts and letters that would have been the envy of any university scholar. He lay for hours and listened to Judas interpret Teutonic thought and relate abstract ideas to their life behind bars.

Tomorrow Punches would need to cash in the jewelry and silver. Judas always handled the merchandise and split the proceeds with Punches. They were partners of a long-distance kind. Punches did the actual thefts, but the entire concept and planning had been Judas' idea. Just a few scores here and there. Nothing to alarm the sheriff or rouse the public to action.

When the West Solomon High Stallions had a road game, a good portion of west Solomon pretty much emptied. A team roster and a phone book were the only research materials necessary for the thefts. Judas had scoped out Solomon for a couple of weeks last year when the Hobbs police were sniffing too close to his operation there. He figured, and correctly so, that Oat Smith would never connect the two events–an away football game and the thefts.

"I like your little burg," Judas had said during his visit. "There's much potential. Bring in some better looking hookers, create a marketing plan for the drug trade, and *mein Gott*, the gambling operation here is run shoddily. It could be a gold mine. I hate to see such a lack of efficiency. It really *pisses me off*. You make the trains run on time or you cut their dick off. The trains will, I guarantee you, run on time."

Punches could start a vehicle quietly, which he did. He blended into the night, moving almost imperceptibly in the first hour of the new day. He watched for signs of Oat's white Explorer or one of his deputies' cars. Yesterday Oat had barely made his presence known, unlike the previous week when he seemed to follow Punches everywhere.

In his experience, this sudden stillness from the law was like the eye of a hurricane. Oat's temporary absence indicated to Punches that the shit was ready to hit the fan. He had been busted several times and on each occasion been lulled into complacency and carelessness when the police seemed to disappear and lose interest. They were a sneaky bunch of bastards.

He had never been busted at night though. And never when he worked alone. Only in the groggy stupor of daylight had Punches been caught and only through the ineptitude of one or another partner in crime. They would be apprehended, squeal so loudly the cops would have to cover their ears and wham!–he found himself spread up against a wall or down on the ground with the click, click, click of guns and handcuffs ringing in his ears.

Just bad memories, he thought. Nothing would go wrong tonight. In his rearview mirror he read the Kiwanis' WELCOME TO SOLOMON–WISEST LITTLE TOWN IN TEXAS sign. Punches relaxed a bit and found time for self-congratulations. He unzipped the money bag and dipped his hand into the stash of small bills. He had committed a number of offenses in Solomon, but the crimes against his brother were the worst–and the most satisfying.

Richard had given Punches access to a company credit card in order to buy gas or food or other small items they might need from time to time. What Punches discovered recently from Judas Conroe was that he could obtain cash advances with the McDonald Wrecker Visa card. Up to five hundred dollars a day. Of course, that uppity bitch Mazel kept a close eye on the one set of books, and the opportunity to embezzle funds never came about. That is, until Richard's death. And Punches knew where the second set of books was hidden. Every day since his brother's shooting, Punches had transferred funds to a company called

Rebel Wrecker–a dummy corporation he had set up with the long distance assistance of Conroe.

Five thousand dollars filled the bag on the passenger seat. Though Judas had advised him to only transfer cash every other day to avoid any chance of suspicion, Punches had cashed in every business day without fail. So, Judas' half of the cut would be one thousand two hundred fifty dollars, and he would never be the wiser. What Judas didn't know couldn't hurt Punches.

He had closed the Rebel Wrecker account earlier in the day and left McDonald Wrecker holding a five thousand dollar credit card debt. His nephew (if he even was his nephew), Clovis, was in for a big surprise. In a sense, Punches was just getting what he felt he should have coming to him all along. His inheritance.

If he hadn't threatened his brother after discovering how Richard was skimming money from the county contract, Punches would never have been written out of the will. All he wanted from the scam was a few hundred dollars a month. That wasn't unreasonable, but Richard went crazy. He beat the crap out of Punches. Richard threatened to kill him if word ever got out about the contract.

So Punches resolved to bide his time and patiently await whatever opportunity for vengeance would arise. Now, here he sat with a bag full of cash by his side and a brother buried a couple of miles back. A short stop in Hobbs and then, on to Las Vegas. Things were going so well he considered stopping when he got to I-20 and buying a new bumper sticker. Maybe an old standby like 1-800-EAT-SHIT or I'M TOO SEXY FOR THIS CAR. Sometimes life can be so good, he thought.

As soon as that notion dashed through his mind, he regretted thinking it. Never, never, never be happy about anything. It brings bad luck.

Sure enough, from behind and approaching fast, two headlights and what Punches imagined as the dark outline of a sports utility vehicle. Complete with something on top. Lights, maybe. He was torn between making a run for it or pulling over to take his chances. Reaching deep into the money bag, he pulled out his .38. If Oat arrested him for murder, he could make it stick and no way could he handle jail time if he knew he was never coming out again.

He looked for the darkest place possible to come to a stop. Long flat stretches of nothing faced him, dotted here and there by an occasional light or random billboard. He decided whatever happened would take place here in the Shaggin Wagen, not outside. The car lights behind him were moving somewhere near a hundred miles per hour and would be upon him in less than a minute. Easing down the window, Punches began to sweat even as the chilled north wind blew across his face. He started to check his gun and make sure it was fully loaded. Pulling it onto his lap, his other hand flipped the interior light switch, but it remained dark. He remembered then removing the bulb for his midnight move.

There was no more time. The brights reflected in his mirror and almost blinded him. Never, never, never think good things, he thought again. Slowing the Shaggin Wagen, Punches edged onto the road's shoulder and beyond to where it was darker still. To the hardpan, where nothing could take root, where living things go to die.

23

THE FOOD CHAIN

Clovis peeked through the small, square window of the jail-house door and saw two prisoners reading girlie magazines: one, a *Hustler*, the other, *Swank*. No wonder recidivism was such a problem, he thought.

The Solomon jail had become high-tech, post-modern. Oat Smith even opened one of the cell doors with a handheld remote. What surprised Clovis most were the clear Plexiglas walls. No more iron bars like when he had spent a couple of nights in there for the offense of making it to third base with Regina Phelps at Reese's Lookout. Not a crime for which someone usually winds up in jail unless Regina Phelps' father happens to be the mayor of Solomon.

He watched Oat give one of the prisoners a telephone, which they then plugged into the cell wall. The man with the *Swank* exchanged his magazine with Oat who first offered him a *Sports Illustrated*, a well-worn swimsuit edition. The prisoner shook his head no and pointed to another item on the cart–*Cosmopolitan*. How times have changed, Clovis thought.

As Oat walked toward him, Clovis made his way back to the chair where he had been sitting for the past half hour. Oat threw open the door and went directly to the ashtray on his desk.

Picking up the burned-out stogie he said, "If their goddamn attorney catches me smoking back there, they'll hang my ass for abusin 'em. Can you believe that shit?" He fired up what remained of the chewed up mess and blew out a couple of designer smoke signals. "And if I don' jump and run eva time they call, they'll have the ACLU after me. Sometimes I don' know if I'm runnin a jail or a fuckin retreat. Waitin on drunks and preverts. Shit."

Clovis nodded while Oat straddled the side of his desk. "Sheriff—"

"Oat, son," the sheriff interrupted. "Call me Oat. Did ya follow all this, son?"

"Well, sort of. I think what you described sounds an awfully lot like, uh, well…"

"Spit it out, son. Ya among friends here."

Clovis shifted in his chair, leaning forward near the front of Oat's desk. Speaking in confidential tones, something just stronger than a whisper, he said, "Oat, the way you explain the operation, well, it sounds like a kickback scheme to me."

Oat drew from his cigar for a long time. When he blew out the smoke, he did so in an exaggerated manner, an incredulous look crossing his face. He took away the soggy, shredded tobacco from the corner of his mouth and stubbed it out between the P and J of PJ's Gentlemen's Club. A no-shit-Sherlock grin appeared as he unwrapped a fresh Roi-Tan extracted from the pocket next to his sheriff's badge. He bit off the end and spit it into the trash.

"Now ya know, I can see how a fella might think that very thing when ya first hear it. But if it was a kickback, hell, I'd have to arrest myself. That kinda sounds like self-abuse to me."

Oat took two matches and struck them simultaneously. The cigar end blazed and he continued talking as smoke rolled out of his mouth. "Kickbacks? Kickbacks? Tha's something might happen ova in Dallas. Not here. What we do here has been goin on a long time. Since befo I became sheriff. We call it a MBA around these parts."

"An MBA?"

"Mutually Beneficial Agreement. That's how things get done out here in the boonies. The old-fashioned way. Ya scratch my nuts and I'll let go of yours. It's the way God intended the free market to work."

"But there are laws against it. It's not really, you know, a fair system."

"Fuck a bunch of fairness, boy," Oat answered with a sudden sternness. "Ya never get ahead in life waitin for somebody to treat ya fair. Ya grab what's open to ya. It's like the food chain, son. Little fish eat littler fish. And the big fish eats whatever in the hell it wants. It's survival of the fittest. Ya swim with the sharks or ya live like a ol' mudfish, waitin there at the bottom of the lake, neva knowin when some scrap is goin to fall your way. I figured, ya bein Richard's boy and all, well hell, I figured ya knew all this. Ya gotta look out fo number one."

"But where does the money come from? Somebody's paying for all this fake wrecker service you're billing out. Where's it come from?"

Oat stood away from the desk and looked straight down at Clovis.

"The money don' belong to nobody. Comes from public funds. It ain' like Richard and me's been stealin from anyone. Some comes from local money, some from the state, even some from the feds. I don' know where it all comes from. I just know it's there. And ya should get your share befo somebody else gets it first."

"But that's stealing, Sheriff. It's tax money. That money is supposed to be going somewhere else."

"Goddamn it, son. Problem is if I don' take that money, some other asshole will. Some swingin dick in Austin or Washington sees some unused money and they's goin to snap it right up from under your nose. Times are hard. Local funds ain' what they used to be. Big fish are swimming lower and lower to fill their bellies. Better to keep the money around here with you and me than let some slick piece a shit steal it away from us.

"Look here now," Oat continued. "I ain' tryin to talk you into something that nobody else does. Look around ya. Everybody's got a little deal on the side. It's Texas for Christ's sake. It don' hurt nobody. Anyway, McDonald Wrecker couldn't survive without the grease. When ya look at it that way, it's healthy for local bidness. It...how do ya say it...it *simulates* the economy."

A red light flashed on the wall behind Oat and a bell sounded overhead.

"Goddamn whiny bastards won't leave me alone. Excuse me while I go wipe their asses for 'em."

Clovis wondered if he would ever find work in which something illegal or immoral wasn't going on. He had listened to Oat's convoluted logic for almost an hour and on the surface of it, the scam wasn't hurting anyone directly. But this was a criminal operation and Clovis' involvement in it would not be a mere case of complicity.

When Oat reentered the room, Clovis thought he looked a bit calmer. "Aren't you worried about getting caught?" Clovis asked. "Aren't there audits, people coming around to look at where the money goes?"

The ease of Oat's laughter released some of Clovis' tension.

"Is that what's worryin ya? Getting caught? Let me ask ya, who in the hell gives a rat's ass 'bout what happens out here? Huh? Nobody, that's who. Nobody's eva looked twice at this two-bit operation and they neva will. That is unless ya go and turn yourself in. Some people around here have like a...a...a...compulsion to turn theyselves into the law eva now and again. Seems like we got more than our share here in Solomon. You're not one of 'em, are ya, son? It could be real unhealthy for our local economy. It could be real unhealthy period...for you or those close to ya."

With some effort Clovis maintained his composure, but the threat jarred him. The fact that Oat involved himself in a scam or two didn't surprise Clovis. Good old boys always carried the potential for getting into a little mischief, sticking in their thumbs and pulling out some plums. And Oat Smith was good old boy through and through. What shook Clovis was the potential evil behind the homespun philosophy and rascal smile. The man appeared capable of much more than mischief.

"No, sir. I wouldn't do that. I understand that what's being said here is private and confidential. Whatever went on between you and Daddy Two is your business."

"Well, son, I was hopin it would be our bidness—you and me. I don' wanna have to mess with some stranger to get this goin again. Sure as hell didn' wanna mess anymore with that piece a shit Punches. But I will if I have to.

"Another thing ya consida is this: if ya lose the county contract, ain' nobody goin to buy McDonald Wrecker. Ya might as well close the doors and declare bankruptcy. And sure as shit, if ya don' do bidness with me, there won't be no goddamn contract. No threat, just fact."

"Oat, give me a little time, please. I just can't say yes or no right this minute. I haven't been around here long enough to really know what's going on."

"I'm missin the money bad, son." The cigar moved from the right side of Oat's mouth to the left as he crossed his arms. "Tell you what. I'll give you one week from today then its shit or get off the pot. Understand?" Oat extended his hand, which Clovis shook firmly while remaining seated. "We done then, right?"

"Well, you said you'd update me about what happened to Daddy Two."

The red light flashed over Oat's head, and the bell went off like a muffled doorbell.

"Fuck 'em," Oat said, waving his cigar at the jailhouse door. "It would be easy to get a conviction on Punches cause he's such a lowlife bastard and nobody can stand him. Mr. Tannyhill, on the other hand, is a long-standing pillar of the community, a big contributor to the arts. And anyways, we couldn't seat a jury that wouldn' have at least a couple of ole boys who owed him money. If history repeated itself, probably the judge, too. He'd be a hard one to find guilty."

"What about the woman you saw at the funeral?"

"Dead end," Oat said. "She was just visitin her granny's grave. You might have knowed her—Rainey Day. Lived over on Cloverdale?"

"No, I don't remember."

"Mighty cute granddaughter," said Oat, "'bout your age." He rolled the Roi-Tan to the center of his lips and smoke snaked out from both sides of his mouth. "If I was a litle younger..."

Clovis ignored Oat's extraneous talk about the girl from the funeral. He wanted to know more about Daddy Two's murder but had not heard much in the way of evidence one way or the other. All Oat gave him was a bunch of loosely-connected explanations of supposed happenings. "So, why would Punches or Tannyhill want him dead?"

"Well, for that piece-a-shit uncle of yours, the *motif* was simple revenge for getting cut out of the will. For Mr. Tannyhill, it was all the money Richard owed him. I neva would a believed one man could get in so deep to his bookie. I seen the books. It was more than serious money."

"All that money you and Daddy Two split from the wrecker business. He lost all of that?"

"Three or four times ova."

"How could that be?"

Oat rose from his chair and came around the desk to help Clovis out of his chair. He put his arm around Clovis' shoulders and walked him toward the door.

"That's why Mr. Tannyhill is a very wealthy man. Most men are like ya daddy. When a man gets some extra cash, skimming it off the top or however, it's like play money. And men use that kind of money on women, booze, or gambling. I guess ya could throw drugs in there nowadays, too. Ain' many men can resist pissin money away on one of them things."

Oat eased him out the door. Clovis took a step away from his grasp before turning around.

"So, what about you?"

"What the hell ya talkin about? I didn' have no reason to kill ya daddy."

"No, no, no. I was talking about which one of those things gets all your money. Women, booze, gambling?"

"Eva damn one of 'em, son. Eva damn one."

1991
Early October

The discontented believe their regrets are about the past.
Mason Cooley

24

UNFINISHED SYMPHONIES

"**F**acilitative communication is in its embryonic stage, Mrs. McDonald," said Dr. Terence Barnstable. "Our work with severely autistic children is well-documented contrary to what the critics might say. However, I see it stretching beyond those boundaries. There's no telling how many people are in what you referred to as a *veggie-state*, people who could be put back in touch with their fellow man through our assistance."

Mazel had been quickly entranced by the young professor that Manuel Daza introduced to her. Words rolled effortlessly from his lips and carried an infectious energy. And, too, an aura of passion surrounded him. A belief in his work so deep, it resonated through each rich baritonal syllable.

He reminded her of Professor Al Pozzo when she first noticed him at Texas State Tech Agricultural & Military College. Though she had been a secretary in the Humanities, Mazel rarely had contact with professors outside of the English department. They dominated her time and generally made her job miserable.

One week though when most of the English staff had retreated to a conference, Al Pozzo from the Philosophy Department walked in with some typing he needed right away for a book–*the book*. Mazel finished it quickly, and Al returned to her desk frequently with his typing needs or sometimes just to flirt.

Speaking now, Dr. Terence Barnstable possessed an indefinable twinkle in his eye that made liking him the only option. What he did with this facilitative communication sounded far-fetched, especially for someone in Al's condition. Still, she enjoyed listening to him.

"Now everything I'm telling you is based on theory and is yet to be proven through any clinical trials with somebody in Dr. Pozzo's situation. All I can tell you is how some of these children have benefited from being able to make contact with the world again. Not through speaking or writing but by a trained facilitative communication technician guiding their hands along a keyboard, punching out a word here and a sentence there. It's better than where they were. Alone, isolated, no means of making the ideas that might be swirling in their heads...no means of letting them out. Until now."

Dr. Barnstable took Mazel's hands and wrapped them inside his own long and sturdy fingers. His tone of voice lowered so deeply that it seemed to reverberate from every wall, surrounding her with a seductive confidence.

"We must keep this between ourselves, however. Neither the Tumbleweed Rest Home nor the university have granted approval for me to undertake anything like this outside of the children's wing. Particularly considering the patient involved, we must maintain secrecy. No one can know besides the people right here."

From across the room, Manuel Daza nodded his head and gave her an approving wink. Al wasn't going to talk.

"Mrs. McDonald–"

"Call me Mazel, Doc. Please. It makes me feel a little younger."

"Very well then, Mazel. You may find this odd, but Dr. Pozzo is the reason I chose this career. I know his book, almost by memory. It is such an inspiration. His words relate to me like nothing I've read before or since. If I could unlock his mind, his spirit, just for a moment..."

"That sounds wonderful, Doc. Could you–"

"I feel as if fate has brought me here. As if my life is somehow linked with Dr. Pozzo. I understand he had a second book outlined in his head. A book–"

"Could you–"

"–of even greater depth and scope, if that's imaginable. If we could communicate, with just minimal responses, we might be able to give the world his final offering. It would be like Schubert or Bruckner coming back to complete their unfinished symphonies."

"Could you hand me some tissues?" Mazel asked. "He's drooling more than usual today."

"Certainly, Mazel. I apologize for going on like that. It's just that–"

"You're passionate about your work. No need to apologize. It's a wonderful attribute and too rarely seen. I saw it in Al at times. He was captivating in those moments. Positively enchanting."

"Thank you for those kind words, Mazel. I want to–"

"Could you–"

"–unlock and restore these people to some–"

"Doc!" Mazel interrupted with greater urgency. "The tissues, please."

***

Mazel slid a match across the striking surface of a matchbook and lit the Gauloises.

"I'll tell you what's in the em-bionic stage," Mazel said to Al after Dr. Barnstable left the room. "It's not facilitative communication. It's communication, period."

She placed the French cigarette between Al's quivering lips, allowing the cigarette to dangle there for a few seconds before taking it back.

"We talk and talk and talk, and we never get around to what we really want to say. Like with me and the boys. There's no signal from the heart to the rest of the body. The feelings go from the heart to the brain and there, they get all mangled up. It's like the heart beats out a message on some tribal drum, and the brain only operates in MS-DOS. Those signals are so messed up by the time they get down to the mouth…is it any wonder that everybody I know owns a gun? By the time you hear yourself speak, it's like Chinese or something.

"Your heart is going 'wait a minute, that's not what I meant.'

"And your mouth says, 'not my fault, I only spit out what the brain gives me.'

"And the brain yells back, 'I've got a thousand things going on at once. Heart–stop with the tom-toms.'

"I mean, how can we communicate with each another? What's inside of us won't even agree to what it wants. And it's no democracy in there, I tell you. Anarchy is more like it. Anarchy and chaos. And all the heart is trying to say is, I don't want to feel so damn alone anymore."

Al Pozzo's sucking sound seemed to increase in volume so Mazel placed the Gauloises again between his lips.

"Clovis is moving back home with me. At least until he decides what to do with the wrecker business. Punches up and ran off yesterday. Nobody has a clue where to or why."

Mazel monitored Al's cigarette but left it in place.

"I went ahead and unpacked some of Clovis' old things. Got that Farrah Fawcett poster and put it on the wall like he used to have it.

"And the trophies. I got them out of the box and dusted them off. Baseball, football, basketball, soccer, bowling. Lots of bowling trophies. Swimming, dressage, Kiwanis Man of the Year, cross country, country dancing, clogging, ballet.

"I'll never forget the first trophy he bought. Clovis was four years old. We stopped at a garage sale. He picks up this beat up old target shooting trophy and says, 'That's me, momma. I shoot guns. It's me.'

"From then on, whenever we had a little spending money, he would go out and buy a trophy. I'd watch him play football in the backyard with Bubba. Then he'd go into his room and have this ceremony. I peeked in on him a few times. He'd stand on a stool like when they win a medal at the Olympics. He'd stand there and announce how many hits he had or how many goals he scored. Then he would pick up a trophy and make crowd noises. Aaahhh, Aaahhh. Like that.

"The whole thing was so cute, you know. But it was sad, too. Because Clovis never could do enough to satisfy Richard. He played on all these sports teams and I'd be so proud, but Richard, he never had a good word to say. He'd climb on Clovis for not being as good as someone else's kid or some other such nonsense."

The light had gone out of the Gauloises so Mazel removed it and flushed it down the toilet.

"Why he turned on Clovis, I don't know. Maybe it was because Richard couldn't see even a speck of himself in the boy.

"Anyway, Clovis ended up earning his own trophies. A whole bunch of them from Pee Wee League all the way through high school. But there's not a one of them left. I asked him what happened to them, the ones he played for, the ones he had earned. He said he gave them all away. Gave them to little kids in the neighborhood. I asked him why.

"He said, 'So, they can have big dreams like I did.'

"I said, 'But you earned those. They're your dreams–come true.'

"And he said, 'No, Momma. Those trophies make me think of nothing but Daddy Two's foot up my butt, or his face all red and screaming at me. No, Momma. Those trophies were a nightmare.'

"Then he stood in the middle of his room and stretched his arms toward the shelves and shelves of other people's trophies and said, 'These meant more to me than the ones I earned. These were my dreams. And Daddy Two never had a place there.'"

***

Mazel heard someone softly calling her name.

"Miss McDonald. Miss McDonald."

It had to be Al. He was the only one in the room. A miracle had taken place. Al Pozzo was back from the living dead. He was calling her name. A cigarette between his lips, calling her name.

"Miss McDonald?"

Don't be so formal, Al. It's me–Mazel. And Doc Barnstable thought it would be a longshot for you to peck out a word or two. And here you are talking, Al. But what's with the accent?

"Mizzzz McDonald?"

"Mizzzz McDonald?"

Manuel Daza's hand jostled her shoulder, and Mazel opened her eyes. Stretching her arms slowly overhead, she extended her fingers and wiggled them around.

"Oh, gosh, Manuel. I was really out of it, wasn't I?"

"It's almost dark."

"Thanks. And thanks for bringing Dr. Barnstable by. He seems like a nice young man."

"I think his heart is in the right place."

Mazel rose from the chair in which she had been sleeping, a crease running across her cheek where a hand supported her head. She bent to pick up her parka and by the time she straightened, Manuel was holding it for her. Slipping her arms through easily, she thanked him. She stroked Al's face.

"You weren't a bad man, Al."

There was no good reason for it, no buildup or twinge to warn her, no rising lump in her throat. She just started crying. Manuel wrapped his arms around her.

"What's wrong, Mizz McDonald?"

"You know," she said through sniffles, "I've told you for years to call me Mazel."

"Just doesn't seem right. I came to like you as Mizz McDonald."

"Your choice, Manuel."

He did not respond but only loosened his grip as Mazel's crying grew quieter.

"I was dreaming when you woke me up. Al was calling my name. It made me so happy. Like all the burdens of life had been lifted from my shoulders. Such a wonderful feeling."

Manuel lifted Mazel's face with his hand until she looked him in the eye. "Every day we live, we gather up more problems, more worries. We think we get over them, but they become part of us. They attach themselves to us—like barnacles. We forget they are there, but they are. And they weigh us down. Some days you can't smile and you don't know why. It's the barnacles, dragging you down. So when you dream like this, sometimes the problems disappear and the soul is clear. It's a joy like no other. Then you wake up and nothing's changed. Only you remember the feeling in your dream and you want it back. But the barnacles have covered it up. It's a rude awakening. I'm sorry I woke you from this."

"They're only dreams, Manuel."

"Where I come from they say we live to dream. Dreams are the reward for making it through the day."

"So when Reverend Yates would say someone has gone to their final reward..."

"They've gone into their eternal dream, free from whatever problems they had. It's their final reward for making it through life."

"No heaven or hell?"

"What would be the point? Could there be anything better than the eternal dream?"

"Heaven, maybe."

"Isn't the dream always better than the reality? Nothing real can match our dreams."

"What about Hell? Is it the eternal nightmare?"

"No, Mizz McDonald. We shield ourselves from it. But the nightmare surrounds us...*all the time.*"

25

THE GAWKERS AND THE CAGE

Tannyhill could remember a time when he waited with anticipation for the arrival of mail. Now the wait was routine and
habit. Dressed in a bathrobe, sipping his first cup of espresso,
he would read the *Solomon Chronicle* by his expansive living room
window. Upon hearing Mac Bailey's aging mail truck, he would
rise from his chair and leave the room until the mailman's grinding gears were exiting the circular caliche driveway.

Mac Bailey might have been a nice enough guy if he had
only learned when to stop talking or had something of interest
to say. The man would drone on about the nuances of postal
service, what type of lure his cousin Jesse used when fishing Lake
Bismarck, or his alcoholic brother's patent infringement case
against LifeCall for their trademark phrase, "I've fallen and I
can't get up."

As usual, when Tannyhill heard the mail truck downshift, he
proceeded to stand. At least he attempted to stand. Too late did
he realize that his left leg was asleep and he fell to the floor.
Tannyhill barely had enough time to crawl behind the drapes to
avoid being seen by Mac Bailey.

Instead of just leaving the mail in the box alongside the driveway, Bailey rolled out of his truck and limped to the front door.
Tannyhill peeked through the sliver of space between the drapes
and the wall. He watched as the mailman hammered the brass
knocker a few times. Then Tannyhill eyed him standing in front
of the living room window and peering in.

Trapped, Tannyhill thought. No other escape existed. Bailey cupped his hands on the window just a few feet from where Tannyhill stood behind the curtain. Finally the mailman walked back to his truck, but instead of leaving, he unwrapped a sandwich and placed it in his lap. Mac Bailey looked toward the expansive living room window as he consumed his lunch.

Tannyhill could not even crawl to the other side of the living room without being noticed, so low was the window to the floor. He inched his back up the wall until he more comfortably settled on the carpet. Chinese dragons seemingly piled to his sides as the sash loosened and his robe opened to reveal his too-ample belly. He moved the skin from side-to-side and squeezed it tightly from his navel to his hip bone. Yet, the skin always settled again in the same place and in the same mass as before. Trapped.

Tannyhill rubbed his stomach in a repetitive, circular motion, slowly round and round, each cycle stretching lower and lower, now and then striking his penis a glancing blow. Ten minutes had passed, and Mac Bailey continued to fill his mouth with what looked to be a giant jelly roll. Tannyhill stretched his penis until he could see almost half of it rising over his stomach. Either his belly was too big or his penis too small. Trapped.

The brief flirtation with his penis caused him to think of Margo. If Tannyhill had a phone near, he would call her. He might even tell her that he loved her. Margo was the one facet of his life in which he felt liberation, a newfound freedom to be himself. Not that he didn't appreciate the freedom he enjoyed working most days from his home, sleeping late, listening to opera. But it came with a price. The damnable settling of accounts, meeting the losers to collect his money, meeting the winners to pay it out and hear them gloat.

The doorbell rang out the familiar eight notes of Beethoven's *Ode to Joy* accompanied by the brass knocker clanging out its incessant tone. Mac Bailey had returned to the door unnoticed while Tannyhill was distracted with love and other matters. He stopped moving his hand around his body and became still.

"Mr. Tannyhill," Mac Bailey called out. "I've got a special delivery letter for you. Just sign the receipt on it and leave it out in the mailbox so's I can pick it up tomorrow. I'll leave the letter under the doormat here, OK? You enjoy the rest of your day now."

When he peeked through the drapes again, Mac Bailey turned the engine and the mail truck gave an initial lurch down the long driveway. Tannyhill rolled to his hands and knees, his nose near the glass. He crawled like that from one side of his expansive living room window to the other, watching Mac Bailey disappear from view.

I detest the gawkers but I love the cage

The obscure opera lyrics inspired Tannyhill to raise his voice, grab hold of the major scale, and not let it go until he reached some resolution. As his once-refined tenor inched upward, more confident with every note, he felt the exuberance that drove him to become a Voice major at Dartmouth. But then his voice wavered at G and cracked on A. He tried twice more with the results worse each time. The C5 that he always hoped to achieve was a dream lost forever. Trapped.

***

The anonymous letter at his fingertips reeked of olive juice and mayonnaise. Tannyhill checked the postmark–Solomon, TX. This twisted letter was a measure of madness. He reread the text again as if by doing so the menace would lessen, or his fears recede.

Dear Viktor Tannyhill,

A former business associate, Punches McDonald, a despicable cockroach of a man, informed me of your desire to retain a collector of debts. I accept the position and I am prepared to begin immediately.

Your line of work can call for some rather persuasive techniques. My methods of putting on the squeeze are unsurpassed and can draw blood from a turnip, so to speak. Turnips and beets are such classic vegetables and so unappreciated by normal men. I would wager that you share my passion for them.

It is our misfortune to live in a time when those of Punches' ilk have triumphed. The morality of the vulgar man reigns. It is up to men such as ourselves, Viktor, to correct the current course of history and forcefully rectify the errors of human evolution.

I present myself to you as a skilled, discrete collector of debt and minister of death. What I lack in artistry is more than compensated for by my craftsmanship and precision. My preparatory work is beyond the pale.

For example, you, sir, live in a splendid ranch house with many unkempt but exquisite acres. I have observed you lounging in a leather chair through that magnificent window overlooking your estate.

Viktor, you have a fine collection of firearms. I admire that in a man. You seem to be missing, however, a .38. More precisely, a lemon squeezer. I would have made you aware of that fact but you were snoring heavily at the time I made this observation.

Perhaps this letter has taken you by surprise. Possibly, you are at this very moment thinking of a way to dismiss me when I approach you in person. Allow me to dissuade you from such a notion.

Somewhere beneath the grounds of Tannyhill lies a Hooters cap belonging to Punches McDonald. A few drops of my former partner's blood are on the bill of his cap as well as a missing .38 lemon squeezer. A small mound of ash fills the remainder of the hole.

If one were to uncover this mound of earth, one would easily deduce that Viktor Tannyhill is a murderer. Do not concern yourself at present. I believe no one with the exception of myself could ever find these items.

In closing, I must ask you to burn this letter on your front lawn immediately. Its smoke will be a certain color and when I see this smoke, I will not need to disturb you further this day. Do not hesitate. Do it now. I will contact you again later, if not sooner.

Sincerely,
Felix Krull (pseudonym)

Tannyhill did as instructed and a south wind took hold of the incredibly dense green smoke, lifting it over and beyond his rooftop. He returned right away to the living room and pulled the drapes closed to his expansive living room window. His eyelids closed tightly for a moment as he tried to think of something, anything besides the fear gripping his gut.

Walking by his father's rifle and gun cabinets, Tannyhill eyed the empty space where he had recently returned the .38 lemon squeezer. He had taken it to Oat when they went through their masquerade of Tannyhill being a suspect in Richard's murder. He had even fired it per Oat's instructions the night before being paraded in front of the chicken-fried-steak-sated Kiwanis. Unlocking the glass-encased handgun display, he removed the Colt .45 military with the walnut textured grip. From the bottom drawer of the cabinet, he found a seven round clip and pushed it into place.

He needed time to think through the situation, this demented threat. After placing the Colt on the night table next to the stereo remote control and settling into his bed, Tannyhill, like any good bookie or assessor of odds, took stock of the risks involved. He began evaluating options as they came to mind. The queasiness Tannyhill felt was similar to the days when he had to leave his home, the days he had to collect and pay the gamblers–but more so. How ironic, he thought, how his desire for a collector to rid himself of the almost debilitating anxiety of leaving his house, now brought about an even worse, unparalleled, gut-wrenching upset.

The only moment of relief he experienced for the next several hours occurred with a flash of anger when Tannyhill recalled one of, what seemed at the time, the least threatening lines of the green-smoked letter.

"You son-of-a-bitch," he said aloud. "I do not snore."

***

"Baby," Margo cooed, "don't worry about it. It happens to everyone."

Tannyhill held the receiver to his ear with the aid of his shoulder. His right hand still held his faltering staff. "Not to me, it doesn't," he mumbled.

"You've got a lot on your mind, Vic. You need me to be your friend tonight, not your lover. Tell me what's got you so upset. Did one of your clients give you a bad time?"

"I'm sorry to disappoint you, Margo. I could tell you were really into it tonight."

"Oh, baby. I'm into it every time I'm with you."

Tannyhill knew he shouldn't say it, but the words came in a rush. He felt as powerless to stop their flow as he was to attain an erection this night. "How many guys have you said that to?"

A suffocating silence followed. Whose life didn't have a defenseless area where another could inflict terrible pain. On the surface Margo was tough and did not apologize for the seamy nature of her work. Still, she wanted the same things as everyone else. She wanted love, and she desired a purity in that love. But Margo had a past. And though she and Tannyhill didn't ignore her past, neither did they allow it to affect how they felt about one another now.

Tannyhill had broken this tacit understanding by making her feel cheap and common. Justification for the remark came from tonight's impotence, which was no justification at all. Margo couldn't be blamed. Nobody had ever excited Tannyhill the way she did. Even the women he had touched, kissed, and entered could not compare with the exquisite beauty of Margo in his ear.

"God, Margo, please forgive me. I didn't mean it."

"You know, Vic, there's not much I haven't heard come out of a man's mouth." He could hear her lighting a cigarette and realized that there was another detail he did not know. What brand did she smoke?

"Men can be vile and violent. They can try and make you feel smaller than a tick on a beetle's butt if you let them. I don't know why so many of them are mean. I stopped trying to figure that out a long time ago. It might have something to do with what you're going through right now. They feel impotent about their work or with their families. They get powerless so they find some woman who they can rip one way or the other.

"But you know, I made my bed and I have laid in it for a long time now. I will take these assholes' money and let them get nasty with me. And yeah, I'll tell them what they want to hear. But when they put that phone down, I forget about it. Lots of men need that and that's the way of this sick old world.

"But that's not me, Vic. That's how I've made my living but that's not me. This is me, baby. Right here, right now. How I am with you is the way I...me...is the way *we* are. At least, this is the way I want to be. And you help me be the way I want to be.

"So, please, don't bring up my work again. Somehow when it comes out of your mouth, I don't feel so good about myself anymore."

Tannyhill rolled to his back and stared at the ceiling. "I am so sorry, Margo. I won't do it again."

"It's alright, baby. I just want you to know where I stand."

"I'm so tired," Tannyhill said. "I've got so much to tell you, but I can hardly keep my eyes open."

"Well, maybe tomorrow. I'll let you go."

"No. Don't go. Please."

"Okay, Vic. Switch the phone onto speaker."

"Do what?"

"I'm going to spend the night with you, sweet baby. Now switch the speaker on and I'll do the same here."

Tannyhill did as Margo instructed and rolled again to his back.

"Close your eyes now." Margo's voice sounded as if it was coming from a cave, but it comforted him just the same.

The next thing Tannyhill knew, Margo's voice was gently tapping him awake. He looked at the clock and discovered he had been sleeping for at least a couple of hours.

"Vic," Margo whispered. "Vic, baby."

"Yes, ba–by."

"Roll over on your side. You're snoring."

26

RUBY TUESDAY

Blinking yellow traffic lights set the rhythm of Clovis McDonald's 1:30 a.m. drive to work. His final one. Sipping on a can of Dr Pepper, he alternated the radio between sports talk, UFO talk, and the Blues Hour. His eyes glanced from one side of the road to the other, ever-alert for the barfly being forced out of its hovel as it neared closing time. At this hour, there was no way to drive but defensively.

Unable to catch a thread of anything resembling intelligent conversation or a blues song that he liked, Clovis pushed a cassette into the tape deck. The struggling speakers ground out a muffled rendition of "Me and Billy the Kid." Yeah, he wore his gun all wrong. Yeah, and he shouldn't have shot that Chihuahua. And who in the hell shot Daddy Two?

As he approached the storage units where the newspapers would soon arrive, he found himself mesmerized by the alternating lights and message board across the street.

FRESH GIRLS–TOPLESS-$2 SHOTS–FRESH GIRLS–TOP-LESS-$2 SHOTS

The PJ's Gentleman's Club chain served free coffee after one a.m. and for a while, Clovis had taken advantage of their generosity at least once a week.

FRESH GIRLS–TOPLESS-$2 SHOTS–FRESH GIRLS–TOP-LESS-$2 SHOTS

One of the FRESH GIRLS, Ruby (if that was her real name), had become friendly with Clovis even though he never slipped a dollar in her G-string. She would look his way while dancing, not with the counterfeit, come-hither crap she hooked the others with, but a solemn or wistful gaze that thoroughly captivated Clovis. One night she asked him for a ride after work explaining that another dancer, Jade (if that was her real name), had become sick during her shift and driven home in Ruby's Firebird.

He told her of his mini-warehouse across the street and that he would be tied up until about three, but he could swing by for her then. She laughed a wily, I-know-something-you-don't-know laugh and said she would just walk over and meet him.

He had said, "It's pretty dark. It even gives me the willies when I'm back there all alone."

She kissed him on the lips for the first time and whispered, "I'm a big girl. I know my way around." Ruby didn't look like a big girl. Her body, yes. Well-defined curves and angular hips had matured far beyond her girlish face. She reminded him of the freshman and sophomore girls he once went out with at TSTA&M.

A couple of hours later, he had been sweeping the mess of leftover papers, straps, and polymer bags left behind by his carriers. He kept telling them to clean up their own garbage but never pressed the point too much. Bending in the corner for the last bit of refuse, Clovis had been startled by her voice and bumped his head into the wall.

"Let's go, hon," she said.

"Hop in the truck," he answered, rubbing the small knot already protruding from the top of his head.

She shook her head no, saying, "Where we're going, you don't need to drive."

In a Metallica T-shirt, jeans, and sneakers, Ruby appeared sexier than in the high heels and G-string she wore inside PJ's. She reached for his hand and they took a romantic-like stroll down row after row of storage sheds. They continued on to the final row and into the far corner where a tall cyclone fence with a barbed wire top stood, and the mini-warehouses ended.

"This is about as far as we can go," he said.

"Oh, I hope not," she answered, revealing a key on the chain around her neck. She opened the warehouse on the end, number 101, and when she turned on the overhead light, Clovis simply said, "Wow!"

The queen-size bed had not a crease or lump under its checkered spread. Candles ringed the walls and as she finished lighting them, Clovis was dazzled by her sexy silhouettes reflected against the concrete blocks. Ruby switched on a floor fan by the overhead door before pulling a rope and closing the door itself.

"Unbelievable."

With a look of satisfaction, she had moved to the far corner of the room and said, "Watch this." Slipping her fingers between two blocks, she began working her hands slowly from side-to-side. When she had worked the block free a couple of inches, she gave one hard pull and it came out of the wall.

"Ventilation. There's another one in that corner." Ruby pointed.

Clovis inched the block back and forth as he had watched Ruby do. In his haste, he smashed the tip of his ring finger between the blocks. The pain caused him to wince and bite his lip. From behind Ruby said, "Excuse me," and he turned to face the totally unclad dancer. The pinched finger became a distant memory.

"Let me pull that thing out," she said. But for the next several hours, the concrete block remained untouched.

Sleep came in sweaty, fitful snatches that first night. Clovis' beeper went off around eight. He remembered burying his head deeper into the pillow and had been surprised to catch a whiff of lemon-scented fabric softener.

"I've got to go," he had mumbled. "I'll take you home now."

Ruby rolled to her side. "Go on. I'll catch a ride later. I'm too tired to move."

Clovis dressed and removed the concrete block he had worked on hours before. He returned to the bed for a goodbye kiss. Ruby had stroked his face.

"I'm sorry to hit you up for this, hon, but I don't get paid until Friday, and the tips have really sucked this week. Do you have something to tie me over?"

Clovis had slid the wallet from his back pocket and opened it. A fifty, a ten and three ones. She grabbed the fifty and said, "Can you come by again next Sunday?" He nodded.

Clovis and Ruby made love every Monday morning for almost two years and each time she asked for something to tie her over until Friday, and each time he handed her a fifty dollar bill, and each time she refused the ride home. She never offered to pay him back and he never asked. Somehow, she never made him feel like a customer. If anything, cradled inside her long, tawny legs, Clovis felt necessary and needed. He looked forward to Monday mornings.

However, two weeks ago, she did not show up. She hadn't been at work all week either, one of the bouncers told him. Nobody seemed to know where she was or if they did, they were not telling. Clovis had checked PJ's for a solid week with no luck. He didn't understand why, but he sensed that she would not be coming back.

The blare of a car horn and the bright lights in his rearview mirror shook Clovis from his thoughts of Ruby. He cut the wheels right and lurched across two lanes into the narrow mini-warehouse driveway. The newly installed security gate did not adjust well to rainy weather. Storms that had passed through earlier in the evening were now playing havoc with the control panel. Four or five times he put in the code with no accompanying reaction from the gate. Finally, the chain started to inch its way across the drive.

From behind he heard the sound of an engine but no lights. He tapped his brakes to get a better view of what was there and saw the familiar outline of not one, but three Fort Worth police cars, all with their lights out. When the gate clanged to a stop, Clovis passed through much faster than normal. Turning into his row of sheds, he breathed a sigh of relief as the three cars moved on. In a minute, however, as he lifted the warehouse door, sirens echoed loudly from one of the back rows.

He ran and with each row of sheds passed came an increased feeling of dread. When he reached the final row, Clovis came to an abrupt halt and peeked around the corner. His heart sank as a half dozen or more cops filled the area by the far end of the fence. Something was out of place though. They were not going in and out of 101 as he had anticipated. They were bringing people, what looked to be teenagers, out of a shed on the other side of the row. 104 or 106, maybe.

He leaned his back against the wall, an emotional release easing the sudden stress. From the other end of the drive, he heard the grinding of truck gears–the Daily News had arrived.

***

The newspaper business had changed since the days when Clovis chunked the *Solomon Chronicle* from his Huffy bicycle. Kids had been eliminated from the paper route business and in their place stood a breed apart. No adult rolls out of bed at 2 a.m. and is happy about it. All needed the income from delivering papers. Some had day gigs while others depended on the route money until they could find a regular job. None of his carriers were in good financial shape, and most were near desperation. The work place at 2 a.m. was as hard as nails. The occasional doughnuts or pizza that Clovis brought in sometimes lightened the mood but only for a short time.

He had grown to loathe the business and would not miss it. The *Fort Worth Daily News* took advantage of these folks at the last and lowest end of the newspaper chain. Not only did they work seven days a week, three hundred sixty-five days a year, they also had to collect money from the subscribers. And if they couldn't collect the money, the carrier took the loss.

The system was entrenched and archaic and who knew if it would ever change. An easy fix, one Clovis had suggested, would be to simply pay the carrier for each paper delivered. Leave the collection of money to the newspaper chain instead of the least powerful link in that chain–the carrier. Guilt had accrued in Clovis' gut like credit card interest. His link was the next-to-last in the chain and its name–complicity. Clovis fought what battles he could, but he was young and no one listened. In the end, management ruled and that was that. His choice boiled down to either do the best he could within a rotting system or quit. That this was his final night in the business felt good.

When the next hour passed uneventfully, Clovis was grateful. Some carriers came and went and said good-bye. A few asked questions about the cops and Clovis told them what he had seen. Speculation among his crew ran the gamut from murder to white slavery. Somebody even mentioned that a right wing militia group had been running weapons through there.

Tippy Holden, who had been on his route less than a month said, "The cops have been real busy back there lately."

"What do you mean?" asked Clovis.

"Don't you ever read this piece of crap we deliver?" Tippy walked to the stand of back issues that Clovis kept on the side wall. Tippy's attitude had already gone south. Clovis figured he might last through the week if that long, but that would no longer be his problem.

"Looky here," said Tippy, pulling out the Metro section of last Tuesday's edition. "It was a mini-whorehouse."

Clovis took the paper and opened the door of his pickup for better light. A photograph showed a woman with her head down being led away from a building with the number 101 stenciled above it. The caption read, EXOTIC DANCER ARRESTED IN MINI-WAREHOUSE.

He sat motionless in the cab of the Dodge Ram until all of his carriers were gone. A host of police cars ambled to and fro until daylight. When the activity died away, Clovis walked slowly to Ruby's place. A strip of yellow tape surrounded shed 104. He attempted to lift the door of shed 101, but it wouldn't budge.

Moving to the side of the building, Clovis felt along the borders of the two cement blocks that he had learned to remove without pinching a finger. Only this time they could not be moved. Freshly sealed.

He leaned his head against the wall and with his finger, traced round and round one of the blocks. By repeating this motion time and again, Clovis could deflect what was going on within himself. Simple, repetitive motions.

Clovis never knew if he had been in love before, so he concluded that he had not. And paying a stripper for sex in a mini-warehouse could hardly qualify. But for all he knew, Ruby was as near to love as he might have come. There had been an ease between them, a comfort level, a bond unlike what he knew with any woman before or since.

Maybe it was their limited expectations that made these things so. They only expected that the other be there in the wee hours of Monday morning. What they were before entering or after leaving shed 101 mattered little. Still, Clovis couldn't help but be surprised. Surprised by this great and seemingly overblown sense of loss. After all, what had he expected? For this kind of feeling to exist outside of shed 101? How unrealistic.

***

Clovis intended to grab a few hours of sleep before throwing his clothes and a few other belongings into his Dodge Ram for the drive back to Solomon. He didn't expect to see Bubba stuffing a cardboard box full of pots, pans, and towels when he opened the apartment door at seven in the morning.

"I don't need all that stuff," Clovis said. "I told you to keep it."

Bubba folded the top of one box and sealed it with several strips of adhesive tape. Without looking up, he began filling another box with plates, glasses, and silverware.

Clovis looked around the living room and saw a sealed box labeled "Stereo." Another box read "Bed" and another "Bath."

You could criticize Bubba for his bull-headedness, his gambling, his anger issues, thought Clovis, but the boy had some packing skills. The question now was *why?*

"What are you doing?" Clovis asked. He removed the newspaper-ink-stained jacket that he intended to throw in the dumpster on his way out.

Bubba wrapped a couple of TSTA&M beer mugs in paper towels before looking up. "I ran out of newspapers," he said. "You got any left in the truck?"

"No," Clovis answered, "I left them all at the warehouse. If I had known-"

"Hell," Bubba interrupted, "I didn't know when you left here."

"Know what?"

"Know that I'm coming with you," Bubba said, as he slammed the Presto Fry Baby into the bottom of the box. "I still think it's a mistake." He rose and opened a cabinet, sweeping their meager canned goods, crackers, and chips into a box in seconds.

"It's not like we're leaving any great thing here though," Bubba continued. "It's not like Arby's will go into a panic when I don't show up tomorrow. Some other idiot will run my shift and get a twenty cent raise. Whoop-de-fucking-do."

Clovis retrieved the Frosted Flakes from a box that Bubba was filling up. He needed something on his stomach to more easily go to sleep no matter how tired he felt. "But I thought you were going to move in with that new girl?"

"Eh, she's too stuck up. Just like the rest of 'em here. What about you and Ruby Tuesday? You guys have been together a long time. Aren't you going to miss her?"

"It's Monday, not Tuesday," Clovis said. "And she didn't show up this week. Or last week. I think it's over." He poured milk into the bowl of cereal but did so too quickly. Milk spilt onto the counter and dripped to the floor. "Yeah, I'm going to miss her."

Bubba drew the adhesive tape several times over the box of kitchen items and food. "There's a lot of fish in the sea, little brother. Just show them your hook and they'll jump on your dinghy."

Clovis ate a spoonful and spoke as he crunched. "When I left here, you weren't even speaking to me. I thought you hated the idea of me going back to Solomon. And what about Oat and Tannyhill and Scott Austin and all those people you don't want to see?"

"Look," Bubba said, "you always scared the crap out of me when you loaded a car on the winch. I'm better at it than you are. I'm just going to protect your sorry ass until you wise up and sell the damn thing."

Clovis had been hesitant to bring up the subject but did so now. "What about Oat? What about the lemon squeezer you have in the truck?"

Bubba secured the bottom of an empty box with three long strips of adhesive. "What about it?"

"Daddy Two was killed with one."

Bubba laughed as he flipped the box over and began filling it with cleaning solvents, still wrapped mouse traps, and other disgusting things from the cabinet below the kitchen sink. "There was a gun show that came to town about five years ago. One guy had fifty-some-odd lemon squeezers that he was pretty much giving away. Hell, everybody I know picked one up. That's a lot of fucking suspects."

"So you, for sure, didn't have anything to do with Daddy Two." Clovis took the bowl with both hands and drank the last of the milk.

Bubba placed some flashlights and beat-up old rags in the box. "I hadn't seen him since last Christmas, right after his prostate surgery. He was lying in bed, bitching and moaning about his catheter bag and the pain. I even remember the last words I said to him. Same thing he said to me when I was ten after I broke my arm."

"What was that?"

Bubba stopped emptying things from beneath the kitchen sink, stood up, and placed his hands on the counter.

"Hush up your whining," he said with a growl. "Stop being a goddamn pussy."

1991
Mid October

Evil men have no songs.

Friedrich Nietzsche

27

OVER-CUMINED

As she stirred the tortilla soup, Mazel felt the unusual sensation of another smile. For two days and now the third night after Bubba's and Clovis' return home, smiles occurred with such regularity that her facial muscles ached. She held her breath to hold the savory aroma a bit longer, relishing the moment with stillness, wanting no more than this. Exhaling between parted lips, she felt her shoulders relax and rolled her neck in a wider arc than normal.

Home. She had dreamed of this. Caught scraps and crumbs of it at times. When the boys were small, all year long they would stick loose change in their big-headed Mickey Mouse bank. Then on New Year's Day, they would open the Mouse up, separate the coins into unruly piles, and wrap them in penny, nickel, dime, and quarter rollers while watching the parades on TV. Richard was usually gone the whole day with all the wrecks from the night before. It was their most peaceful time together. But even then, the tyranny of Richard reigned, his return inevitable.

Mazel turned her head away from the stove top when Bubba opened the back door. "God Almighty, that smells good," he said.

Clovis trailed in after Bubba and asked, "What is it?"

"You said you like spicy stuff," she answered. "Tortilla soup."

Bubba opened the silverware drawer, retrieved a spoon, and took a step toward the pot.

"Uh, uh, uh," Mazel said, angling her way between Bubba and the soup. "Go on now and get clean. Unless you want to move that broken down La-Z-Boy out to the curb first."

Both boys grunted. "We're exhausted, Momma," Clovis said. "We'll do it tomorrow."

"That's what you said yesterday," Mazel countered, but without resolve in her voice. "Wash real good under your fingernails. No woman likes a man with grimy fingers. Now move along."

"Just a taste?" Bubba asked.

"Move along."

She listened to the boys' work boots thudding on the wood floor toward the other end of the house. Their muffled conversation sounded like music to ears that for too long heard little but echoes.

Mazel had never been a great cook. She had catered to Richard's tastes, which were elemental: meat, potatoes, an occasional vegetable though nothing more exciting than string beans or an ear of corn. Bread. White bread with margarine dolloped on it. And something sweet every now and again. Mostly pecan pies and the occasional peach cobbler.

Since the boys return home, however, Mazel's culinary creativity had been unleashed. The boys favored Cajun and Thai. They even doused their spaghetti in Tabasco sauce. So she unearthed recipes calling for spices, the ones that sat solidifying in their tiny containers for who knew how many years. Bubba said he liked it when small beads of sweat appeared on his cheeks and under his eyes while feasting on a particularly peppery entrée.

Tonight's meal looked simple–a large bowl of soup, yet its aroma was racy and tempting. Mazel dashed another helping of cumin into the pot, but the lid popped off and half the container poured into the soup. Able to scrape some of it out, she still worried that too much had sunk below the surface. She added some flour and a can of Miller Lite to the mix believing they would help minimize the effects of the spice jar blowout. After all, a little cumin goes a long, long way.

Clovis returned to the kitchen first with his dark hair wet and slicked back from the shower. "Am I doing these right?" he asked, waving several towing invoices at Mazel.

"Did you use the blue invoices for the county business?" she asked, while removing the soup ladle from a drawer.

"They're in order," he said, "at the bottom of the stack."

"And the white ones are for the regular business?"

"Right." Clovis offered up his bowl to Mazel who made sure to scoop out good size chunks of chicken into it. "I'm sorry I mixed those two up yesterday, Momma."

Bubba entered the room pushing his head through the tight neck of a TSTA&M White Buffalo t-shirt. "Hey, what's with the numbers on those invoices anyway? None of them end in two or three?" He grabbed a bowl and held it toward Mazel just as Clovis had.

"You wait till we're seated, young man," she said to Clovis who was already blowing the steam from a spoonful. "Richard rolled dice behind that dive bar, The Hole in the Wall. You know, you throw a two or three and crap out. It was a superstitious thing with him. As long as I've been doing his books, he never filled out an invoice ending in a two or three." She spooned out her bowl last, mostly veggies and tortillas and very little chicken. "Have you found the county books yet?"

"Not yet," Clovis answered, "but we haven't had much time to look. Why did you keep them separate?"

"That's the way he wanted it," Mazel said. "I offered to keep both sets but your...Richard insisted on keeping the county contract books."

"As soon as we find them, you can do both sets," Clovis said.

"If you're not used to it," Mazel said, taking a seat at the kitchen table, "the skips on the invoices can be confusing. Your Uncle Punches never got it down."

"That son-of-a-bitch," Bubba said. "Nice time for him to hightail it. Do you think he might have run off with the books, too?"

"I don't know why," Mazel replied. "It wouldn't do him any good. Except maybe for spite."

Everyone waded into their soup at roughly the same time. Mazel thought it very tasty but possibly too spicy. "I may have over-cumined it a little," she offered. Another spoonful and another quickly followed. Then the afterburn, stripping the lining of her tongue and causing her esophagus to contract.

"Over-cayenned it is more like it," said Bubba.

Her coughing came in fits, and the Dr Pepper offered no relief.

"You going to be alright?" Clovis asked, before he began coughing.

She nodded her head in the affirmative. Bubba rapped his hand on the table a couple of times. "Good God, Momma, what kind of peppers did you use? My mouth is on fire."

"Jala (cough, cough)…jala (cough, wheeze)…jalapenos."

"Did you scrape out the seeds?" Bubba asked before sneezing.

"Do what?" Mazel enjoyed their dumbfounded expressions before laughing to let them in on the joke. "I spilled a whole jar of cumin in it. Thought I got most of it out (cough, cough), but I guess I didn't."

"Bubba's right," Clovis said, "it's the cayenne and the peppers." Clovis left the table and walked down the hallway.

"I'm sorry," she called out after him. "I'll call out for pizza or something."

He returned right away carrying a box of Kleenex to the table while he dabbed below his eyes with one. "I love it, Momma. I like food that's a challenge."

"Me, too," Bubba said. "I'm going to finish this here and go back for seconds."

Mazel coughed slightly and cleared her throat. Taking a Kleenex, she wiped the corners of her mouth and then her forehead. A second Kleenex caught a couple of tears as they escaped her eyes. Home.

The telephone rang first followed by the doorbell. Clovis' beeper sounded and someone pounded hard on the front door.

The cacophony of beeps, rings, chimes, and knocks intruded on Mazel's moment of peace, triggering another coughing spell.

"What the hell?" Clovis said, as he unsnapped his beeper. Bubba walked down the hallway and said, "I'll get the phone." Mazel pushed away from the table and went to the front door where the knocking had entered its second round.

"How do, ma'am," said Oat Smith.

"Sheriff," Mazel acknowledged. "What brings you around here?"

"Well, they's some news about Punches. Can I come in?"

"We just sat down to dinner."

Bubba touched her shoulder from behind. "Momma, there's an accident out near the interstate. One of the cars is blocking traffic so we've got to head out."

"They's another tow job needs done tonight," Oat Smith said. "You boys swing by my office when ya finish with the wreck. Ya gonna need my help finding this otha one."

"What about Punches?" Mazel asked.

"This here otha vehicle is hid under a bunch a brush on Bill Todd's ranch. It's the Shaggin Wagen. No sign a Punches but they's blood splatta'ed all ova it." Oat Smith removed his stiff-brimmed hat and smiled at Mazel. "That dinner in there sure has my stomach juices a pumping, ma'am."

"I'll go fix you a container to take home," Mazel said. "The boys can bring it when they meet up with you."

"That's mighty nice of you, Miss Mazel. Mighty nice." Oat moved the hat to his head and walked to his Explorer.

"What the hell?" asked Clovis, when they closed the front door. "Punches dead, too?"

"Sounds like it," Bubba said. "Maybe the county books are still in the van."

"Can't you boys finish your dinner before you go?"

"No," they answered simultaneously.

"This interstate thing is kind of an emergency," Bubba said.

"Got to go now," Clovis added.

While Bubba and Clovis changed into their work clothes and boots, Mazel unloaded the entire batch of tortilla soup into a large Tupperware container. She returned to her chair at the kitchen table, but she couldn't get back the serene state of mind so abruptly disturbed just minutes ago. The boys headed straight toward the back door and waved.

"Wait a minute," she said. "Take this to the Sheriff."

"We would have eaten it," Clovis said.

"You're just being nice," Mazel answered, as she reached for her purse on the china cabinet and retrieved a twenty. "Here, go get you something to eat that won't leave burn marks down your gut."

Bubba took the bill, and they turned toward the door.

"Wait a minute." Mazel rose from her chair and went to the spice rack. She pulled out the Ground Cumin and Cayenne Pepper containers. "Put that down a second," she said. Clovis set the Tupperware back on the table. Mazel opened the lid and poured in unhealthy portions of each spice.

"He's going to have steam coming out of his ears," Bubba said.

Mazel wanted to regain that feeling of peace, that moment when it was just the boys and her, that minute when they appeared to be what she dreamed a normal family might actually be. Maybe that moment would come again, but there were never any guarantees. Damn the intrusions. Damn the beepers. Damn the telephone. And damn that Oat Smith. She held out the Tupperware bowl to Clovis.

"Serve him right."

28

SOME NON-ESSENTIAL BONE

"Tannyhill." He wedged the phone between his shoulder and ear while crossing out what he now considered an ill-conceived pick on his weekly schedule of football games.

"Yes, sir. This is Fred Delaney."

"Congratulations, Fred. This has got to be a band director's dream come true–playing in the Jingle Elf Parade. Long overdue, my friend, long overdue."

"Well, thank you kindly. It's people like you who support the program that makes it all possible."

"Always has been a pleasure to help out in any facet of the university's music program. If a young person loves music, they ought to be allowed every chance to succeed."

"We're so fortunate to have a benefactor like you around. That's why I'm somewhat reluctant to ask for something else."

"You need help with new uniforms for the parade?" Tannyhill asked. "No problem. I've had a windfall here recently, and I'd be willing to give it all away for a good cause like this."

"It's not...we don't need the money right now."

"What is it then?"

"Well, we've got a singer to do *Oklahoma!*" Fred Delaney said. "That's what the parade committee wanted us to play. And he's OK, you know, but this is going to be on cable TV and–"

"What can I do?"

"I think with some better instruction, some coaching, he could do an outstanding job. I know you've had a lot of experience. I'm just wondering if you would consider helping him out."

"Fred, now is a bad time for me. I really can't make it into town for a while."

"Well, he could come out to your place."

"No, no. I'm sorry. I, uh, I can't do that either at this time."

"Well, OK, Vic. I understand. Thanks anyway."

"Sorry, Fred."

Minutes later, Tannyhill dialed Fred Delaney's office at TSTA&M.

"Fred, how about you have your vocalist give me a call?"

"Thanks for reconsidering," Fred Delaney said. "That's a load off my mind. Then you'll see him soon?"

Tannyhill sang a few strong bars from Escamillo's high tessitura in the third act of *Carmen*. "How was that?"

"Uh, very nice. Great voice, Vic."

"I mean the sound quality. Was it clear?"

"Yes, sir, just like we were in the same room."

"You see, I can give your man lessons over the phone. You can do just about anything with a telephone these days. Have him give me a call."

"OK, Vic. Thank you. I'll have someone bring the music out to you."

"No. No, I'll give you my fax number. Nobody comes out here for any reason. Alright?"

"OK."

***

With bookies, life is fixed. Invariable. The margin of victory is always the same. You even out the bets, lay off the heavy end, balance the scales. Profit is built into the vig, the ten percent a losing bettor pays, like a commission in the world of legitimate business. A wise bookmaker sleeps well at night without the worry of games yet to be played on the coast. No matter how the ball bounces, his take is constant. Stable.

Vic Tannyhill lived according to these precepts. Balanced in his affairs, Vic's emotional pendulum didn't sway to and fro. At best it would on occasion vibrate lightly like a tuning fork, but for the most part remained motionless. Fixed.

Tannyhill had difficulty adjusting to the abrupt swings of fortune now dominating his life. Moods oscillated, expanding and contracting like an accordion–a dreadful instrument to Tannyhill's mind. He felt like one of his clientele–winning with a huge underdog, or being decimated, losing what looked to be a sure thing. Tannyhill could not handle this kind of action.

On one hand, he had never been happier. Not leaving home, rising from bed but for the barest of necessities, Tannyhill was finding his center. Though tending toward agoraphobia, he held little concern that his lifestyle was in any way a problem. He just liked being alone. People wore on him, physically drained him.

Physically, Margo drained him, too, but in a different way. A way he craved. He would phone her, or she him, up to seven or eight times a day. Not every call ended in orgasmic spasms, but they were all good.

Their relationship wasn't built on sex alone. Tannyhill had been surprised with Margo's breadth of knowledge on any number of subjects, including music. Though she had some sketchy knowledge of opera, her true love was the stage, show tunes. As a child her parents had taken her to Dallas for a Rodgers and Hammerstein. She said she had never gotten over the ecstasy of those three hours.

No, their relationship wasn't built on sex alone. But damn, it was good when it went there. Margo's voice could be husky or sweet, tart or wholesome. Whatever voice she chose struck Tannyhill's chord. And the pillow talk afterwards, the tender cooing in his ear and then, sleep.

When he awoke, satisfied beyond any previous hope, he awoke alone. And there, right then and there, was the point where Vic knew he wanted this relationship to last. Never before had he gone to sleep with a woman and actually wanted her to be there when he awoke. Forced smiles and clumsy hugs leading nowhere. Wishing they were gone or that he had crept away during the night.

Not these days though. When Tannyhill awoke from an encounter with Margo, he missed her voice. If he awoke early enough, he would say *Buon giorno* and she might still be on the line to answer. Usually though, Margo was already about her day, and he would call her right away with the same greeting. He longed for her and wanted more. That was the first indication he was falling in love. The first of many.

On the other hand there was Felix Krull, pseudonym.

***

Instead of collecting from the losers on Tuesday and paying the winners on Wednesday and instead of driving from one meeting spot to another, Tannyhill had reduced his outside exposure to Wednesday afternoon at the dimly lit, round-backed booth near the rear exit of Sorrento's Bar & Grill. Though collections spiked the week after Oat Smith brought him into jail in handcuffs, it didn't last into the second week. His clients were betting against the possibility that Tannyhill might have murdered Richard McDonald.

He kept the meets short, not encouraging any discourse other than that having to do with the straightforward transaction of money. His last scheduled meet this Wednesday walked in a few minutes late and apologized as he approached Tannyhill's booth.

"I'm sorry, Mister Tannyhill," Bubba Albright said. "There was a car parked across someone's driveway. Kind of a rush job."

Bubba removed a small wad of bills from his jeans pocket and handed it to Tannyhill.

The outside of the wad looked promising to him with a couple of twenties but the interior quickly dissolved into a ten, a couple of fives and more ones than he cared to count at the moment. "Bubba, this only covers about a quarter of what you lost last week."

"I know, but there'll be more coming in. I don't have any expenses now except the truck payment. I'll bring more next week, I promise."

Tannyhill motioned for the lone waitress on duty. "Marion, would you bring us two of your cleanest glasses with double shots of the DoubleWood?"

"I've got to run," Bubba said, his hands on the table starting their push away.

"We need about five minutes to discuss your debt."

Bubba settled back into his seat.

"Nine thousand dollars is a lot of money," Tannyhill said. "I get no joy out of seeing a young man in that kind of a hole and digging deeper." He stuffed the money from Bubba into his ledger book. "As I see it, we've got some options." He keyed the locks on his bulky briefcase. It sprang open revealing his Colt .45 military issue.

Bubba's eyes widened at the sight.

"That's not one of the options," Tannyhill said. Marion set their drinks on the table while Tannyhill moved a twenty toward her.

"That man at the bar bought these," Marion said. She turned around and pointed at an empty barstool. "Well, he was there a minute ago. Anyway, he tipped me and everything, so we're good."

"No name?" Tannyhill asked.

"No, just cash money," Marion answered. "I don't recollect seeing him here before. Kind of tall, cheap sunglasses, some creepy looking tattoos on his arms, reading a book. Sound familiar?"

"Not really. Thank you, Marion." Tannyhill took a glass, held it below his nose, and inhaled the single malt. "Bubba...what the hell is your given name any way?"

Bubba retrieved the other glass, skipped the sniffing of the Scotch's scent, and downed half of the large shot. "Cecil." He coughed a couple of times. "I prefer Bubba."

"Fine." Tannyhill passed a small sip through his lips. "Bubba, I'm going to give you some options that I believe are more than fair. One, and the option I highly recommend, you work for me doing my cash transactions."

"Do what?"

"You do what I'm doing now. You collect from the losers and pay out the winners. I credit you one percent of the total net, and we work your debt down."

"How much is that per week?" Bubba sipped the Balvenie this time.

"About two hundred dollars. It would take almost a year to work off what you owe me."

Bubba leaned forward and tapped his fingers on the table as he spoke. "You're telling me that you'd trust me handling all that money."

Tannyhill laughed. "It's not a question of trust. It's a question of mathematics. I know exactly what's coming in and going out. There's no way to hustle me and get away with it. And if you tried to run away with the cash, then the item in the briefcase does become an option."

Bubba smiled at Tannyhill. "I don't mean any disrespect, Mr. Tannyhill, but you seem like too classy a fellow to kill someone."

Swirling the Balvenie DoubleWood around his glass, Tannyhill pointed his index finger toward the ceiling. "See that?" Bubba leaned back his head. "Any idea what that is?" Tannyhill asked.

"Looks like somebody smeared brown paint up there," Bubba answered.

"That somebody was my father and that's not paint." He sniffed his glass again before taking another sip. "One person ever stole money from him. My father took a fungo bat and split his head open. It sprayed like Old Faithful. I was eleven and sitting right here. You only think you know what I'm capable of doing. My father paid Sorrento to keep that blood on the ceiling as a warning. Nobody has ever even tried to steal anything from me."

Bubba stared at the ceiling a while longer before saying, "It sounds like a deal to me. Did you have any other options?"

"Yes, I hire someone else to do my collecting. I cut you off from betting, and the collector rides you like a cheap claimer until you're paid off."

"Like I said," Bubba repeated, "it sounds like a deal to me. When do I start?"

"Come by my house next Tuesday at noon." Vic considered his sleep pattern. "On second thought, make that around two. Until Tuesday then?"

"Just one question, Mr. Tannyhill." Bubba dragged the back of his hand across the opposing cheek leaving a bit of grease from the last tow job in the process. "This is a real fair deal for me and I appreciate it." He hesitated.

"What's the question then?"

"Why me? Why are you giving me a break?"

Tannyhill considered his answer for a while. "In part, it's a practical move. I'm making some big changes in my life, and frankly, I don't want to be bothered with the collecting any longer."

Bubba moved his body around in the booth and the Naugahyde reacted with an otherworldly noise that only emanates from coated vinyl. "There are other people you could get to do this. We don't know each other that well."

"But I knew your father for a long time."

Bubba bowed his neck. "Richard was *not* my father."

Tannyhill continued. "Honestly, I don't know how he came up with it all. I never thought the wrecker business could bring in that kind of cash. But still, he died owing me money."

"Wait a minute," Bubba said, "you don't expect me to work off his debt, too, do you?"

Tannyhill shoved the shot glass on the table from one hand to the other and back. "Absolutely not. Your...Richard and I worked that out long before he died."

"So, he worked his debt off?" Bubba questioned.

"In a sense. We covered all the bases in case something happened to him."

Tannyhill took all the sugar packages from the table's container and shuffled them from one hand to the other.

"Bubba, I never intended to be what I am. In some measure, for better or for worse, we all end up imitating our fathers. That's just the way men are wired."

"Doesn't apply to me," Bubba said.

"Do you have any idea how many times Richard came here from a wrecker job and handed me a wad of bills? He even put the larger denominations on the outside just like you."

"It's different," Bubba answered. "It's circumstances."

"It's a trap," Tannyhill interjected. "I struggle every day not to be like my old man. When I'm not paying attention, he finds his way back into me. The blood on the ceiling...that's my legacy."

Bubba stared at Tannyhill without moving.

"Look at where we are and what we're doing." Tannyhill bowed his head, closing his eyes. "This could be Art and Richard sitting right here thirty years ago."

"But we're different than them," Bubba protested.

"Don't you see? We simply imitate what we saw growing up. Not that we want to. It's just too easy to fall back into. What was their habit is now our habit."

Bubba rose from the fan-backed booth.

"I'm changing my life all around," Tannyhill said. "You should think about doing the same."

"What's the line on Tech at UT?" Bubba asked.

"Hasn't moved. Still eight and a half."

"Give me fifty on Texas," Bubba said.

"That's not a good bet."

"Well, alright then." Bubba shifted his weight from one foot to the other. "Give me fifty on Tech."

Bubba walked toward the exit. Tannyhill called out, "That's not a good bet either."

***

"I already accepted that position."

The voice snaked its way over the fan-backed booth–firm, menacing, but not loud.

"Felix Krull, I presume," Tannyhill answered. "Thank you for the Scotch." The shrill sound of Naugahyde announced Vic's movement as he began to slide out of the booth.

"Stay there, Viktor," the man said. "If I see you over here, there'll be some more blood on that ceiling."

Tannyhill settled back into the vinyl. He could feel beads of sweat popping out all over his face. His forehead, he imagined, must look like a sheet of bubble wrap. He called out, "Can I at least return the favor and buy you a drink?"

He heard the rattle of ice in a glass and saw a hand at the end of his booth.

"I paid Maid Marion to take a break," the voice attached to the hand said, "but I had the foresight to order us another Balvenie. Take it."

Tannyhill leaned sideways to retrieve the glass. The rolled up sleeve of Krull's shirt revealed a few inches of wrist and forearm. Some type of vine-like tattoo thickly covered what he could see of his skin.

"Thank you," Tannyhill said, as he took a quick sip, attempting to calm himself. "Should I continue to address you by that rogue's name?"

"Ah," came the reply, "I saw *Death in Venice* on your bookshelf. I hoped you were familiar with Felix Krull. Are you a fan of Thomas Mann?"

193

"I'm not a big fan of one hundred word sentences." Tannyhill sipped again at the drink and wondered if this tact of chumminess would work. "*Magic Mountain* almost destroyed my appetite for fiction. When I got to the end of a sentence, I couldn't remember where I began."

The laugh that rose over the booth sounded much like the voice, harsh yet restrained. "Genius takes effort, Viktor. Anyway, *Felix Krull* was a much easier read."

"Not really," Tannyhill said. "I didn't find anything to like about the character. That everyone bought into his con games and all the women adored him, well, that seemed like a load of crap to me."

His breathing became shallow as the seconds of silence between the booths grew.

"I see your Ivy League education was a failure, Viktor."

"People call me Tannyhill or Vic. Viktor sounds way too pretentious for someone from Solomon, Texas." When the voice didn't respond, he continued. "And when it comes to the Ivy League, Dartmouth barely hangs on by its fingertips. Obviously you have a great education though. Where did you go?"

"Huntsville."

"Oh, Sam Houston State. The Bearkats. That's a fine Texas school."

"I'm sure it is," the voice said, "but I was housed in the Walls Unit down the road. You know, the one with the fence, the concrete and barbed wire. The state gave me a full scholarship there for six years."

This time Tannyhill remained quiet, closed his eyes, and waited for the voice to speak again. The jab into the side of his thigh caused him to lurch forward in pain. He reached for whatever pierced the skin but was restrained by a strong hand.

"Do not mistake my congeniality with weakness," the voice said into his ear. Felix Krull, whoever this man was, withdrew the knife point and released his hand. Tannyhill eyed the switchblade, its tip red with his blood. The man swiped the knife with a cocktail napkin before snapping it back into place. "A quality knife oil will shine that up again," the man said. "*Scheisse*, Viktor, I barely broke the skin. You bleed like a stuck pig."

The man wore a baseball cap low on his forehead, a pair of dark sunglasses, and a scraggly beard. His appearance was similar to a lot of blue collar men around Solomon. Tannyhill worked to look as unfazed by the stabbing as possible. The blood felt warm on the palm of his hand pressed against his black Levi's.

"What do you want?" Tannyhill asked, in a slightly shaky voice. Considering the pain shooting through his leg, it was the best he could do.

"We're partners now," Krull said. "Ever since Punches told me about your gambling enterprise, I've been scoping you out. I don't believe you're maximizing your profits. In fact, I think you run a shoddy operation. The deal you just offered that kid Bubba, for example. That shows a real chink in your armor. You can't do that when you live on *this* side of the law.

"You see, the way to handle that is to break some non-essential bone. Some bone that won't stop him from working but will hurt like hell when he does. Then if he still doesn't get the picture, you move on to…essential boneage."

"What if I don't want a partner?"

"That ship has sailed," the man said, as he held up a finger with a thin line of blood dripping from its tip. "It's sealed in *blut*." The man pushed out of the booth. "I'll be in touch."

"Wait," Tannyhill said. "What do you want? You can't–"

With his back to Vic, the man held up his left hand and interrupted, "Stop right there." He turned and removed his sunglasses. Tannyhill could see two teardrop tattoos next to the outer edge of his right eye. "I can do anything I want. That is the way of the superior man. I said I will be in touch."

"But I–"

"Would you rather I start with some non-essential bone?"

29

A WINDY DAY

"**S**o's you boys is pardners?"

Clovis had become too familiar with the soggy Roi-Tan slogging its way from one side of Oat Smith's mouth to the other. What turned his stomach though were the occasional bits of wet tobacco adhering to his lower lip or sliding down to rest somewhere on Oat's chin.

"So's ya brotha knows what's goin' on here?" Oat addressed Clovis again.

"I'm standing right here, Sheriff," Bubba said. "And yeah, I know about the phony–"

"Whoa, whoa, whoa," Oat interrupted. "Put a sock in it. We don' talk about these things 'less we know the coast is clear. Shut my door and have a look see if anyone's around."

Bubba walked a few yards into the office before stepping back in and bringing the door to a close. "There's a lady at the desk just outside your office."

"Tha's jus' Miss Shenkman," Oat said. "She don' hear so good. That's why I hired her."

"What does she do?" Bubba asked.

"Dispatcher."

"That's Wilma?"

"In the flesh," Oat said. "No one else out there?"

"No."

"Alright then," Oat said, "you boys take a seat." He stayed at the front of his desk and scooched himself onto the edge.

Looking down at Clovis, Oat shook his head back and forth. "Not anybody else you told, right?"

"Right."

"Are ya sure?"

"Yeah, I'm sure."

Oat faced Bubba. "And you?"

"Didn't tell a soul," Bubba answered.

"You didn' tell ya momma?"

"No."

"How 'bout Miss Nancy Lee?" Oat asked. "What exactly you been sharing with her out at the Dillard?"

Clovis noted Bubba's back straightening and the muscles in his forearms tightening. "We haven't told anyone, period," Clovis said. "So can we get on with this?"

"I been trying to get on with this since ya Daddy died," Oat said. "Are ya on board with me now or are you gonna get off the pot?"

While Clovis struggled with the mixed metaphor, Bubba asked, "How exactly does this deal work?"

Oat smiled as he stood and patted Bubba on the shoulder before moving on to the chair behind his desk. "Now that's the kind of question I've been waiting to hear. I bet you boys are startin' to feel the pinch. Got some bills be comin' due, I imagine. Or maybe Mr. Tannyhill is wantin' a little taste of his money back."

"Jesus," Bubba said, "does everybody in this town know everybody's business?"

"Oh, hell, son," Oat answered, "there's just one secret I care about keeping. And that's this right here, right now, in this room. Richard and me had us some conflations ova the years." Oat held his index finger in the air. "But the one thing I could count on was: he knew how to keep his mouth shut. Now that piece a shit brother of his was a different story. He got what he deserved."

Clovis asked, "Have you found his body yet?"

"Not yet." Oat stretched one boot onto his desk followed by the other boot crossing it at the ankle. "But there ain't no question he's dead. You saw all the blood in that van. Someone popped him two or three times. I'm guessing in the head."

"So, anything on who shot Daddy Two?" Clovis asked. "Did you check any more on that girl watching the funeral?"

"Aw, her Grandma Rainey died a coupla months back. She was jus' out there visitin'. Cute little old gal. I thought I told you that already."

"You did. Just wondering why she was hanging around."

"This could be all tied up in a bow if I collude that Punches killed his brother." Oat struck a couple of matches together and relit his burned out stogie. "But that all depends on if you boys are gonna work with me or not."

"What does that mean?" Bubba asked.

"That means ya had no good reason to be here. But ya was in Solomon the night Richard got shot." Oat leaned his head back and blew out a huge plume of cheap smoke. "It wouldn' take much to make a case against ya, Bubba."

"But there's no evidence," Bubba said. Clovis watched Bubba's hands as they gripped the arms of his chair. "And hell, I didn't do it. I never came anywhere close to the house."

"Don't matta," Oat said. "Evidence don't matta either. You was humpin Scott Austin's wife, and he's a legend 'round here. He took us to State ten years ago. Then you was eatin' burritos right before ya daddy was killed. Now that just sounds cold-blooded, don't it?"

"He wasn't my daddy."

"And there's your motif," Oat grinned at Bubba. "Ya hated the man. And he didn' like you none either."

Clovis rose to his feet as soon as he saw Bubba jump out of his chair. Bubba's face reddened and his fists clinched. Clovis placed a hand on his shoulder, but Bubba brushed it off.

"Tha's it, boy." Oat blew smoke toward Bubba's face. "Let loose a that temper of yours. Can only help build my case against ya."

Bubba turned and bolted out of the Sheriff's office. Clovis followed behind but stopped at the door and drew it to a close. He returned slowly to his seat.

"Alright, Oat. How exactly does this deal work?"

***

Standing just inside the rusty screen door of Sorrento's, everything seemed to grind to a halt for Clovis. A cue ball paused against the rail, "Car Wheels on a Gravel Road" faded to a close on the jukebox, popping grease quieted to a slow sizzle, and loud, boozy voices muffled themselves into reserved conversations. Clovis felt like he had walked into the eye of a hurricane.

He asked the dozen or so people at the pool tables and around the bar if they had seen Bubba. A few shook their heads no. The rest of them went back to what they were doing. And the still life that had been Sorrento's shifted slowly, one frame at a time into normalcy.

Clovis didn't really know of many other places to look for his brother. It had been a couple of hours since Bubba stormed out of Oat Smith's office. Clovis paged him again but didn't believe that Bubba would answer.

Without a moment of transition, the smell of a grease-laden grill was replaced by the overwhelming aroma of vanilla and new crayons. Clovis turned toward the screen door at his back and heard an enchanting, earthy rasp from the other side.

"Hey, are you just taking up space or what?"

He saw no face but instead a headful of black and tangled hair blowing across the eyes of a woman who had already tweaked his senses of smell and hearing. In one hand she held a guitar case and in the other, a fistful of cords.

"Please?" she asked with a bit more agitation.

"Sure, yeah, sorry." Clovis pushed wide the squeaky door as the woman squeezed herself and her equipment through the opening. "Need some help?" he asked.

She propped her guitar case against the closest table and tossed the cords onto a chair. Turning hard on the heels of her hiking boots, she locked eyes with Clovis and stepped toward him. "Yeah, you can help. Just hold the door open for me, okay? You look like you'd make a good doorstop."

"Doorstops R Us," he said, with a nervous laugh.

The guitar player took a folded up Texas Rangers cap from the back pocket of her jeans and fit it snugly on her head, further obscuring her face from his view. "Well, alrighty then," she said and walked to the back of a shiny black Silverado. She began grappling with a speaker column.

> There's a wall between us but it's not what it seems
> It's only made of concrete and barbed wire

Lucinda Williams' voice had returned to the jukebox. Clovis assumed this was the "cute little ol' gal" that Oat Smith had mentioned, the girl Oat had seen at Daddy Two's funeral. Clovis noticed a flyer on the wall outside of Sorrento's that showed Windy Day sitting on a bar stool with a guitar in hand. The photo wasn't very clear and the ball cap covered most of her face as well.

He looked back to the pickup and noted the lack of progress she had made with the speaker. "You need a little hand?"

She pushed a few stray hairs from one side of her face, squinted, and seemed to study his face for a few moments. "You know what they say about a man with little hands?"

Clovis allowed the screen door to slam shut and jumped into the bed of the pickup. He pushed the heavier than expected Peavey speaker to the edge of the tailgate. "Do you speak to all of your friends like this?" he asked.

"I would if I had any friends."

"Small wonder." Clovis held onto the top of the speaker column as she eased it onto the sidewalk. He still couldn't make out her face from this angle.

"Who asked for your help anyway?"

"Well, you did," said Clovis, "and I take being a doorstop pretty damn seriously." He slid off the tailgate, lifted the speaker by the handle, and tried his best to make it appear as if it didn't feel like the heaviest thing he had ever lifted in his life. She grabbed the base of it and they moved it inside Sorrento's as Mr. Sorrento himself held the door open for them.

They returned to the pickup without speaking and repeated the process with the second column.

"Sorry I was a little snippy with you," she said. "I appreciate the help."

Clovis wiped a few beads of sweat from his forehead as he sat on the edge of the stage. "That's alright." He stared at the floor and tried to catch his breath.

"Can I buy you a beer?" she asked.

"I'm looking for my brother. Maybe later."

"Alrighty then," she said. "Thanks again, doorstop."

When Clovis looked up, she had her back to him and was already plugging a cord into the preamp. "I've got a name," he said, pushing himself away from the stage.

"I cover that song," she said to Clovis. "Hey, Mr. Sorrento," she called out, "where's the electrical outlet?"

"Under the table on the right of the stage," he called back from behind the bar.

"Your right or stage right?" she said.

"My right," Sorrento answered.

"Thank you." She kept her head down and crouched under the table to her left.

"You cover what song?" Clovis asked. He took a couple of steps in her direction.

"'I've Got a Name.' Jim Croce wrote it. It's a beautiful song." She struggled with the fit between the preamp prongs and the outlet. "Well, piss up a rope!"

"Can I help you?" Clovis asked.

"No, I got it." She pushed herself up from the floor. "I broke a fucking nail." She flipped the switch on the back of the preamp and a red light glowed brightly.

"My name is Clovis McDonald." He addressed the back of her head.

"Oh, my goodness," she said. She removed her baseball cap and flipped it on the table.

"What's wrong?" Clovis asked.

"Nothing. Just a…just a twisted cord is all."

Clovis could tell she was brushing the hair out of her face. She seemed to be wiping sweat away with her sleeve, but it was difficult to tell as she still had her back to him.

"I'm Windy Day."

"I figured that out from the poster," Clovis said. "Unusual spelling."

"Unusual family."

"Yeah, well, whose isn't?"

She turned to face him, and for a moment Clovis vaguely sensed some kind of recognition though it passed. She looked to be around his age, maybe a few difficult years framing her dark brown eyes with premature wrinkles. He felt an urge to cup the cheeks of her round face into the palms of his hands and tell her everything would be alright.

Her attire appeared designed to cover, instead of accentuate, parts of her body. It didn't matter to Clovis.

"You know what," he said. "My brother can take care of himself. How about that beer?"

"Clovis McDonald," she said. Windy shook her head and stared at him as if he was an old friend. "This calls for a shot of tequila and a Tecate."

Clovis tried to not look like a lovesick puppy, but he failed.

"Hey, hey, hey," Windy said. "Nothing like that is ever, and I mean *ever* going to happen between us. Never. Get that look out of your eyes right now."

"Okay, sure. Just a friendly drink. That's good." The words passed through his lips, but his heart didn't follow.

Windy took a step toward the bar and said, "I'll order the drinks and be right back. Don't go anywhere, you hear?"

Clovis leaned against the stage again.

He watched admiringly as her jeans couldn't hide the well-rounded hips, those melon-esque cusps of perfection gliding past several bar patrons. He had noticed, also, that her wrists were quite a bit thicker than those of Ruby Tuesday in Fort Worth. Her forearms seemed muscular with a matching, small sunburst tattoo on the underside of each. He watched as she rested an elbow on the bar, talking to Mr. Sorrento. Her distinct laugh echoed throughout the aged wood room.

That sense of familiarity struck Clovis again. Something about her nose, maybe. The fleeting recognition held neither a positive nor negative connotation. It just was. Sketchy, nonspecific, veiled. Then fading, dissipating, a shadow, gone.

1991
Late October

When a thing is funny, search it for a hidden truth.
George Bernard Shaw

30

COMFORTABLE YET DISTINCTIVE

Mazel tapped a cigarette from the pack of Lucky Strike Lights and another from a pack of Gauloises. She placed the Gauloises in the corner of Al's mouth, pressed his lips together tightly and attached a small strip of adhesive tape to his cheek and chin. Lighting his and then hers, Mazel aligned an ashtray in his lap under the cigarette.

"Don't know why I didn't think of it sooner. You were always partial to anything French, weren't you? Can't say they're cheap or easy to come by. They smell awful. Gauloises must be French for day-old fish heads."

Al's sucking sound began, so little as not to be noticed unless you were listening for it. He stared out the window, a thin line of drool snaking its way past his taped lips, but somehow, with the Gauloises dangling there, Al appeared more dignified.

"I know you weren't expecting me today, but I've got some trouble at home."

Mazel stared out the window and occasionally tapped Al's ash into the container below. Whenever Al's cigarette would burn out, she would go through the lighting, pressing, taping, and aligning process again. Several times she moved to the edge of her chair and made sounds as if starting to speak. Then she would sit back and stare blankly out the window.

She wished Manuel Daza would come through the door. But this was Saturday, his day off. Come to think of it, she had never visited Al on a Saturday. The Tumbleweed Rest Home had a different vibe today—more visitors, fewer regular staff members, everyone's movements seemed forced, superficial, and out of kilter.

"Bubba is in jail."

Clovis had called around dinnertime last night to say he would be home late. She had asked about his brother, and Clovis said that Bubba would be home later, too. She dozed off while watching Johnny Carson. When Mazel jerked awake after midnight, she checked their rooms. Her mother-worry kicked in right away. The rest of the night she called their beepers countless times but to no avail.

"Oat Smith called early this morning. Said that Bubba was drunk and got into a fight at PJ's."

How many times, she wondered, had she warned them about going to PJ's Gentlemen's Club? Richard had stumbled home from PJ's for years reeking of cheap gin and even cheaper perfume. Early in their marriage he would return home randy and with a slightly drunken, seductive charm. But that alluring quality wore away quickly as did his desire for Mazel. By then, the absence of passion was more than mutual.

"Clovis finally called this morning. He didn't know anything about Bubba being in jail. Said he met a girl and they stayed up all night talking. I told him that he could have at least called me back. Said the battery died on his beeper. He didn't consider I might be worried.

"Anyway, Oat is going to let Bubba out around four. Clovis is running behind at work so I'll need to go pick him up." She slouched lower in the chair and leaned heavily against the left armrest. "Should be some interesting dinner conversation tonight."

Mazel stubbed out the Lucky Light from which she had only taken a couple of drags. Al Pozzo smoked his last Gauloises a few minutes ago.

"Maybe it's because I didn't get any sleep but...the feeling, like I want to shut down...I don't want to feel that, you know?

That's why I came to see you today. I could have just crawled back under the covers. Not for an hour or two but for days. Like the depression after the accident.

"I couldn't stop thinking about Enrique being dead. I couldn't stop thinking about giving the boys different fathers. I couldn't stop thinking about you. And then I couldn't stop thinking about every little mistake I ever made in my life. I thought about all those things until I couldn't think straight. So, I shut down. And I don't think anyone understands how tempting that is when all these bad thoughts come rushing in. You just want to sleep and turn them off.

"I felt it kick up today for the first time in a long while."

For the remainder of the visit, only Mazel's occasional snore would awaken her and keep the room from being completely quiet.

***

Having exited the Tumbleweed Rest Home, Mazel's vision of a lone man sitting in the darkened corner behind Dock Two startled her. She turned to reenter the building when the man said, "Mizz McDonald?"

"Manuel?"

Emerging from the dock shadows, she could recognize the face but not the attire. "In all these years, I don't think I've ever seen you in anything but a uniform. You look totally different."

"It's all my wife ever see me in," Manuel responded. "It's Cubavera. Most of my shirts are. Comfortable yet distinctive."

Through her sour mood, Mazel couldn't resist a short laugh. "Something your wife said?"

"No, just a fact."

"What are you doing here? Shouldn't Fermina be serving you some fried worms about now?"

Manuel stood next to Mazel and extended his elbow, which she accepted. "Let's walk," he said.

"What about Al's Agnostic Angels?"

"Small crowd today. They look peaceful enough. But we'll walk the back ground so nobody sees us."

"Sounds good to me," she said. They exited the dock area and meandered down the walkway through the desert flora. Sparse and beautiful, mostly hearty.

"I wear this shirt and jeans, because this is who I am. I want you to see the real Manuel one time. For what must be said."

"This sounds serious. How did you know I was here?"

"Karen was charge nurse on the last shift. She call. No one remember seeing you here on a Saturday. She thought something might be wrong."

Mazel noticed Manuel glance behind them. She placed her free hand on his arm as they walked. He acknowledged her touch with a smile, albeit something of a sad one. "Why didn't you come on inside?"

"Patty's on duty now," Manuel said. "We are not so *simpatico.*"

"She's probably just upset that I didn't bring her usual allotment of Kit Kats," Mazel said. "Patty always has a burr up her ass about something. Anyway, this was kind of an impromptu trip."

"That's why I'm here. You always call when you're coming out."

"You could have called me from home," she said. "There was no reason to get dressed up and come down here."

"I beg to disagree with you. We are friends of a type, but there are levels of friends. For today, I must see you and wear what I wear to tell you some truth. Deeper friends should reveal deeper truths. I am more than my uniform allows you to see. The uniform hides many things."

"God, this really must be serious."

"Best if we sit," he said, leading Mazel to a wooden bench a few yards off the path.

"I'm speaking to you, friend-to-friend," he stated. "I care for you very much, as much as any woman except for Fermina and my daughters."

"Thank you, Manuel. I'm honored."

"Don't speak too soon. What I tell you now is hard to say, but it is for your own good." Manuel shifted his feet to and fro and squeezed his hands together. "Mazel McDonald, you are what we call *ensimismada*. It means you spend a lot of time thinking about your life and your problems. It means -"

"Cut the crap, I know what it means. You're telling me I'm self-absorbed."

"No, no, no." Manuel fidgeted with his fingers, crossed and uncrossed his legs. "No, no, no." He stood up and looked across the mesa. "Alright, *si*, but not exactly."

Mazel watched him stare into the distance but did not respond. It did feel different to hear Manuel speak like this outside of the Tumbleweed. She knew him to be direct in his comments to her. But on the inside, in his uniform, in his position as an orderly, Mazel felt somehow insulated from his words.

This revelation would have knocked Mazel off her feet if she had been standing–she felt superior to Manuel inside the building. But outside, well, Manuel had been absolutely right. His words carried more weight here. They penetrated to the core here. His words rang truer here.

"You can't get over the past. I tell you this inside, but you don't hear as well in there. I stand sometimes and listen to you talk to Dr. Al. You shouldn't live with so much regret. It drags you down. It drags your boys down."

"What gives you the right to eavesdrop on Al and me?" she asked.

"Listen to what you just say. It's not you and Dr. Al. It's you... talking to yourself."

"What...you think...I know...Goddamn it, I know that."

"It's you thinking." Manuel looked Mazel in the eyes. "It's you thinking of the same mistakes, the same regrets. For the last twenty years."

"But it helps me," Mazel offered back. "It keeps me going."

"It keeps you going *nowhere*."

Mazel grasped the bench rail and tried to stand but didn't have the strength to push herself up. She turned her head away from

Manuel, away from the Tumbleweed, and looked to the semi-barren land instead. The urge to shut down, the urge to climb to the roof, to look over the edge of the five-story Tumbleweed Rest Home, the urge to face the abyss again, the urge to fall and never rise–

"It keeps you from living."

Mazel rose shakily from the bench, and Manuel steadied her with both hands holding her just above the elbow.

"Your *penitencia* was over long ago. It is time now for *salvacion*."

When Mazel stood, she checked her watch for the time. Three-twenty three. "Bubba is getting out of jail at four. I've got to go."

"What?"

"Another time," she answered. "Can you help me to my car?"

"Yes."

Manuel escorted Mazel to the car with their elbows locked together. "I had much more to say," he said. "Are you okay to drive? I can take you. It will give us more time."

She slid into the driver's seat and held the door open. "I'm okay. I'll be back in a couple of days. We can talk then."

"Miss McDonald, I'm sorry to upset you." Her took her left hand that rested on the steering wheel into his hands. Kneeling by the open car door, Manuel kissed the back of her hand and then pressed it to his cheek.

"It's okay," she said. "I'm not mad at you." His teary eyes met hers. She couldn't remember seeing him so emotional. "Really Manuel, you should be in charge of this place. You understand much more than those people inside."

"I understand nothing. I am what I am. Nothing more." He kissed her hand once more before letting go, standing, and backing away from the car.

"And what, pray tell, is that?"

Manuel opened his arms to the north and south, his face a faint rainbow, a wan smile with a tear at its edge.

"Comfortable, yet distinctive."

31

LIFE ON THE LINE

"**O**at, isn't there anything you can do?"

Tannyhill tapped out a couple more aspirin onto his nightstand and swallowed them with a swig of Maalox. The head and stomach aches had been around since his encounter with the man identifying himself as Felix Krull, never going away, medicines only lessening the severity.

"Do you want me to come out there and arrest you again?"

Tannyhill started to dismiss the notion out of hand but stopped before he answered to consider how it might shake out. A temporary solution, he decided. At some point, he'd have to face the man again. Oat Smith said his law enforcement friends thought the man sounded like an ex-convict named Judas Conroe. Based his operation out of Hobbs, New Mexico, but had disappeared recently. Oat had said the detective in Hobbs was thrown off by the second teardrop tattoo for a while. One represented his first kill and manslaughter conviction. The second teardrop, the detective surmised, must be a more recent kill.

"No. Thanks for the offer though. Can't you just find him and arrest him?"

"How would I find him? Unless I come out there and live with ya til he returns. Might be a nice change a pace for a coupla of weeks or so. The ol' lady has had a burr up her ass lately. Whatcha think?"

Tannyhill could think of a fate worse than death–being around Oat Smith for any extended length of time. "Sorry, Oat, that won't work. Any suggestions on what I should do? I feel like a sitting duck out here."

"I tell you what, Mr. Tannyhill. I'd carry one of ya guns at all times. If you're taking a crap, have a gun inside the commode. You eva see *The Godfather*?"

"See what?"

"The *Godfather* movies. They tape a gun inside the crapper and bam, bam, bam, he comes out shootin'. That's the way to do it."

"Yes, I see," Tannyhill said. "He caught them with their pants down, so to speak."

"Say what?"

"Never mind." The throbbing in Tannyhill's head intensified. "So you're saying I should put a gun in every room. In drawers, under my pillows, on the bookcase."

"And in every crapper."

"Yes, Oat, of course. I will have no unarmed toilets."

"Don' take no chances. It sounds like this ol' boy won't give you no warnin next time he shows up. Aim for the heart and then put a couple in his head."

"So, you're saying I should kill him?"

"I'd be glad to do it fo ya, but I'd have to know when he's a comin. If he tells ya, call me. I'll come out and blow the shit out of him. Maybe ya could knock some debt off a ol' Oat's account. Maybe even clear it off for me."

The pain in Tannyhill's head now jabbed through his eyes. He pinched the bridge of his nose between his thumb and forefinger. "Sounds like a paid hit when you put it that way."

"No, sir," Oat responded. "It's legal. They's even a legal name for it—*quid pro quo.*"

"Thank you for the offer, Oat. That's real considerate of you."

"No problem. Wouldn't be the first time I shot a man. Nothin to it really. Just relax your finger and bend it a couple of times. Do ya think ya can do it?"

"I think I can," Tannyhill answered.

"Just keep repeatin that, sir. Ya gotta believe in yourself. Just like the story I read to my grandchildren. My favorite book in the whole world. Exceptin' for the Bible, of course.

"What's that?"

"*The Little Engine That Could.* Remember what the train says when he's trying to get up the hill with all those Christmas toys?"

"I don't guess my father ever read that one to me, Oat. What did he say?"

"I-think-I-can, I-think-I-can, I-think-I-can…"

***

"…I-think-I-can…"

But not without Margo. Whether his pendulum swung to the good side or bad, he wanted Margo with him.

Some relief for his churning interior came by attending to the particulars of his work–picking games, recording messages for the phone lines, itemizing bets from degenerates. Yet he couldn't shake the menacing shadow of Judas Conroe. A creak, pop, or any other house settling sound led Tannyhill to survey whatever room he occupied for the nearest gun hiding place.

Only when he spoke with Margo could he, for a time, lose himself. Their individual fantasies merged, transforming into a reality more genuine and better defined than any existence he had known before now. Tannyhill's need for her grew during this period of adversity, beyond what he had ever experienced with any other woman. In fact, during their dreamy pillow talk last night, it slipped out.

"I love you, Margo. I love you."

He winced during the long silence, stomach gnarled in anticipation of her response. Picking up the stereo remote, he had hit himself in the head and the CD's changed: *The Barber of Seville* to *Rigoletto*. Then her wholesome, Polly Purebread voice–the perfect choice.

"I love you, too, Vic. I love you, too."

The buzzer of the microwave and the telephone rang simultaneously producing a startle effect that buckled Tannyhill's knees. He reflexively opened the refrigerator door and reached next to the Gouda for the Ruger 9mm. Upon realizing the sounds' origins, Tannyhill stopped the microwave and then checked the caller ID. Damn, the chicken primavera would have to wait.

"Tannyhill."

"Hello, sir. This is Grant Glassford. Professor Delaney asked me to give you a call."

"Yes, Grant, I'm looking forward to working with you. I've read in the *Solomon Chronicle* where you're a big hit."

"That's in front of a few thousand people, sir. They're more interested in getting to the restroom and buying a hot dog before the second half starts. This Jingle Elf parade, I mean, a lot of people are going to hear me."

"Listen, Grant...and please stop calling me sir, alright? I like the ring of Tannyhill and without the mister attached to it."

"Yes...yes, okay."

"When Pavarotti sang at the Metropolitan Opera, do you know how many people were there?"

"No, sir. Sorry...Tannyhill."

"No more than what you see at halftime."

"But that is something of a different audience," Grant Glassford countered.

"They drip on their pants and zip up just like we do out here."

"But they know and understand music."

"They're about the only people left in the whole country that do." Tannyhill opened the refrigerator door again and placed the Ruger 9mm next to the Gouda. "But they're not going to be watching the Jingle Elf Parade. I know it's a big deal for you, but it's in Chicago. Do you know anybody there?"

"Not really."

"You'll be lucky if several thousand people hear you sing. Just like halftime."

Tannyhill calmed the young man, and they began practicing scales. Grant's voice had a fine quality and resonance. If he had been trained professionally at a younger age, he might have been operatic quality. The longer he listened, the more Tannyhill could recognize his own voice coming through the line.

"Your phrasing is a bit off there, Grant. Break it up a bit. You're singing the line as a whole—*where the wind comes sweeping down the plain.* Make it two phrases—*where the wind,* pause, *comes sweeping down the plain.* Pretend you're Sinatra or Willie Nelson. Push those words together and cram them in tight."

Grant Glassford took telephone instruction well. By the end of their first session, he was ready for more. "Can we go over this again tomorrow?"

"No, no, no. Practice what we've gone over and call me on Friday. Don't overwork your voice. It sounded like you were getting a little thin there toward the end."

"OK."

"L-A," Tannyhill prompted.

"H-O," came the immediate response.

"M-A."

In unison they sang, "*Oklahoma! OK.*"

He liked this kid.

***

"Hello."

"I love you," Tannyhill said into the telephone.

"Well, I love you, too," Margo Chandler replied. "Who are you?"

Tannyhill laughed as much as a worried man with a worried mind can laugh. "You just went up another notch in my ears."

"Maybe you should bring me back down to earth, Vic. I get nose bleeds at these heights."

Margo knew nothing of Felix Krull or Judas Conroe or whatever he called himself today. Tannyhill didn't want to worry her now.

He wanted her voice to sparkle and then gradually glide to a gamy, itching rasp. He yearned for Margo's slow, sensual pirouette of patois. He craved those minty words melting in his ear as they passed through the fiery kiln of her mouth. Was there anything that could bring more joy, more elation, more satisfaction to Tannyhill than the titillation of Margo's voice? She was…she was opera. A lyric opera unfettered by the standard repertoire of grand opera. She was Diva.

Tannyhill might wish to be confined within the walls of his home, but his libido desired to be un-caged. If need be, to soar with Margo and risk flying too near the sun.

Love and music, these have I lived for…

He needed her in his life *forever.*

"Margo, I've been waiting all of my life for your voice. To pierce through this dusty old heart no matter how thick. Margo Chandler, will you marry me?"

"Ooohhh, Vic. I would marry you, but I don't know what you look like."

"I may have a solution for that. How about if we keep things pretty much as they are? You keep your place and I'll keep mine. We won't really change what we're doing now at all."

"Wait a minute. We don't live together, but we're still married?"

"Yeah, the beautiful people in Hollywood do it all the time. Some of them rarely see each other, but they're married."

"You might have used a better example," Margo laughed. "Those folks don't seem to stay married forever."

"Solomon is a long way from Hollywood. We would have a real commitment."

Margo paused for a while. Tannyhill could feel his heart thumping and could see his shirt bouncing with every beat. "If anyone heard you saying this," she finally said, "you'd be committed alright–out to the Tumbleweed. This is as crazy a thing as I ever heard. I swear."

"And you are the sexiest swearer in existence," Tannyhill replied without hesitation. "Phone sex, that was a crazy idea, too. Look how it all worked out for you."

Tannyhill thought of a close and began his delivery.

"Think about all the advantages a marriage like ours would have. If you're in a bad mood or want to be alone, instead of having to deal with me, you just don't answer the phone. We could grow old together and never worry about wrinkles or liver spots."

"I could grow to the size of a house," Margo said, "and you'd still think of me as–"

"–absolutely the most beautiful woman."

"No bad breath."

"Or holding in your gas."

"No fights over the remote control."

"No joint checking."

"No faking an orgasm," she said, "though I'm damn good at it."

"No worry about performing. Not that it ever happens to me. Uh, just that once."

"Vic, you know this idea is growing on me."

"There's a ring set I've seen," Tannyhill said, going for the close. "I'll monitor the Home Shopping Network tomorrow and as soon as I see it again, I'll call you. I hope you like it."

"A real diamond, right?" she asked. "I had someone try to pass off zirconium as a diamond when I was younger. I twisted his nutsack so tight he almost choked on them."

Tannyhill broke into song. His spontaneity surprised him as did the Rodgers and Hammerstein melody on his lips.

> Bali Ha'i, may call you
> Any night, any day
> In your heart, you'll hear it call you:
> Come away, come away.

Margo responded, "I'll marry you, Vic. But how exactly is this going to work?"

"I've already thought it all out. You have conference call on your phone, right?"

"I do," she said. "Hands free, too. You know, so I can use my hands for more important things. What are you wearing?"

"My Dartmouth t-shirt and a pair of Levis."

"Details, Vic." Margo's voice stepped off the cliff and glided downward from one erotic crag to the next. "I need details, more details." Her breathing grew heavy and rhythmic. "Tell me more."

"Ooohhh, my Diva."

32

A MASTER YO-YO'ER

Clovis fought the urge to inhale a slice of Frank 'n Steins pizza before his mother or Bubba joined him in the kitchen. His Momma had taught them to wait for other people to be seated before digging into your food. She had been lying in bed when he arrived home a few minutes ago with two Monster pizzas. Weenie and Monster were the only sizes the pizza joint on the square offered.

Bubba had just finished showering off the taint of jail when Clovis entered the house. "I'm fucking starving," Bubba had called out from the bathroom in response to Clovis' arrival.

Mazel entered the kitchen first, eyes rimmed with smudgy black areas extending across her temples and down her cheeks from a combination of tears, mascara, and eyeliner–a sight Clovis had become all-too-familiar with while growing up. She placed a slice of pizza on a paper plate, sat at the table, and took a bite. "Could you get me a DP?" she asked.

Clovis couldn't stop looking at his mother taking a second bite, breaking one of her few, but cardinal, rules of etiquette.

"Clovis? DP?"

"Sure, sorry Momma." By the time he returned with two cans of Dr Pepper, Bubba had joined them and was stacking his plate with five or six slices of pizza.

"Wouldn't you like to be a Pepper, too?" Mazel asked Bubba with a distracted, singsongy lilt.

"I'm going to my room," Bubba answered.

"Sit down, boys," Mazel said quietly. "We need to talk."

"I'm tired," Bubba said. "I'm going to lay down."

Clovis grabbed a slice of pizza and watched Bubba take a few steps out of the kitchen and into the hallway.

"*No!*" Mazel yelled. "No, come back here right now."

Bubba stopped, his back to the kitchen. Clovis could hear the crunch as Bubba took a bite of pizza before turning around.

"Well," Bubba said, "since you put it that way, Momma." He returned to the table and took a seat across from her.

Clovis thought he could still detect a hint of alcohol seeping through Bubba's pores.

"So, Clovis, tell me again why you were out all night," Mazel said.

"I'm sorry I didn't call, Momma. I was listening to some music at Sorrento's, and then I got to talking with the singer. We just sat in the back of her pickup and all of a sudden, the sun was coming up."

"That sounds kind of romantic," Mazel said.

"That sounds kind of lame," Bubba said, through a mouthful of pizza. "You're up all night with a musician, and you don't get laid? I didn't think that was possible."

"Did you find any romance last night, Bubba? I hear the Solomon jail can really put a shine on your ass."

"Tell me you got a hand job, at least," Bubba said.

"Bubba," Mazel yelled, "stop it." She looked at Clovis and said, "The both of you."

They ate in silence for a minute. Bubba went to the refrigerator and returned with a Pearl Lager. Clovis popped the top of his Dr Pepper and said, "She's a really good singer. And she writes a lot of her own stuff."

"What's her name?" Mazel asked.

"Windy Day. Windy with an 'i', not an 'e'."

Bubba snorted derisively, and Mazel tossed her half-eaten slice of pizza onto the paper plate.

"What did Oat Smith say when he let you out?" Mazel placed her elbows on the table and leaned toward Bubba. "Why did he say you all were business partners?"

"I don't know. Why don't you ask Clovis?"

"Richard and Oat always had their heads together," she said, "like they were up to no good. Neither of you better be up to anything with that man. You can't trust him."

"I got everything under control, Momma," Clovis said, in a low monotone.

Mazel jumped up and grabbed some paper towels from the roll next to the kitchen sink. She went to Bubba's side and dabbed at his nose. "It's bleeding again."

Bubba took the towels from his mother. "I got it," he said, leaning his head back.

While washing some blood from her fingers at the kitchen sink, she asked, "What do you mean, you've got it under control?"

Clovis didn't want to answer directly. He didn't want to outright lie either. What he could do was tack around the truth, sail a few bits of fact into the mix, and hope to navigate through the questions without revealing much of anything.

"Oat just wants us to catch up on the county billing. That's all."

Mazel dried her hands on a kitchen towel hanging from a hook. "So why did he say 'you all' were partners?"

"Grab me a couple more towels, Momma," Bubba said.

Mazel ripped them from the roll. "I prefer requests to demands," she said, handing them to Bubba.

"Oh," Bubba said, "like your request to come back and sit here for dinner?"

Clovis' stomach turned a flip. "Excuse me," he said, after a belch erupted with a low-pitched, contralto resonance. "Bubba, could you at least cool it while we eat?"

"So," Mazel said, returning to her chair, "what caused the fight last night?"

"Aw, fuck it." Bubba pushed his chair out forcefully as he stood. "I'm going to my room." He placed three more slices of pizza on his plate while still holding the paper towels to his nose with the other hand.

"Who hit you?" she asked. "Were they in jail, too?"

"I was out of my mind drunk, Momma," Bubba said. "Does it really matter?" He walked out of the kitchen for the second time.

"Bubba!" Mazel called out. "You're acting just like your father."

Clovis hoped that his brother would continue walking down the hallway without saying a word. But Bubba stopped in roughly the same place he had in his initial attempt to flee the kitchen. He came back to the doorway.

"What caused any fight I ever got into? From first grade to now, to the day that I die–it's you, Momma. I'm always having to stand up for you."

"You don't have to…" Her voice faded to silence.

"Hey Bubba," Bubba said, "your momma is looking fine. Let me know when she's having another two-guys-in-a-day special."

Clovis had been confronted his entire life with the same kind of taunts, from the same group of kids, then teenagers, and now adults of Solomon, Texas. He never figured out a way to make it stop except sometimes with his fists, when he couldn't stand to hear another word.

Bubba threw his bloody towels into the trash bin. "Or how about, what happens when two penises go into one vagina? Nine months later, two dicks come out."

Clovis leaped out of his chair and rammed his shoulder into Bubba's ribs. They fell onto the floor with Clovis shouting, "Shut up, shut up, shut up!" They wrestled in the narrow hallway, essentially rolling a half-turn into one wall, then a half-turn into the other. Their grunts of exertion went on for nearly a minute until the gun went off. They froze in place for a few seconds and then jumped to their feet.

Mazel stood with a pistol pointing downward. Clovis moved toward her and saw a small hole in the kitchen floor. She set the gun on the table and sat back in her chair.

"The one thing that always kept me going no matter what," she said, "was how you two got along. How you two stood up for each other, how good a friends you…you *had* to be. From the day that you were born, because you didn't have a choice. Because your mother was a total basket case. Certifiable."

"Stop it, Momma," Clovis said.

"Yeah, please," Bubba said. "Please stop."

"I told Al today that I have that feeling again," Mazel said. "Like maybe I want to shut it all down. Or climb up on the roof to get away."

Clovis and Bubba sat at the table. Mazel picked up the half-eaten slice of pizza, brought it to her lips, and set it back on the plate without taking a bite.

"What can we do, Momma?" Clovis asked.

She pushed her chair back and leaned toward the china hutch to retrieve her pack of Lucky Strike Lights. She lit one and moved an ashtray to the table in one coordinated, graceful, well-practiced scoop.

Clovis noticed a trickle of blood again on Bubba's upper lip. He retrieved a couple of paper towels.

"Thanks," Bubba mumbled.

"I need one thing right now, boys," Mazel said. "I need the truth, the whole truth, and nothing but the truth. Or so help me God, we're just going down the same road we did when your father was here."

Bubba rose from his chair and went running down the hallway.

Clovis apologized for his brother. "Sorry, Momma." He walked down the hallway after Bubba.

He came back to the table in a couple of minutes.

"He'll be back soon," Clovis said. "He just had to throw up, that's all."

***

Clovis had always been a master yo-yoer of the truth. As quickly as he would slide a morsel of fact down the string, he would yank it back into his grasp. When sharing the whole story carried the weight of pain or consequence for either himself or the party hearing the whole story, out came the yo-yo. Now you see it, now you don't; now you see it, now you don't.

Bubba called his brother *diplomatic.* He didn't say it in a nice way either. The way Clovis understood Bubba's thinking was this--if you're going to tell the truth, tell it hard and straight regardless of the consequences; if you're going to tell some of the truth but leave out bits and pieces, then you might as well lie. Bubba told in-your-face truths, truths without filters, truths without a net. His lies were bold and heartfelt, lies so good that you wanted to believe them even if you knew they were total fabrications. The only person Clovis knew who Bubba cut any slack from his harsh and direct manner of truth-telling was their Momma.

After fifteen minutes of yo-yoing the story of McDonald Wrecker, the county contract, and the so-called partnership with Oat Smith, Clovis looked to Bubba. His brother had merely nodded and said, "Uh-huh," as Clovis strategically maneuvered the spool of truth, down and up the string. Bubba bit his lower lip and looked as if he might need to throw up again.

Thus far, the soft-pedaled story appeared to keep his mother thrown off balance. She asked questions of Clovis but had yet to get to the heart of the matter--its risks and its illegality.

"Why can't the county just pay you more for each tow job?" Mazel asked. "Why do you have to write these bogus invoices to get all of your money?"

Clovis took a sip of DP before speaking. "You know how government works. They keep the payments for a regular tow kind of low so they can look good. Then they can back door the real cost to us through another channel. This kind of thing goes on all the time."

"Is it legal?"

"If you look at it from a *prima facie* sense," Clovis struggled for the right words, "then you might consider the business arrangement to be somewhat irregular. However, there has been a tacit agreement between McDonald Wrecker and Oat Smith for more than twenty years."

"I don't understand," Mazel replied, turning to address Bubba. "Is it legal or not?"

Clovis watched his brother's fist tighten and release a couple of times before hearing, "Clovis is the one who knows this stuff." Bubba bit his lower lip again. "He made the deal. It's his business, ask him."

"Well, I did ask him," Mazel said, "but he spins everything around like a flamenco dancer. Just tell me the damn truth."

Bubba pushed away from the table and stood. "I don't feel so good." He pushed his chair in and leaned his hands against its back. "And that's the truth."

"Did you find the books for the county business?" Mazel said, ignoring what sounded to Clovis like Bubba's exit line.

"No," Clovis answered. "I think Punches might have got rid of them after he stole the money out of the account."

Mazel lit another Lucky Light. "Then you'll be starting a whole new accounting ledger. No history that this has been going on for twenty years."

"I guess that's right," Clovis said.

"Then to somebody on the outside, it looks like you and Oat just started this little side business. Sounds to me like if somebody gets their feathers in a bunch, they could make you look guilty of some kind of corruption. Have you thought of that?"

Clovis readied his yo-yo spool for a quick dash of truth. "Oat is the law around here. No one has checked the books in all these years. Why would they start now? Anyway, we can't survive without the contract. How much did Daddy Two transfer to you out of that account?"

"Around two thousand a month," Mazel answered.

Bubba yanked his chair into the air and slammed it down on the kitchen floor with enough force to splinter one of the legs. "That son-of-a-bitch!"

"Wha–?" Mazel started.

"Daddy Two was–"

Clovis interrupted. "Don't go there, Bubba."

"Why the hell not? Momma, here's the truth. Daddy Two was skimming another two grand a month and splitting it with Oat Smith. They've been running this scam since we were born. Do you have any idea how much money that is?"

Mazel shook her head from side to side.

"That's over half a million dollars," Bubba answered himself. "Daddy Two's take was half of that. And did we ever see a dime of that money? Hell no."

"He lost it all to Tannyhill," Clovis said, "and Lord knows what else." He crumpled the Dr Pepper can in his hand. "It was just play money to him."

"And us here," Bubba said, "scraping by. I'm glad he got his brains blown out."

"Bubba," Clovis said, "stop it."

Mazel stood and placed her hand on Clovis' shoulder. "That's alright." She moved over to Bubba, put her hands on his shoulders, and looked into his eyes. "I should have got rid of that man a long time ago."

***

Clovis eased off the clutch a fraction of a second too soon, and the wrecker didn't complete its shift into gear. He glided it back into neutral and allowed it to rest there for a minute as the wrecker picked up speed down the extended incline on Ranch Road 2325. Though it was Bubba's night to cover any tows, Clovis figured his brother wasn't in any condition to handle this three a.m. accident call.

Once the barn door had been opened with their mother, once the truth had poked its nose through the confines of its enclosure and sniffed the liberating effect of the whole truth, nothing but the truth stampeded out the door as if the barn was on fire. At times things got testy. Like when he told his mother

228

how Oat Smith forced his hand by threatening to arrest Bubba for Daddy Two's murder. What other alternative was there for Clovis than to accept the fake invoicing setup? His Momma had simply nodded her head in quiet acquiescence and resignation. But Bubba's fist had jammed hard into Clovis' arm. "Why did you have to go and tell her about that?" Bubba said. "There's nothing to it anyway."

Yet Bubba went ahead and explained to his mother about spending the weekend with Nancy Lee Graves. Mazel's advice to Bubba had been similar to Clovis' admonition back in Fort Worth. "If you keep messing around like that, you're going to get your ass shot off."

The wrecker slowed as the road leveled off, and Clovis down-shifted, which caused the wrecker to grind a bit slower still. He saw a pickup truck parked on the far side of a cattle guard. Two heads appeared in the rear window. Just a couple of sweaty teenagers having some fun. He had used this lonely stretch of road a few times himself in high school.

A memory flash of Jenny Hazelton's quadruple-hooked bra strap happened in the same instant as lightning sparked half of the western sky with a strobe light effect. Clovis had just been getting the hang of the wrap-around-two-handed-single-hook-release when Jenny climbed into his Chevy Luv for a ride. The four hooks gave him so much trouble the first time that he had to ask Jenny for help. He remembered it dampened the mood but not for long. They dated until he became so adept at unhooking the massive strap that Clovis could do it with one hand.

He didn't know if Windy Day wore a bra at all last night. Before, during, and after her show at Sorrento's, she wore a black t-shirt underneath an unbuttoned, red, rolled up to the elbows long-sleeved, embroidered cowgirl shirt with pearl snaps. When the wind chilled the night, she retrieved a charcoal gray duster from the cab of her pickup truck.

"You're really into this cowgirl look, aren't you?" Clovis had asked her.

"Actually this was my Grandma Rainey's coat," Windy answered.

Until that time, Clovis thought that Windy Day was a stage name, surely made up, because who would name their daughter Windy if their last name was Day?

"Whoa there, Flicka," Clovis had said. "Your grandma's name was Rainy Day?"

"Yep," she had answered. "But that one was unintentional. Her maiden name was Rainey Corbett. Rainey with an 'e' before the 'y'."

"And your mother?"

"Wasn't married when she shot me out," Windy had said. "Want to guess her name?"

"No idea," Clovis said. "Snow? Cloudy? Have-a-good?"

"Sunny."

Windy had slipped her arms into the duster and stood leaning against the tailgate of her pickup. Clovis felt his heart ka-thump as he eyed her silhouette, lit by a pale moon and the yellow glow of a neon Lone Star Beer sign in the window of Sorrento's. "I had a very strange family," Windy continued. She put a hiking boot on the fender and pulled her way onto the pickup bed.

"You mentioned that before," Clovis said. She settled down beside him, propping her back against the cab of her truck.

"We probably have a lot more in common than you think," she had said.

Thunder rolled with enough force to interrupt his fresh memories of Windy Day. Ranch Road 2325 intersected with Farm Road 3033. A single car accident had occurred off the farm road less than a mile from that point. Nothing out that far except for cactus and deadwood and the occasional abandoned truck parked on the hardpan.

The only two lights that broke up the dark terrain in the distance flickered and then died. Clovis flipped on his high beams and began looking to the south side of the road. The driver hadn't needed medical attention according to Wilma Shenkman, the dispatcher who notified Clovis of the towing job.

What he took as another bolt of lightning lit the southern sky, but this one had a reddish tint. It hung below the clouds and then lazily drifted downward. A flare. About fifty yards off the road, Clovis saw something but couldn't make it out. He came to a stop as the flare floated steadily toward the ground. A car with its hood open was the first thing he could identify. Then slowly he recognized a figure, someone leaning against the back fender.

No road existed to where the car had come to rest. Clovis wondered how or why the guy had driven there. He eased the wrecker onto the hardpan. Small rocks clanged against the undercarriage and scrub scraped there, too. The flare's light weakened and died out. Clovis could still make out the vehicle with the wrecker lights, but it was further off the road than he had thought. Maybe a hundred yards or more.

As he neared the car, Clovis noticed the man waving and calling out. He rolled the window down, clicked off the radio, and heard, "Hey, Bubba! Hey, Bubba!" Maybe this guy knew his brother or maybe he was the type that called everybody Bubba. Clovis positioned the wrecker so the man would be at the passenger side. He raised the window to where it was only cracked a few inches and made sure the door was locked. Something about being this far off the road, the flare, and now the hard exterior of the man approaching the wrecker put Clovis on point.

"Hey, Bubba," the man said again as he attempted to open the passenger door. "Hey, what gives?"

"What seems to be the trouble with your car?" Clovis asked.

Squinting through the opening in the window, the man said, "You aren't Bubba."

"Sorry to disappoint. My brother has the night off."

"I don't think so," the man said. "This is his night on duty. I believe you alternate nights, don't you?"

"Well," Clovis said, feeling a knot forming in his gut, "we've got some flexibility between us. Why do you think it's Bubba's night to work? Do you know him?"

"*Scheisse,*" the man hissed through his teeth and took a couple of steps backward toward his car.

"Do you need a tow or what?" Clovis called out.

The man continued walking to his vehicle and lowered the hood. Clovis watched as he got into the car and started the engine. Then he saw the man pick up something from his dashboard that looked like a gun. Clovis' attempt to slide the wrecker into gear didn't succeed the first time, nor the second. The man rose from his car seat and stood facing Clovis. He yelled, "Bubba owes me money!" He leveled the gun at the wrecker. Clovis finally rammed home the gear shift and was quickly bouncing high on the hardpan.

In his rearview mirror, Clovis saw the man raise his gun into the air. A few seconds later the chunky mess of land all around Clovis was lit like daylight with a reddish tinge. The wrecker bounded onto the farm road, propelling Clovis upward, his head banging into the cab's roof. With a squeal of tires, Clovis was pointed in the right direction.

The flare flickered out to the south, replaced by the strobe-like lightning. A stray burst of rain pelted the wrecker for a few seconds, giant drops pounding the cab with a frenzied intensity. Then nothing but darkness as thunder surrounded him and then grimly moved toward Solomon.

1991
Late October

If you can't get rid of the skeleton in your closet, you'd best teach it to dance.

George Bernard Shaw

33

JUST SHUT UP AND DANCE

I don't want to end up like this, Mazel thought.

To get to Al Pozzo's room from the back dock, Mazel had to pass through a hallway that primarily housed dementia and Alzheimer's patients. From wheelchairs and walkers, their eyes reflected confusion or a haunting intensity, the same kind of look that Mazel might have when absorbed in thought, trying to recall the name of a band that recorded "Up on the Roof." Not the James Taylor version but the earlier one by the same guys who did "Under the Boardwalk." The name floated just beyond reach, taunting her as she stretched for it, only to grasp a handful of air as it danced around yet another bend in her memory. The people she passed might be in a stage where their whole life, all they had ever known might be just as elusive as...

The Drifters.

What a relief to remember. It had been bugging her since she first got in the car and heard the song on KSNM, the local classic rock station. At least the struggle to remember had been a slight distraction from the hard truths that Bubba and Clovis revealed last night. She didn't know where else to go after a few fitful hours of sleep but to see Al.

When Mazel pushed open the door to Al's room, she immediately began talking.

"You're not going to believe what's going on, Al."

She closed the door behind her, struggling to secure her coat on a single peg after her first attempt failed and it slid to the floor.

"Let's see," she said, with her back to Al, "we've got a possible murder charge, stealing money, adultery, gambling. I think we've got most of the major commandments broken or about to be committed. Are you ready to hear all about it?"

"Sounds interesting," came the voice from behind. "I'm all ears."

Mazel spun round to see Dr. Barnstable sitting next to Al Pozzo. "God dammit! You scared me half to death."

"You can add another broken commandment to your list."

"I didn't know you were working," Mazel said, holding a hand to her chest. "I can come back later."

"Nonsense," he answered. "Please sit. I'd love the company."

Mazel had never seen the computers, keyboard, and assorted gizmos associated with Dr. Barnstable's work with Al Pozzo. "How's it going anyway?" she asked.

"It's coming along. We're getting things typed out on the computer, but at this stage, they're pretty much open to interpretation."

"Like what?"

He rose from the chair, patted his hand on the seat, and said, "Come, I'll show you."

Mazel lifted her purse from the floor and slung the long strap over the coat that hung on the peg. The urgent need to speak to Al, to unload all the burdens she heard from Bubba and Clovis last night would have to wait.

It's just you talking to yourself.

That's what Manuel Daza had said to her yesterday.

It keeps you going nowhere.

Dr. Barnstable had been speaking, but his words were just now catching up to her consciousness. "He seems to have a slight aversion to most vowels at this stage. The further I get into facilitative communications, the more I can discern and even predict the development of a patient. Here, look at what we did today."

Mazel eased onto the chair that still permeated the warmth from Dr. Barnstable's prior occupancy. The green letters on the black screen were a phenomenon that Mazel would need to adapt to as a data entry specialist, class II at TSTA&M. She still preferred the resistance offered by the keys of a typewriter. A few weeks remained until starting her new job so she had some time to get used to the feel of a computer keyboard.

hut klwp enuf g4sm uuu.;///d.sw   ,, wqawuzu spl qrqu3y pn rigs/a thkhyueb hyuuw

"Doc," Mazel said, "It's not my intention to offend you, but this is gibberish."

"Ah, to the untrained eye, yes. But Al and I have progressed beyond the initial gibberish period. We are now entering the pre-gobbledygook phase."

Mazel turned her face up to Dr. Barnstable and arched her eyebrows high. "Sounds like you're taking me on a snipe hunt."

"I'm sorry. I don't understand."

"Show me how this thing works," she said.

He lifted Al Pozzo's wrists onto the keyboard and then stood behind him. Dr. Barnstable leaned over, covered Pozzo's hands in his own, and their forearms rose in unison. After ten seconds or so, Al's right index finger with Dr. Barnstable's finger in tow struck the "u".

"He's partial to 'u's," Dr. Barnstable said.

In tandem they then struck two more "u's" followed by two "8's".

"You must inspire him, Mazel. Eight is his favorite number. He types it when I believe he's in a good place."

Mazel said, "How do I know that you're not the one forcing his finger down? You could make him type anything that you want to."

"Come around here and you try it," he answered.

Mazel complied and the doctor wrapped her hands and wrists to Al Pozzo with a Velcro fastener. "Now," he said, "guide his hands about an inch over the keyboard."

When nothing occurred, Mazel looked to the doctor. "Give it some time," he said.

"His arms are heavy. How much longer–" She felt her left index finger following behind Al's finger striking the keyboard while the right finger followed rapidly with two more jabs.

wuu

Before she could speak, her right hand came down again.

8

Mazel's left hand moved and that index finger came down followed by the right.

ai

The left finger landed on the space bar for a couple of seconds. Then the same process repeated and Mazel looked at the green letters on the computer screen:

wuu8ai wuu8ai

"What the hell?" she said. "Get this off of me." Mazel grabbed at the Velcro connections and tore them away, leaving Al's hands to drop on the keyboard.

"I'm sorry, Mazel. I should have prepared you. It can be disconcerting when you first feel his hands move."

"Disconcerting?" Mazel said, rising from the chair. "Disconcerting?" she said louder, almost accusatory. "It feels creepy is how it feels. Like a Ouija board or something. I hate Ouija boards."

Dr. Barnstable placed Al's twitching right hand on Pozzo's lap and then Al's left hand atop the rapidly moving wrist. "I've thought about this frequently." He disconnected the keyboard and its related cords. "Facilitative communication does have its historic predecessors. Planchette writing or fuji from China are forms of spirit writing that date back before the Ming Dynasty."

Mazel retrieved two packs of cigarettes and a lighter from her purse. She dropped the pack of Gauloises on a table next to Al and tapped a Lucky Strike Light out of the other pack. "Spirit writing sounds like Ouija board crap." She lit the cigarette, leaning against the window frame while staring at the mesquite tree that Al always seemed to be watching. She rubbed the back of one hand with the other repeatedly as if trying to scrub something off.

"It's taken far more seriously than a children's game," the doctor said. "There are books of the Tao that were conceived entirely by spirit writing." He rolled the computer equipment cart to the side of Al's chair. "In a sense, we've modernized fuji through these incredible advances in computer technology. The one primary difference being that I'm actually attempting to unlock the minds and spirits of those still living."

Mazel went through the ritual of lighting a Gauloises, inserting it in one corner of Al's mouth, placing an ashtray in Al's lap, and taping his lips together next to the cigarette. "It still sounds like a bunch of hooey to me." She sat in the chair next to Al again and watched some smoke ease from the side of his mouth that wasn't taped.

"I always felt a strong pull from the Ouija board," she said, "like it was out of my control. But the damn thing always gave me the answer I wanted. It gave me hope. And for a while, I forgot all about the disappointments. At least until reality would step back in and kick the living crap out of me."

"Now *that's* a bunch of poppycock." The doctor crouched in front of Mazel. "My father preferred the term 'poppycock', because it wasn't as slangy as 'hooey'. Being a book editor, he was particular about such things. Regardless, hope and disappointment are merely psychological constructs. The world is neutral."

"You think I shouldn't have hopes or feel disappointment?" she asked.

Dr. Barnstable straightened up and pointed to the computer screen.

wuu8ai wuu8ai

"I see hope there," he said. "But if it's disappointment, I'll experience the feeling and then go on."

"What if every time you get your hopes up, like I did with my boys coming home, then it backfires and becomes as bad as ever?" Mazel moved the ashtray under Al's chin and knocked a long ash into it.

"Then you go on and try something else," Dr. Barnstable said. "Do you know what I see here?" He pointed at the monitor again.

"Gibberish or gobbledygook?"

His index finger jabbed at the screen, his fingernail clicking against the glass. "I see pattern. He substitutes 'u' for 'o' all the time. He never strikes the 'o' or the 'L' keys."

"So?"

"So, I think this is saying 'you' where it says 'w-u-u.' I believe '8' is the most positive number we have. Certainly the most spiritual with its beginning and its ending arriving at the same place. And on its side, '8' is the sign for infinity. The '8' symbolizes good things such as hope, love, and understanding."

"You certainly see a lot more in a typewriter than I ever saw," she said. "And I suppose the 'a-i' is something meaningful, too?"

"Not so much. Since he refuses to use the 'L', he substitutes the next closest thing–'i'.

Mazel shook her finger at the keyboard. "Wouldn't the closest thing to an 'L' be the number '1'?" "He never uses the numbers '1' or '0'," Dr. Barnstable said, "which makes perfect sense if you think about our book. The deterioration of humanity through the use of the computer, the relentless choice of either '0' or '1' with no other option, the loss of mankind's ability to struggle against–"

"Hopelessness," Mazel interrupted. "I remember. I typed Al's manuscript at least a dozen times."

Dr. Barnstable nodded his head and appeared ready to say something more but didn't.

"What?" Mazel asked. "Why are you biting your tongue?"

"Nothing."

"Well," she said, "don't stop now." She tapped another lengthy ash from Al's Gauloises. "What's your take on what he typed there?"

"Your hands were guiding so the 'you' he refers to is–you, Mazel. The 'ai' at the end is how Al refers to himself. My interpretation of this is a simple emotional connection that Al feels with you. It's a very positive reaction to your presence."

Mazel removed the cigarette from Al's lips and tamped it out in the ashtray. "Sounds like you see what you want to see."

Dr. Barnstable again almost spoke a couple of times but didn't. Instead he walked toward the door but stopped short. "I'll leave you two alone. Don't worry about the equipment. I'm coming back later to do some more work."

He opened the door and hesitated with the handle in his hand.

"It's better than me not seeing anything," he said. "Doing something, even if it doesn't work out exactly as I plan, is better than relying on hope alone. Disappointment meets either path. But doing something, anything, is the only chance we have to overcome–"

Again Mazel interrupted.

"Hopelessness."

***

Once alone with Al, Mazel off-loaded the entire gamut of problems facing Bubba and Clovis. Expressing herself to him helped Mazel clarify the issues involved and their interconnectedness. However, something seemed a little off in their conversation. She kept hearing Manuel say, *it's just you talking to yourself. It keeps you going nowhere.*

On one level Mazel had always understood that she was just talking to herself. She wasn't completely oblivious to the fact that Al had not responded to her for twenty-five years. But since Al was physically there, she never felt alone or that she was dealing with everything on her own. Al was right there, drooling and twitching and lately, even smoking. She didn't feel like some damn fool sitting around talking to herself. But Manuel's words kept ricocheting through her mind and caused her to feel less connected to Al Pozzo today. Instead of imagining Al listening and absorbing what she said, Mazel's words seemed to bounce back to her like an echo from a well.

"And last but not least," she said, "Clovis brought up the subject of a DNA test again." She walked into the restroom and deposited several Lucky Strike Light and Gaulouses butts into the toilet and flushed. "Only this time, it's a real possibility." After Mazel sat back in her chair, she wiped some drool from Al's lips and dropped the tissue into the trashcan at her feet.

"The cost has finally come down to where it's affordable. Not that we have a thousand dollars laying around somewhere. Even a few years ago, the price was outrageous. But now…"

It keeps you going nowhere.

"Miss McDonald?"

Mazel heard the voice behind her, familiar but like everything else this day, just a little off pitch. She hoped to turn around and see Manuel Daza standing in the doorway.

"Who are you?" she asked, eyeing the white-clad, fortyish man.

"I'm the new orderly," he answered, "Jack Tillich." The door closed behind him as he shifted bedsheets from one arm to the other. "I was wondering if I might be able to change Dr. Pozzo's linens."

"Isn't this Manuel's shift?"

He placed the bedsheets on the night stand next to Al's bed. "I'm sorry but this is my first day. I don't know everybody yet. Do you want me to ask Patty?"

"No, that's alright." So many things off-kilter, sideways, disjointed. "I need to stretch my legs anyway." Mazel started to rise but one of her hands slipped off the armrest, landing her back into the chair.

"Are you alright?" Jack asked, moving to her side. Mazel didn't resist the new orderly's assistance in getting to an upright position.

"Just embarrassed. Thank you."

She walked to the ward desk where Patty sat staring at a computer screen. Mazel rested her elbows on the tall stand separating nurses and orderlies from patients and visitors. Though not facing Mazel directly, she thought that Patty could certainly see her standing here. Mazel cleared her throat, shifted weight from one foot to the other causing her to sway, and moved her folded hands up and down on the counter. Patty's profile, however, remained still.

Mazel held onto the counter ledge, extending both arms to stretch her back. A purposefully loud moan of exertion traveled through her open lips.

"If you want something," Patty said, "you need to ask me." The nurse didn't move her gaze from the computer screen. "I don't respond to all that stuff you're doing."

Mazel knew Patty to be abrupt on occasion, but this seemed a bit much. "Do you know -"

"I hate this computer," Patty interrupted, still staring at the screen. "It's more trouble than writing out the reports. What was wrong with the old way?"

"I don't-"

"That's a rhetorical question." Patty turned toward Mazel and rubbed the eraser head of a pencil against her cheek. "He'p yew?"

Mazel rushed her words in hopes of not being interrupted again. "Is Manuel working today?"

Patty shook her head from side to side and smirked. "He never worked when he worked here."

Mazel's stomach knotted. "What?"

"Manuel Daza was lazy and shiftless," Patty replied. "The only reason he got away with it for so long is because he's a Mexican. He knew how to keep his mouth shut around his betters."

The knot in her stomach spread to a tightness in her chest. "That's not true. He works hard. What are you talking about?"

Patty eased back in her chair and crossed her arms, a look of self-satisfaction spread across her face. "Him and Francisco failed their drug test. They got fired."

Mazel's held firmly to the counter ledge as her knees buckled. "Do you have his address? Maybe his phone number?"

"Wouldn't do you any good. He's probably already skedaddled back over the border. It was either that or jail."

"Jail?"

Patty pushed her rolling chair back to the computer desk. "We always have come up short on the drug inventory. Makes sense that the two guys who tested positive are guilty. Dr. Masters turned them in to the sheriff. Arrested Francisco but Manuel was already gone."

Mazel's body trembled and her hand on the counter ledge began to shake. Her mind raced haphazardly. She could not think of anything to do, nothing to rectify what had gone so suddenly wrong. Would she ever see her friend again or had he vanished forever?

"You had to know he was using," Patty continued. "All that laid back, mystical BS he spouted off. Just the drugs talking. He was so full of it."

"What about his family? Fermina and his girls?"

Patty turned away from Mazel and stared at the computer screen. "What about them?"

"Did they go with him?"

A nurse handed Patty a sheet of paper, which she signed and handed back. "All the talking you two did, all the time he wasted in that room with you, I figured you knew more about him than that."

"Knew what?"

Patty rubbed the eraser against her cheek again. "They left him a long time ago, ten years or so. I heard they went back to Mexico. They weren't legal, you know."

Mazel barely made it to the toilet of the women's restroom across the hallway. She closed her eyes to the mess she had made, flushing and flushing again. The loss of Manuel left her feeling hollow, shelled-out, without a center. It didn't matter if he used drugs, did it? It didn't matter that he wasn't truthful. It didn't matter that he might have stolen some pills. He was her friend.

Friends of a type.

That she might never hear Manuel's voice again left her feeling an enormous sense of loss. But then, Mazel felt the sting of betrayal. Her all-knowing friend had filled her with beautiful stories, family stories, and salt of the earth wisdoms that turned out to be mirages, mystical illusions, sleight of hand magic, drug-induced fantasies signifying…signifying what?

We live to dream.

Signifying that Manuel needed to reveal his dreams to her as much as she needed to hear them? As much as she needed to reveal herself to Al Pozzo?

You are speaking to yourself.

Maybe he masked his pain with drugs in the same way Mazel tried to ignore hers by withdrawing, by allowing herself to close down when it hurt so much that she couldn't put one foot in front of the other. His stories, like *Aesop's Fables*, had morals. Maybe they were hard truths earned through the pain of losing his family, his Fermina. The suffering of his real world replaced by a beauty and truth in his imagination.

Nothing real can match our dreams.

He would only tell her his dreams. He couldn't bring himself to tell her the truth about his life. Mazel flushed the toilet for what she hoped was the last time.

We shield ourselves from it.

Shield ourselves from what? The barnacles? Hell? The eternal nightmare?

The nightmare surrounds us—all the time.

Mazel exited the stall and pulled a handful of paper towels from the dispenser. One of the towels became entangled inside. She attempted to rip it out, but the dispenser came out with the towel and fell to the floor, a tinny crash that echoed in the restroom. For the first time in her life, Mazel understood what it meant when somebody said—I didn't know whether to laugh or cry.

Having already cried, she decided to laugh. Mazel laughed at the sight of the dispenser on the floor with the roll of towels still rolling toward the other side of the restroom. She laughed so hard that she doubled over and clutched at her chest.

There is great music there.

So what if the only person who ever heard the music inside Mazel was a drugged-up, thieving, illegal immigrant who spun beautiful stories, homily-like tales manufactured out of whole cloth?

Mazel composed herself for the walk back to Al Pozzo's room. She ran her fingers through the growing streaks of gray hair that she saw in the mirror. She tore a paper towel from the dispenser on the floor and blew her nose. Observing herself a final time before exiting, Mazel's face didn't exhibit any consistency. Anger, loss, confusion. They all were there. But what lay beneath?

There is great music there.

After leaving the restroom, Mazel felt compelled to stop at the nurse's station. Patty stared at the computer screen as Mazel rapped on the counter ledge with her knuckles.

"Hey, Patty. You've seen your last Kit Kat from me."

***

When Dr. Barnstable reentered Al Pozzo's room a half hour later, Mazel made it known that she did not want to engage in communication–facilitative or otherwise. Being the type that likes to wag his jaw just to fill empty space, he tried to engage her in conversation a couple of times but to no avail. On the third try, she snapped her fingers loudly, twice, before his second word could follow the first. The room remained silent after that except for the occasional tapping of keys by the forearm writing team of Pozzo and Barnstable.

Pozzo and Barnstable. There was something familiar with the pairing of their names. Like Rowan and Martin, Martin and Lewis, Lewis and Clark. It sounded like they belonged together or had been together. The short-lived thought passed away as the weight of Manuel's fate clouded her mind once again.

She fought to dismiss him.

She wanted to revel in his betrayal.

She wanted to be the aggrieved one.

She defended herself to herself.

Yet, more and more her thoughts traveled in Manuel's shoes.

How painful was it to drown your voice around your *betters*?

How painful was it to wrap yourself in a shell too small for a soul of such substance?

How painful was it to submerge yourself, to float so you didn't make waves?

How painful it was…talking to yourself.

To go nowhere.

To let things keep flowing in the same direction; same as it ever was. Floating, adrift.

Dam it.

Goddamn it, dam it. Make it stop.

Not by shutting down. But by shutting down the river. By damming the rapids that lead to the falls. Making it stop. Make it change direction before sinking and going nowhere.

It keeps you going nowhere.

She retrieved her coat and purse from the peg on the back of the door.

"Are you taking your leave?" asked Dr. Barnstable.

"Yes," she answered. "How's it going with him now?"

"Not too well I'm afraid," he said. "I don't think he wants me here. He keeps telling me to go."

"How do you know that?"

"Look here." Dr. Barnstable tapped his finger on the computer screen.

Mazel leaned in as she placed one arm through her coat sleeve.

> gu gu gugu gu gu gugugu gu gu gu gu gu

"Goo-goo?"

"No. Remember he doesn't ever use 'o'. Instead he uses 'u' for 'o'."

Mazel finished donning her coat and laughed. "He doesn't want you to go. He wants me to get off my ass and do something for a change." She stopped at the door. "I'm not coming back here for a while, Doc. I'm trusting you to take care of Al during my absence."

"What?" asked Dr. Barnstable.

"I've been spending too much time here lately." Mazel took a full pack of Gauloises from her purse and tossed it toward Dr. Barnstable. "Give him one of those when you two have a good day."

Mazel dashed from one hallway to the next, a lightness in her step that she had not felt for some time. She didn't know what she was going to do yet, but she was going to do something. Something to help her boys, something to save herself.

Salvacion.

Passing through the dementia and Alzheimer's area, she slowed her pace and observed the faces of those in the hallway. They all seemed to reach for memories and come away grappling with wisps of scenes, some real, some imagined. A woman in a wheelchair stretched her elbows away from her body at the sight of Mazel and began flapping back and forth like a chicken.

"Chicken dance," Mazel said repeatedly as she traveled down the corridor. She clapped, waved, flapped, and shimmied her way through the canes and walkers and wheelchairs.

"I don't hear the music," a man said, holding onto his IV stand.

"*Put your hands on your hips,*" a woman sang. "*And bring your knees in ti-i-ight.*"

The orderly alongside the woman looked at Mazel and shrugged, "She hears 'The Time Warp'."

"*But it's the pelvic thru-u-ust…*"

"I still don't hear the music," the man yelled again.

"Shut up, you old fool," said the woman, the one who started the flap.

"Just shut up and dance."

34

THE BARITONE MUST DIE

When Vic Tannyhill peeked between the drapes and the expansive living room window, he expected to see Bubba Albright. They had an appointment, Tuesday at two. Instead it was Bubba's mother. He wouldn't bet the house on it though. Her hair now had great streaks of white and her once chiseled, angular face appeared more rounded. It had been what, five years? Maybe ten?

Richard would have Mazel at his side sometimes in an attempt to elicit sympathy from Tannyhill. Other guys who owed him money would at times bring a child or two. Those without a wife or children might bring a tiny nephew or niece and pass them off as their own. When no human family was available, they brought sad-eyed, long-faced dogs.

"This here is why I can't pay you right now," they had said. That would be the cue for the gambler's prop to go wide-eyed into a thousand mile stare toward oblivion. "I'll pay you, that's for sure, but (insert wife's, child's, nephew's, niece's, dog's name here) had (to go to the hospital, lost her job, got pregnant, generally fucked up royally) and that's where all my money went."

The first eight notes of Beethoven's *Ode to Joy* rang again as the woman withdrew her finger from the doorbell. Getting to a point in his life where Tannyhill would no longer have physical contact with other human beings seemed to involve seeing a lot of human beings. The Reverend Yates earlier today, Clovis

McDonald, now Mazel, then one or two more visitors tonight–
the second contingent on what was to happen with the first.

Fortunately, Tannyhill wore clothes, unlike most days when
he donned one of three outfits–a seersucker robe for summer, a
terrycloth robe for winter, and a silk robe for phone dates with
Margo Chandler. He reluctantly walked to the door, his Lucchese
Crocodile Belly Boots striking the entryway marble floor with
much more resolve than their owner actually had.

"Why Mazel McDonald, what an unexpected pleasure. What's
it been–ten years or more? You look exactly the same now as you
did then."

"You don't look so bad yourself, Vic," Mazel said, "but let's
cut the crap. We need to talk business. Can I come in?"

Tannyhill pulled the door open wider and stepped to the
side. "Please, by all means." He led her past the living room and
further down the hallway past the gun display cases. They ended
up in the dining room, a formal area in the center of his house
that felt more intimate and safer since the intrusion of Judas
Conroe into his life. Four walls surrounded them with only one
door into the room and no windows.

"That's quite a gun collection," she said, sitting in the chair
that Tannyhill had pulled out for her. "Do you ever have a need
to use any of them?"

"They were my father's guns. For some reason I've been
reluctant to sell them." Tannyhill took the seat opposite Mazel.
"I assure you they're just for show."

Mazel placed her elbows on the dining room table and
crossed her forearms. "Did you kill my husband?"

"Good heavens, no."

"Then why did Oat Smith bring you to jail in handcuffs?"

"One of the most profoundly stupid things I have ever
done in my life." Tannyhill brought both hands to his lips in
a prayer-like motion, expelling a heavy sigh. "I instigated all
that. Somehow I thought that if I looked capable of murder,

the gamblers would treat me with more respect. So I asked Oat to bring me in and make it look like I was a real suspect. It was all a ruse."

Mazel leaned back in the chair, her arms crossing her chest. "That's what Bubba said. He said he didn't figure a man like you would actually shoot anyone."

"You see," he said, "that's exactly my problem. If I know Bubba, he didn't put it in such genteel terms either, did he?"

"He owes you money. I'm not going to make it any worse on him."

"Is that why you're here? About Bubba's debt?"

"Actually, I'm here about Richard's debt. I want to make arrangements to pay it to you. Over time, of course."

"You don't have to do that. I've written it off."

"But I want to pay it, if you'll meet my terms."

"Terms?"

"Yes," Mazel said. "I don't want Bubba working for you. He's in enough trouble as it is. He doesn't need to be doing anything illegal on the side."

"Would you like a drink?" Tannyhill rose and moved a wine glass near the port decanter on the butler's sideboard.

"No, thank you."

"I was trying to do Bubba a favor." Tannyhill poured two fingers of port into the glass. "I don't want to see him end up in the same situation as Richard." He took a sip and returned to the table. "By the way, my condolences for the loss of your husband."

"Here's my offer," Mazel said. "I start work in a few weeks. We can pay you a hundred a week until Richard's debt is paid off. In return you don't use Bubba as a collector, and you don't allow him to gamble anymore."

"I'm truly amazed that you are aware of all this." He swished some port around his mouth and swallowed before continuing. "Most men don't tell their wives or their mothers anything about their gambling problems."

"The boys and me had a come-to-Jesus meeting the other night. There were too many damn secrets holding us all back. I'm clearing them out so we can get on with things."

Tannyhill downed the remainder of the port. "Do you have any idea how much time it would take to pay off Richard's debt?"

"I don't know for sure. A couple of years maybe?"

"Try a couple of decades." He rose again and repeated the glass-port decanter sequence. "Do I look like a fool, Mazel?"

"I certainly didn't mean to offend you. It's just...I got to do something to protect my boys."

Tannyhill leaned against the butler's sideboard, his eyes intensely focused on her. "Your husband's debt is paid in full, including a fair market interest rate on the principal payoff."

"I'm really lost." She pointed to the serving tray. "Do you mind? I think I'll have that drink now."

He poured the two fingers in silence and brought the glass around the table to Mazel. "Many years ago, in exchange for letting Richard continue to gamble and continue to lose, he and I came to an arrangement. He would pay me what he could every week, but the remainder went into my account book. When it reached five thousand dollars, I had him purchase a life insurance policy. Then we would start the process for the next five thousand dollars and the next insurance policy."

"So, you did have a reason to want him dead," Mazel said. "A lot of men would kill for that kind of money."

"Ah, there's the rub, Mazel. Richard knew I didn't have it in my heart to kill someone over money. He played me. I played him. We both got what we wanted in the end. Win-win."

"And I got nothing," she said. "Do you have any idea what your line of work does to us innocent bystanders?"

Tannyhill returned to the other side of the table, his shoulders stooped a bit, the heels of his boots clicking softly on the hardwood floor. "The cost to others has been weighing more and more on my soul."

"So what happens between us?" she asked. "How much does Bubba owe you?"

In the background, the CD of Wagner's *Parsifal* became stuck, looping and looping as the baritone kept hitting the same note that Tannyhill considered flat. "Excuse me." A couple of minutes later he returned with a remote control that he lay on the table. Down the hallway, Klingsor resumed his conjuring of Kundry to seduce Parsifal.

"Let's do this." Tannyhill brought his hands together with one loud clap. "I could redeem myself in part if I forgave all of Bubba's debt, but that would not allow any redemption to shine on you or Bubba. So, what if you and Bubba pay me a hundred a week for one year? I give you a nice discount, you pay me half of the money Bubba owes, and we all feel a little better about ourselves."

"And you don't let Bubba bet again, right?"

"Right," he answered, "but I can't stop him from going through somebody else."

"And you call off whoever you have collecting money. Clovis said the guy is crazy."

Tannyhill bit into his lip. "Clovis told me the same thing."

"What?"

"He stopped by here earlier today and told me what happened with the wrecker call the other night. You should be proud of that young man."

"What do you mean?"

"Clovis offered to help pay me off, too," Tannyhill said. Mazel didn't speak but looked at him questioningly. "He said he could come up with two hundred dollars a week. If you were only going to come up with one hundred, where's he coming up with the other hundred every week?"

Mazel shook her head several times as if clearing away some cobwebs. "So, you and Oat Smith are pretty good friends?" she asked.

He grunted out a couple of laughs. "I wouldn't say we're friends. But Oat and I have a longstanding business relationship. We're on good terms."

"If I could ask of you just one more thing." She cleared her throat and her right hand smoothed some hair back and off of her forehead. "It's concerning Clovis and Oat Smith."

***

With his back to the wall and sitting on the floor of his bedroom closet, Vic Tannyhill couldn't resist the occasional impulse to slide a hand down his leg and touch the holstered Colt .45 military edition. How else does one spend their night awaiting the arrival of Judas Conroe?

Two plaid coffee thermoses were to his left along with a couple of Black Beauties obtained through one of his clients. He figured a combination of Sumatran coffee and speed would keep the buzz going all night. To counter the urinating effects of coffee, Vic had several large containers with screw-on lids, which would be thrown out first thing in the morning. He couldn't take the risk of revealing his hiding place.

Sweet Maid Marion from Sorrento's had phoned his betting line late last night and left a message: "That guy was back in here tonight. So I listened in like you asked. He was in your booth telling a guy that he was taking over your business. Sounded really drunk. He said that you were taking an early retirement effective tomorrow night. Then Jackie Everts wanted to sit in the booth I was in, *his* booth, so I had to stop spying. So, Mr. Tannyhill, you will take a hundred dollars off of Larry's account, won't you? If there's anything else I can do, just give me a holler. Oh, by the way, I did try to call your house but the line was busy. Good night."

Of course, the line was busy. He and Margo had been sleeping.

Marion's story received some corroboration with the unexpected visit from Clovis McDonald this morning. Aside from wanting to help settle Bubba's account, Clovis told Tannyhill of his three a.m. encounter with the flare-shooting wild man, the man who said Bubba owed him money.

The relentless looping of a Wagner's Greatest Hits CD playing at even a low volume helped keep him on edge. This particular recording had a Brunhilde who screeched in the upper register like her toes were being pinched too tightly in her boots. No sleep in Valhalla with that tortured voice, and no sleep for Tannyhill as he fingered his .45 again.

Rarely did Tannyhill's gaze stray from what he could see through the slight opening of one of the closet's double doors. Illuminated by the digital displays of the clock on the mahogany-stained nightstand and the various components of his CD player, he observed the lumpy mass in the center of his bed. Having formed a collection of sheets, towels, and throws into what he thought was a rather believable semblance of his sleeping body, Tannyhill hoped it was lifelike enough to fool Judas Conroe. Through the speaker phone came the additional enhancement of consistent and, at times, exceptional volumes of snoring-Margo. Though completely unaware of his intentions, she provided a key element of credibility to the bedroom scene.

Everything had been calculated and rehearsed. A snack plate of smoked Gouda, prosciutto, grapes, and croissants occupied a shoe shelf on the side wall of the closet. A squeaky hinge had been doused with some WD-40. He disposed of the two closet light bulbs that turned on automatically with just this slight crack of the door. The design of his set even included a pen and the weekly schedule of games laying in the middle of the bed as if he had been overtaken by sleep while working on his picks.

Tannyhill fingered the Uzi Pistol to his right, a back-up in case the Colt jammed. If Conroe did arrive this night, Tannyhill had meticulously planned that Judas would never leave. Yet the edgy gnaw in his gut made him aware *that the best laid schemes o' mice an' men, gang aft a-gley."*

When winds came in hard from the north or the northwest like they were blowing tonight, a whistling would echo down the hallway and into Vic's bedroom. He never could find a repairman who was able to locate the problem, because they usually disagreed as to what the specific problem was. The seals, the sash, the windows, who knew? He had learned to live with the haunting sounds, which were partially subdued by the operatic pieces that played on low volume during his sleep. On high alert tonight, the mournful whines and occasional creaks and groans of his house had Vic regularly tensing and reaching for his holster.

Nothing in Tannyhill's life had prepared him to deal with the sizzling nerves and fraying resolve of this night in the closet. Not the hours of distress prior to voice recitals, auditions, performances–all seeming rather meaningless in this moment of life and death.

What had Vic ever known about death, in particular a violent death, other than what he had seen on stage? A mortally wounded tenor on the floor sings that he is dying while others bemoan his approaching death by singing that the tenor is dying. The deaths were interminable, some lasting twenty minutes or longer. Deaths were either tragic or transplendent depending on whether you were watching Verdi or Wagner. Deaths opened the gates of Hell or the doors of Valhalla. The librettos of death were all similar, but the music, the musical motifs were exhilaratingly *diversi*.

What seemed unfair in operatic deaths were the multitudes of tenors and sopranos who bit the dust. The tenor must survive this scene tonight.

The baritone must die.

***

Tannyhill detected a change of atmosphere, the positive pressure of air escaping from the house. A sudden ache in his right ear put him on alert. He rose to his feet as he had during several false alarms tonight. In his right hand was the Colt .45; in his left hand was the CD remote control. His left index finger rested on the volume control that he planned on using to distract Judas Conroe.

No sound came from the hallway or the bedroom but in the pale blue digital light at the foot of his bed stood the baritone. Conroe's arm rose from his side. In his hand, a gun that Conroe aimed toward the lower portion of the sheets, towels, and throws in the bed.

"You sure are a sound sleeper, Viktor," Conroe said, "and you snore like the fatuous pig you are."

The back of Tannyhill's left hand rested on the closet door, ready to open it and finish this business but for one problem–he couldn't feel his legs. He had stayed awake on the closet floor, but his legs had gone to sleep. The tingling sensation ran down both legs as he steadied himself by placing his right hand and pistol on the door jamb.

"Wake up, partner," Conroe continued, "we've got a little piece of business to transact."

Tannyhill lifted his right leg into the air and wiggled it around. When it returned to the ground, a thousand tiny pin pricks shot through his foot. He repeated the twisting movements with his left leg experiencing the same results.

"Look, I believe a man ought to be awake when he gets killed. Now wake up or I'm going to set off your alarm by putting one in your fat ass. Do you hear me?"

Loud and clear. Every time Judas spoke, his tone and volume escalated. Some feeling returned to Vic's right leg, but his left remained lifeless.

"Well, Vic, it's 4:10, ante meridiem. Time to wake up and die!"

The crack of the gun's report caused Vic to flinch. The second shot did the same.

"You awake now, Viktor? Sounds like we found a cure for your snoring."

As carefully as Vic had calculated this whole scene, he had not considered the possibility of his legs going to sleep nor did he remember to push the mute button on his telephone. Margo's screams were shrill and piercing and dead legs or not, Vic had to act now.

He pushed open the door and began firing at the back of Judas Conroe. One of the shots knocked Conroe forward and headfirst onto the mass of sheets, towels and throws. His gun landed on the floor, scuttled over the wood, and crashed into the baseboard. Margo continued screaming.

Tannyhill stepped out of the closet, but his left leg was still numb. The Karastan Ashara rug cushioned his fall. He immediately rose to his knees with the pistol and the remote in his hands. His first thought was *Thank God for New Zealand wool* followed by *why the hell am I thinking about wool?*

Conroe moaned but had not moved. Vic stayed on his knees and maneuvered around the bed to the mahogany-stained nightstand.

"Margo, Margo. It's me. It's Vic. Calm down. Stop screaming. Everything is alright. I'm okay. Nothing to worry about. It's alright."

Her screams came to an end, but her voice was shaky. "Vic, what...what...what the fuck is going on? What happened? I...I... I'll call the police."

"Margo, I've got it under control. Now listen and do exactly as I tell you. Do not call anybody. Do not call the police. Do not call an ambulance. Do not call anybody. I'll call you back in a few minutes, but I've got to finish this. Do you understand?"

"I...I...I..."

"I'm hanging up now. I'll talk to you as soon as I can."

Tannyhill pushed the speaker button off and rose to his feet that he could now feel.

"Viktor, you never cease to amaze me." Though still face down on the bed, Conroe moved his head to the side and looked at Tannyhill. "A Colt .45? That's why I saw shit flying out of my body. That hardly seems fair, man. I only brought a Glock 19. Granted, I was going to kill you, but I wasn't going to make a complete mess of it. Clean in, clean out. Just holes in the body. In fact, if you would go get it for me, I'll show you."

Conroe slowly drew his right arm next to his body and pushed his head and neck slightly off the bed. "Well, Viktor, good news. I think I might still have a chance. So, what's the next step? Do you call the sheriff or an ambulance first?"

Tannyhill remained motionless next to the bed.

"You know, partner, it's never over till the fat lady sings," said Conroe, his left arm joining with his right to lift him even higher off the bed.

Tannyhill moved the remote control in the direction of the CD player. Raising the volume, the shrill Brunhilde easily reached the opening lines of the Immolation Scene. Tannyhill leaned down where Judas Conroe could easily look into his eyes.

"By definition, Mr. Conroe, the fat lady *is* singing."

***

"Who the hell is this?" Oat Smith barked into the telephone.

"Vic Tannyhill."

"Oh, OK, right." Oat yawned. "Yes sir, Mr. Tannyhill. What can I do ya for?"

"Oat, I need some help."

"Must be something pretty important if you're calling in the dark."

"It is and I'm sorry for waking you. I need what I believe in the business is called a cleaner. Do you know a cleaner that you can completely trust?"

"Well, Mr. Tannyhill, I do my own cleanin'."

"Maybe I should explain. I don't mean a cleaner like–"

"I know what ya mean, Mr. Tannyhill, and I do my own clean up. Only had to do it a time or two. You got something that ya need to go away like it neva happened, right?"

"That's correct."

"Without goin' too much into detail since we're on the phone and all, what exactly are we dealin' with here?"

"I need to get rid of a...of a dead mouse in my bedroom."

"Did you plug that sumbitchin' mouse?"

"Yes, Oat. And it left quite a mess."

"Well, well, well. You are the man, Mr. Tannyhill. Good gravy, I didn't know ya had the stones to drop him. I'm proud of ya, sir, real proud of ya."

"Thank you."

"So what kind of a mess do we have there? Is it a big spill? Hell, are ya alright?"

"I'm fine. It's mostly contained on the bed. A few holes in the wall. Maybe some stuff on the floor and baseboards."

"That mouse is deader than a doornail?" Oat asked.

"He is now."

"Damn, almighty, Mr. Tannyhill. I'm bustin my buttons I'm so damn proud of ya."

"Oat, it was just something I had to do. Nothing of which to be proud. I just want to be sure that...that there's no threat of anyone ever seeing this mouse again."

"No need to worry 'bout that. Who's going to give a shit one way or the otha? A mouse like that had no connections, no relations to speak of. The only person I can think of that might even know what he was doin' is Punches."

"No need to worry about Punches. The mouse scared him to death. Dead and buried."

"Is that a fact?" Oat said. "That is some hot damn good news there. Only thing mighta been better was if I popped that piece a shit myself. But I'm glad to hear he's gone all the same."

"So, I'm thinking we can get rid of a lot of this by burying it. There's a bunch of mesquite surrounding this dried out area about a mile from the house."

"We're gonna burn it all first. We'll figure it out when I get there. Speaking of which, if I get a move on, we might still have some dark left. It's always betta to do this kinda thing in the dark."

"What should I do?"

"Get you some paper towels and sop up the mouse blood on the floor and the baseboards. Then get ya some old hand towels, dip 'em in cold water, wring 'em out good, and start dabbin up what you can. I'll bring some hydrogen peroxide to get the rest."

"Oat, you certainly sound like you know what you're doing. Anything else? I've got a couple of shovels, a double bit axe…"

"I'm always looking for a reason to use my backhoe. I got one of those minis. Let me hitch her up, and I'll be on out there."

"I don't know how I can thank you for this."

"Well, I sure as hell do, Mr. Tannyhill. Clear ol' Oat's gambling account and maybe give me a credit, you know."

"How's a thousand sound?"

"Credit?" Oat asked.

"Credit."

"Can't wait to hear all the details. I'll be out there in no time."

"Thanks again."

"You know what ya are, Mr. Tannyhill?"

"I'm afraid to ask."

"You are the baddest mothafucka in Solomon, Texas."

1992
January 1, 1992

Love is a wonderful institution, but who would want to live in an institution?

H.L. Mencken

35

INDEED

"**W**hat does one wear to a phone wedding?"

Clovis thought he heard what Windy Day said, but couldn't be sure due to the volume of Wilson Pickett's vocals coming from the CD player.

No more lonely nights
When you'll be all alone
All you gotta do is pick up your telephone and dial now
6-3-4-5-7-8-9 (that's my number!)
6-3-4-5-7-8-9

He took a few steps from Windy's living room down the hallway. "Say what?" he called out. She stepped out of her bedroom wearing a white ruffled blouse, a long black skirt, and bare feet. "Is this alright?" she asked, stretching her arms out with palms up.

After two months of being friends with Windy Day, Clovis thought he might be coming to terms with the fact that, for whatever reason she might have, they would never share any carnal knowledge. Yet, seeing her in the hallway made weak his virtuous intent.

"And it's my first time to meet your mother." Windy placed one hand on her hip and rested the other against the door jamb. "Come on, Doorstop, tell me what you think."

"I think you need to explain in some detail why we have to have a platonic relationship."

"Aw, crap," Windy said, "I knew this neckline had too much plunge in it. I'll try something else."

"No, no, no. Your virtue is safe with me. Anyway we're going to be late. Throw on those black lizard skins and let's get out of here."

"I'm not so worried about you as I am your brother," she said, disappearing back into the bedroom.

Bubba had come by Sorrento's a few weeks ago. Clovis introduced his friend between sets, and Bubba couldn't stop flirting with Windy. She finally gave Bubba a friendly, but sharp, jab to the deltoid and said, "You need to learn this quick. You've got the same chance with me as your brother and that's nil, none, nada. Got it?"

"So, you're a lezbo?" Bubba asked.

"If that's what you need to believe."

Bubba still couldn't restrain the occasional come-on line or the sneak peeks at her cleavage. When Windy had returned to the stage, Bubba said, "I'd rank her mid-to-upper middle if she knocked off a few pounds." Clovis nailed Bubba's other deltoid with his fist. "Don't rate Windy on your stupid fuckability scale." Bubba rubbed his arm and had said, "Alright, alright. You two just need to stop punching me."

Clovis now called out to Windy, "Bubba promised he'd stop hitting on you if you stop hitting him."

"I'll stop hitting him if he stops hitting on me," she answered from the bedroom. "And it sounds like you might need a little recommitment lesson yourself."

"It was just a compliment," he lied, and returned to the living room. He sat in possibly his favorite chair in the world–Grandma Rainey Day's antique rocker with carved rope twist designs that Clovis loved to rub his fingers across while pushing himself back and forth.

Many hours he had sit in the rocker as Windy and he easily moved from one subject to the next. A couple of weeks ago he even felt comfortable enough to discuss the McDonald-Albright family history, complete with the twin-sons-of-different-fathers scenario. It surprised Clovis that she had asked so many questions centering on Virgil Albright and the possibility that he might actually be Clovis' father. He adopted the "who-knows-and-who-cares" attitude from Bubba, but Windy hadn't bought into it.

"You want to know who your father is just as bad as I wanted to know who mine was," she had said.

"Did you find out?"

"Yeah," Windy had answered. "Grandma Rainey knew, but she wouldn't tell me at first. I'd ask and she would say, 'he weren't a good man' over and over again. But I think she finally realized she didn't want to take that secret to the grave. I met him once, and she was right–he weren't a good man. I got my answer, and then I didn't care anymore."

"Did he live around here?" Clovis had asked. "Is he still alive?"

"Yes and no," she answered.

"What happened to him?"

"Who cares?" had been Windy's answer. "Let's drop it, okay?"

He heard her striding down the hallway in rhythm to Wilson Pickett's version of "Mustang Sally." Pushing himself out of the rocker, he appreciated that Windy had indeed pulled on her black lizard skin boots.

"Too much?" she asked, holding her arms out and spinning around.

"If Bubba can't control himself," he answered, "we'll beat the shit out of his arms."

"Can you take my guitar case on out to the truck? I'll be out in a minute." With that, she turned and headed back down the hallway.

Though it was New Year's Day, Clovis was comfortable walking to the truck in his corduroy sports coat. In fact, he removed it and hung it on a peg in the back seat of the pickup. A gust of north wind caused Clovis to examine the sky. He saw a solid group of dark clouds inching their way from the northwest toward Solomon.

Windy bounded out of the house with a small box in one hand and a spiral notebook in the other. As soon as she moved into the passenger seat, Windy offered him the box and said, "Happy Birthday."

A small card was taped to the cardboard. It read:

In honor of our first meeting
To a lily among thorns

He pulled out a cast iron door stop in the shape of a *fleur-de-lis*.

"Thank you," he said. "It's heavy."

"That means it's not cheap," Windy replied.

"Now I've got to know your birthday so I can get you something. See what you started."

"October first. That should be easy enough to remember. Exactly nine months after you."

"How strange," Clovis said.

"Indeed."

36

A DOLLAR SHORT

"**O**h, Bubba," Mazel said, "can't it wait for a couple of hours?"
"The winch is stuck," Bubba called out from behind his
bedroom door. "He used a whole can of PB Blaster, but it's not
budging. I can't just leave him out on the highway."

Mazel's hopes for the day were sinking. Driving to the Tumbleweed with Bubba in tow had been the plan. With his job as an
excuse, she couldn't be certain that he would make it there on
his own. "Can't he wait until we're done with the wedding?"

Bubba rushed headlong out of his room with a bag in hand.
Mazel leaned back to avoid a jarring collision, but they bumped
slightly. Just enough for Mazel to get her hands on Bubba's arms
and hold him in place.

"Can't this boy do anything right?" Mazel asked. "How did he
get the winch stuck?"

"Who knows?" Bubba said. "I mean it's Oatie Smith for God's
sake. He's the last guy I would have hired, but we really didn't
have a choice."

Mazel loosened her hold on Bubba. "Mr. Tannyhill and I had
to sweeten the deal with Oat. Hiring his son was a small price to
pay to get you boys out of that mess." She looked at the gym bag
Bubba held. "Are your wedding clothes in there? The ones you
just had on?"

"Yes, Momma."

"They're going to get wrinkled. I'll get you some Downy and maybe some Febreeze."

Mazel led Bubba to the kitchen and into the laundry room. "Grab a couple of towels, too," she said, "and wet one down in case you get some grease on you."

"I told you New Year's Day isn't a good time to have a wedding," Bubba said, as Mazel heard water running in the kitchen sink. "Or to find out who your father is?"

Mazel walked back into the kitchen carrying a spray bottle in each hand. "It's important to me. It's your birthday."

Bubba folded the wet towel and placed it on top of the dry one. "But you know how busy New Year's Day is. And Oatie is just like his daddy. He doesn't have a lick of sense."

She handed the two bottles to Bubba who wrapped them inside the towels. "Just promise me that you'll fix the winch and drive right out there. Promise me."

"I will," he said, with what Mazel perceived as a hint of irritation. "Why do we have to do this at the Tumbleweed anyway?"

"I have my reasons." Mazel felt the promise of the day unraveling. Bubba could justifiably use the work excuse and not show up. "And weddings can be fun."

"A phone sex wedding? Do we stand around and listen to them breathe heavy?"

"It's a *phone wedding*," Mazel corrected Bubba. "Promise me you'll help Oatie and then drive out as quick as you can."

"Promise."

Bubba walked to the front door with the bottles inside towels wrapped under one arm and the bag of clothes in the other. Mazel followed but Bubba stopped before opening the door. "Do you have any idea how hard it is for me today?" he asked.

"I think I do."

"It's not the DNA or the wedding or the stupid winch," Bubba said. "It's New Year's Day. I'd have a bet on every bowl game and be switching channels right now like a crazy man. I'd be so juiced that my mind wouldn't be able to think about anything but football. I miss it. I miss losing myself in a game." He turned around to face Mazel. "I try to watch a game now and there's nothing inside me. I don't care. One team could win or the other team, but I don't care which one."

Mazel stepped forward and wrapped her arms around Bubba. "I'm sorry, son. I'm so very sorry."

He hugged her with a tender grip. "It's not your fault, Momma. I'm the one with the gambling problem."

Mazel remembered trying to comfort Bubba as a child, but those hugs had been met with a rigid countenance that couldn't be reassured. She squeezed him tighter.

"Do you need to call your sponsor?" Mazel said into his chest.

"Nah, everybody in Gamblers Anonymous is going through the same thing today. It's better to stay busy and not watch. It's hard when you don't care who wins."

Mazel stepped back from his embrace. "Bubba, you realize that you're not just talking about football, don't you? I mean, which one it is, you know, who wins…it's always been important. You just never wanted to admit it to yourself. Especially when your choices were, well, pretty lousy. Daddy–"

"Yeah," Bubba interrupted, "there's some good basketball games today, too. I've got to go."

"Wait just a second." Mazel turned down the hallway and went to her bedroom.

"Hurry up, Momma. Oatie might be doing some serious damage to that wrecker."

The weight of the box caused a twinge in Mazel's lower back as she lifted it from the closet floor. This was actually a present for Bubba and Clovis, but Bubba could use a lift right now. "I meant to wrap this later," she said, as she carried it to Bubba, "but you might need it while you're out."

"Radio Shack?" Bubba set down the Downy-and-Febreze-filled towels and his bag of clothes on the catch-all table by the front door. He took the already opened box and set it on the hallway floor. After moving the cardboard flaps back, Bubba lifted the bulky apparatus. "Momma?"

She clapped her hands a couple of times and said, "Happy Birthday." She bent forward and brought out an instruction manual that had already been opened. "This is for you and your brother. After his little scare with that crazy man out in the middle of nowhere, I knew what you boys needed."

"A cellular phone," Bubba said. "These things are like five hundred, six hundred bucks."

"You're telling me," she answered. "I figured this would save you all some time. It's all ready to use. The number is activated and I charged it up. Just plug it into your lighter and you're good to go."

Bubba detached the phone from its large black unit and stretched the cord until the receiver reached his ear. "I'm going to take it out to the truck. I'll be right back."

Watching Bubba jog out to the truck in his work boots reminded Mazel of the few times in his childhood when he couldn't hide a moment of excitement or happiness. It reminded her of New Year's Day with Richard, Daddy Two, out most of the day working while she and the boys would play board games. Then the ritual pouring out of the year's worth of change accumulated in the big Mickey Mouse head piggy bank. Counting out coins into wrappers, sealing them at the ends, and continuously guessing how much money they would end up with until all the tiny pieces of happiness were tucked into place.

When it was over, the sinking feeling tied to Richard's eminent return would begin. But the next day or the day after that, a coin or two could be heard striking the bottom of the Mickey Mouse head. A smile would cross her lips, anticipating the peace of the next New Year's Day.

"Thank you, Momma," Bubba said as he returned. "But you do realize that my present is a day late."

"Well, I was a dollar short," Mazel said. "Anyway, you got to open it and use it first. So you've got that over your brother."

Bubba picked up his towels and clothes and headed back to the truck.

"Hey," she called out, "promise me again."

"I'll be there as soon as I can," Bubba answered. "And if something holds me up, I can call the Tumbleweed now."

"Wait a minute." Mazel went to the kitchen and grabbed the book. She ran out the front door and handed the 'Solomon and Surrounding Areas' phone book to Bubba who was already inside the truck with the motor running. "You keep this with the phone, you hear?"

"Alright, Momma."

"Hurry along but you drive careful." Mazel glanced at the northern sky and felt a tightness in her chest. "I don't like the look of these clouds blowing in. They might have some snow or ice in them."

37

NO COMPLIMENT INTENDED

"So's when I leave here," Oat Smith said, "I take this here marriage license to Miss Margo's house for her to sign, and then drive on ova to Reverend Yates's house with it."

Tannyhill twisted the double Windsor knot tightly and examined the bottom of his tie in the mirror. Just over the belt buckle. For not wearing a tie in years, it had only taken three attempts to find the fashionably correct length. "Yes, Oat, that's it. Your duties as best man will conclude at that point. I appreciate your assistance."

"My pleasure, Mr. Tannyhill. Uh, do ya mind if I partake before the big event?"

"In the dining room on the sideboard, there's a decanter of port. Would you please pour me a glass?"

Oat's boots were already in the hallway when he called back, "Yes, sir."

Tannyhill picked up the stereo remote control from his nightstand and checked again to ensure the music for the wedding was primed correctly. Margo and he had disagreed for days about what should be played. She opted for the traditional *Bridal Chorus* for the beginning and the *Wedding March* for the conclusion. Tannyhill, however, had heard all of the Wagner he ever wanted to hear for the remainder of his days. He pushed for alternatives and finally convinced Margo that Bach's *Air on a G String* was a more fitting and definitely a more beautiful piece to usher in their ceremony. He had no issues with Mendelssohn's romp on a pipe organ to end the proceedings.

The wedding reception music was another story. They had fun with it, finally choosing Wilson Pickett's "634-5789" to be performed by a friend of Clovis McDonald–Windy Day. Tannyhill auditioned others over the phone including his protégé, Grant Glassford. Grant had done a commendable job with his rendition of *Oklahoma!* at the Jingle Elf Parade. However, when it came to rasping out the soul of a blues song, Windy Day had a gift. She had slowed the song down and eliminated the pop element from Pickett's version. She gritted out the phone number in a fevered pitch, then a decrescendo into the verse, followed by the next chorus in an earthy growl.

Tannyhill chose the second and final song of the reception. The "Theme from Shaft." He easily schooled Grant Glassford to sing in a lower register. Grant also obliged his teacher's request to alter the lyrics slightly and include the second half of the multisyllabic expletive omitted in the Isaac Hayes' version.

They say this cat Shaft is a bad mother(fucker)
(Only) talking 'bout Shaft
Then we can dig it

"Here ya go, Mr. Tannyhill," Oat said, handing the glass of port to him.

"Where's your glass?"

Oat reached into his right pants pocket and tugged at something that didn't cooperate in coming out. "I carry my own supply." He gave the object in his pocket a long pull, a hard pull before it came flying out and onto the wood floor. The flask spun round as it clattered across the room, traveled under the nightstand and came to rest against the baseboard.

"Must be powerful stuff," Tannyhill said.

"It's some moonshine my cousin makes." Oat knelt beside the nightstand and retrieved the flask. "Want a sip?"

"No thanks, Sheriff. But I do propose a toast."

Oat cleared his throat. "I didn' prepare nothin'."

"No, no, Oat. This is to you." Tannyhill raised his glass, and Oat Smith followed suit.

"Oat, we've had a longstanding and beneficial relationship over the years. These last couple of months though have seen some extraordinarily trying times. And to your credit, you have stepped up, showing yourself to be a man of reason and discretion."

Oat moved his flask to end the toast, but Tannyhill drew his glass back and away.

"Thank you, sir, for all of your help with the incident involving Judas Conroe. Thank you for concluding that Punches McDonald murdered his brother and putting an end to that business. Thank you for terminating your long and profitable relationship with McDonald Wrecker."

Oat held up his free hand to stop Tannyhill's toast. "You're still giving me a hundred dollars a week on my gambling account, right? Five years, ya said."

"Of course, Oat. Not a problem." He lowered his port and tapped Oat's flask lightly. "I've got more to my toast, but let's have a halftime break, shall we?"

They both took sips and Oat's face scrunched tightly as he swallowed. "That hog feed just doesn' go down smooth like when he used corn meal," he said. "Ya can't cut corners when it comes to makin' high quality shine."

"To continue," Tannyhill said, "I appreciate you agreeing to be my best man in this unorthodox wedding and without questioning why. But why, I must answer. When you leave here today, Oat, I do not intend to see you again. Or anyone else for that matter."

"Why?" Oat asked. "What about your collections and payout?"

"I'm selling the bookmaking business to Spencer Davis up in Lubbock–"

"What about my five years of credit?" Oat interrupted.

"It's all part of the deal. You know you can trust me." He held out his glass again, but Oat didn't move.

"So's you goin' to be a hermit or somethin'?"

"That's one way of putting it, I suppose."

Oat shuffled from one foot to the other nervously. "Do you mind if ol' Oat gives you a holler every now and again?"

Tannyhill stretched further and tapped Oat's tumbler. "Oat, you should call me once a month so we can catch up. My thinking might become, well, complacent if I couldn't hear your point of view from time to time."

"Thank ya for the compliment, Mr. Tannyhill."

"No compliment intended."

The toast completed, both Tannyhill and Oat emptied their glasses.

"So, who do you really think killed Richard?" Tannyhill asked, setting his glass on the nightstand.

"Honestly, I don' have a fuckin' clue."

38

A CHOCOLATE FLAVORED MOON PIE

For a wedding taking place in three locations, Clovis thought everything had gone well. There was the hiccup of septuagenarian Ezzie Yates forgetting the bride's and groom's names at the end of the ceremony. He finally settled on a solution to conclude the vows.

"Do you, Line One, take you, Line Two, to have and to…well, just to have…from this day forward, for better or for worse…" Reverend Yates had said.

Clovis whispered into Windy Day's ear, "Busy signal or no busy signal."

Windy delivered a spell-binding performance of "634-5789" to the audience in Al Pozzo's room, which hopefully had translated well over the phone lines. One of Reverend Ezzie Yates' assistant ministers led him out of the room when he started singing along. Clovis' mother, Dr. Terence Barnstable, Grant Glassford, the new orderly Jack Tillich, two nurses, and a hallway full of Tumbleweed patients gave Windy a rousing ovation when she concluded. Even Al Pozzo appeared to enjoy it as Mazel pointed to his lap and said, "Look, both hands are twitching."

Vic Tannyhill's voice student, Grant Glassford, was now singing the "Theme from Shaft" with a karaoke machine accompaniment. Windy must have thought the sing-along a good idea. She had everyone singing and strutting around the room. Vic Tannyhill's voice rang strong over the phone. Clovis could even hear Oat Smith's twang in the background.

Another hiccup occurred due to Bubba's absence. With him was Nellie Robin's Cinnamon-Apple-Pecan Wedding Cake. But Jack Tillich dashed down the hallway and brought back an armful of Ho-Ho's, Ding Dongs, Twinkies, and a chocolate flavored Moon Pie for himself. They stood around munching on their snacks as Margo and Tannyhill taunted them on the phone with how Nellie Robin had outdone herself with the wedding cakes they were enjoying.

For the finale, Oat Smith gave a rambling toast to the couple. He concluded with, "As a great philosopher once said, the secret of a happy marriage will always remain a secret. Good luck y'all." Everyone touched their plastic champagne cups together and drank the 1990 Krug that Tannyhill had couriered out to the Tumbleweed the day before.

The couple said their good-byes and left on their honeymoon. Margo was flying to Aruba and Tannyhill would call her from the comfort of his home. The orderly and nurses returned to their work while Grant Glassford packaged up his karaoke machine and bid *adieu.*

Mazel asked that everyone else stay. "Doc, would you go get your gizmos and hook Al up?"

"Why?" Dr. Barnstable asked.

"Just in case," she answered. "I mean, he's been typing some meaningful things lately, hasn't he? Stuff you might be able to use in your all's second book?"

"Well," Dr. Barnstable said, "that's still open to interpretation, but possibly."

"Maybe you can run it by your father and see what he thinks," Mazel said.

"My father?"

"He's still a book editor, isn't he?" Mazel asked. "He could edit one more of Al's books."

Dr. Barnstable laughed through a confused face. "How long have you known?"

"Barnstable is a fairly uncommon name," she said. "Now go get your computer and Velcro yourself onto Al."

Clovis would have to ask his mother about the conversation later. He didn't really understand what had just occurred. Though he did notice that something meaningful, some history, just passed between Dr. Barnstable and his mother.

He stepped close to her and whispered, "I thought this was just going to be you, me, and Bubba."

"If it was just us," she said, "we'd go right out and tell these folks. Let's let them in on it from the start. There's nothing to be ashamed of or to hide anymore."

Clovis didn't feel nearly as anxious as he thought he might. Finding out the identity of his father no longer carried the importance it once had. However, he did want his brother here. He wondered if Bubba might blow the whole thing off, find another excuse not to show up, relapse into that hollow state in which he had been so often consumed before they returned to Solomon.

"Hey," his mother called out, holding up a manila envelope. "Someone opened this up. Not that I'm upset about it or anything. I already know. But who was it couldn't wait to find out who Bubba's and Clovis' daddy is?"

39

HERE COMES THE SUN

Mazel placed a Gauloises in the corner of Al's mouth. She went through her routine to ensure that the cigarette would stay in place and that ashes would fall into the large ashtray underneath. Dr. Al Pozzo stared out the window onto the same landscape he had looked upon for almost half of his life. His hands hovered over the keyboard with Dr. Barnstable's forearms Velcroed to him. Al occasionally pecked a few keys while they all waited for Bubba to arrive.

When the door to Al Pozzo's room would open, Mazel still looked expectantly for Manuel Daza. To see him enter the doorway was irrational, she knew, but her heart went there nonetheless. Though the feeling might fade with time, she knew her heart would always go there.

Mazel noticed that Al had stopped his sucking sound so she untaped his mouth and removed the Gauloises. Al's left hand with Dr. Barnstable's accompaniment moved down on one key. The right hand followed with two more jabs. His hands moved in the same pattern again and then another time even faster. He kept repeating the pattern in faster and faster succession.

"Momma, what's he doing?" Clovis asked.

"I don't know," she said. "I haven't seen this before. Doc?"

"Look," Windy Day said. "It's snowing."

Al's gaze never wavered from the view outside his window. But Mazel noticed that everyone, including Dr. Barnstable, was looking there, too. Mazel started to turn but as she did, she noticed the computer monitor. The green images filled the screen with the same three letters.

sunsunsunsunsunsunsunsunsunsunsunsunsunsun
sunsunsunsunsunsunsunsunsunsunsunsunsun

"Doc?"

"He's not a good speller, Mazel. Never uses the 'o'. Remember?"

Mazel looked out the window as the big, lazy snowflakes appeared stationary for a while like a painting of snow instead of the real thing. Under the mesquite tree, that had always been at the center of Al Pozzo's focus, stood a lone figure. Holding a cake box and a couple of towels in his hands, a gym bag slung over his shoulder, Bubba was unaware of the roomful of people watching him. He let the towels fall to the ground next to the tree, crouched down, and sat on them.

Al Pozzo and Dr. Barnstable kept clicking the same three keys. Clovis put his hand on her shoulder and asked again, "Momma, what's going on?"

Opening what Mazel assumed was Nellie Robin's Cinnamon-Apple-Pecan Wedding Cake, Bubba reached inside. He pinched off a bite and scooped it into his mouth. Leaning his body on the mesquite bark, Bubba's head arced back to look at the sky or the snow or something above him.

"Clovis," Mazel said, "your father wasn't a bad man."

The focus of everyone in the room changed from Bubba to Mazel. She moved Al Pozzo's hair back and away from his face. The typing ceased and the only sound in the room was a distant football game being played on a television somewhere down the hallway. Mazel stroked Al's face, once on each side.

"Your father is this man."

40

WHO YOUR FATHER ISN'T

Scattershot ice pellets clinked and clattered against Al Pozzo's window. A sky full of clotting, Cimmerian clouds cloaked the final hour of daylight. Winds whistled through the imperfections of the window's sealing. A chill cruised up and across Clovis' back. He rose from the floor and gathered his corduroy jacket from a peg behind the bathroom door.

Bubba and his mother were down the hallway getting Dr Peppers and a Coke. Windy Day repeated a flurry of notes on her guitar as she sat on the chair near the window. Clovis had heard her work on riffs before, creating fills one time, then changing them slightly with each replay. Placing his jacket around her shoulders, Windy stopped finger picking. She reached for Clovis' hand before he drew away.

"How are you doing with all this?" she asked, without letting go of his hand.

"It's a shock and all, but I think it's growing on me." Clovis looked at Al Pozzo lying on the bed. "Momma said he wasn't a bad man. Better than Richard or Virgil, for sure."

Windy propped her guitar against the wall with one hand and pulled Clovis closer with the other. "You know, that's the first time I've heard you call them anything but Daddy One or Daddy Two."

"Well, neither one is my daddy now." He crouched low next to Windy at her hand's persistent urging. "That quiet fellow over there on the bed is."

She placed her free hand on Clovis' cheek with a tender touch, something that had never happened before. "One of us finally has a father to be proud of. I couldn't be happier for you. I couldn't be happier for both of us." Windy released Clovis' hand and pulled his face to hers with an insistent caress to the back of his neck.

The kiss, he thought curious. The open mouth, a cause of wonder.

"I've changed my mind about you, doorstop," Windy said, withdrawing slightly from their kiss.

"Why?"

"I don't know," she answered. "Things have changed."

"What? That this guy is my father?"

Windy remained a few inches from Clovis' face. Her eyes offered an intensity that Clovis found new–intriguing and persuasive.

"It's not who your father is," Windy said, "as much as who your father isn't."

"But what–"

"Just shut up and kiss me."

Clovis couldn't be certain as to how long they kissed. When his mother and Bubba turned the door handle to enter the room, Clovis found his back against the wall next to the window with not a scootch between himself and Windy Day. By the time they walked completely through the doorway, Clovis and Windy stood apart and were looking out the window.

Bubba set three Dr Peppers and one Coca-Cola on the tray table where earlier, Dr. Barnstable's equipment had been. Mazel filled the remaining area of the tray with pre-packaged white bread sandwiches and potato chips.

"Did we miss something?" Bubba asked.

His face still flushed, Clovis smiled as Windy bent down and picked up his corduroy coat that had landed at their feet.

"Oh, what the hell is going on?" Bubba asked. "What have you two been doing?"

"Just hanging around," Windy answered.

"Just hanging out is more like it," Bubba said, pointing at her blouse, which she straightened. "You said that wasn't going to happen–with either of us."

Windy put Clovis' coat around her shoulders. "He offered me his jacket," she said. "How could I resist?"

"So, you're really not a lezbo?"

Clovis marveled at the strength of his mother's jab into Bubba's deltoid.

"Apologize," his mother said.

"I'm sorry," Bubba responded, rubbing his arm. "Can you all lighten up on the punches? I've still got a bruise from last time."

"Well, stop calling people names," Clovis said.

Mazel put her arm around Bubba's shoulders. "It's not something your father would have done."

41

A THOUSAND, THOUSAND POINTS OF LIGHT

Bubba placed his hands on Mazel's shoulders and helped her rise from the blankets covering the floor. They were taking a well-deserved break from separating coins out of the big-headed Mickey Mouse bank.

Windy Day already occupied one of the chairs in Al Pozzo's room with Clovis standing next to her. She propped the guitar in her lap and started picking a slowed-down version of what Mazel recognized as "She's in Love with the Boy." Seemed like every time Mazel turned on her radio during the past year, she heard Trisha Yearwood belting it out. But on Windy's fingers, the song took on new life with a fresh, soulful rhythm replacing the one worn thin over time.

"I'm going to call dispatch and see how it's going," Bubba said. He bent down and picked up a couple of quarters from the floor. "Going to try and get hold of Oatie, too."

"Do you think he's overwhelmed?" Mazel asked.

"I don't think many people are out on New Year's Day," Bubba answered. "They'd have to be crazy to be out on this ice. Don't start rolling those pennies without me."

Mazel stretched her arms toward the ceiling, interlocked her fingers, and released a cleansing breath as she let both hands glide to her hips. Yes, what kind of crazy person goes out on a night like this? What kind of fool can't wait to see *Thelma & Louise* at the Campus Theatres and at this very moment is driving toward oblivion? Mazel's decision to venture out on a night such as this would always be there to haunt her. But maybe going forward, it would no longer consume her.

She looked out Al's window. The parking lot lighting made the snowy ice on the pavement visible. Dr. Barnstable had called the nurse's station after his drive home to Solomon and warned them that the roads were iced up. When Mazel informed the boys and Windy Day that, for the sake of safety, they would not be leaving until the roads were clear, she unexpectedly met no resistance. She had retrieved the Mickey Mouse bank and coin rollers from the car and congratulated herself on having the foresight to bring them for just such an occasion.

Orderly Jack Tillich brought several blankets from the storage closet and placed them on the floor after Mazel told him their plans. Four folded cots with bedding also stood in the closet area. There were no empty rooms, so they'd be spending the night with Al. Jack said that he, too, was staying at the Tumbleweed to cover shifts for the ones who couldn't make it in due to the ice storm.

Beyond the parking lot, Mazel saw smaller lights dotting the darkened landscape–Al's Agnostic Angels. There used to be so many more of them. Ten years ago, their tents and campsites looked like a thousand points of light. Al's followers still made the mesa glow at night like a beach full of firefly squid that Mazel had once seen in a *National Geographic* at the dentist's office. But now she could see only half a hundred. Still impressive considering they were outside in an ice storm.

Is That All There Is? Getting the Most Out of a Meaningless Existence

Al's Agnostic Angels were devoted to Pozzo and his book. In truth–a truth only shared by Dr. Barnstable, his father, Mazel, and Al–the book owed its existence and its popular appeal to the editor, Quentin Barnstable. Mazel typed enough drafts to see the book turned completely on its head. Before Quentin Barnstable got hold of the manuscript, the work read as dry as kindling, a book meant to impress a few other eggheads, and then die a slow lonely death on the dusty shelf of a university library.

Without question, Al Pozzo's mind had operated at a high level. But his thinking traveled linearly unlike Quentin Barnstable, who could translate brilliance and arc it to a place where it met the minds of the common reader.

Mazel had little doubt of Dr. Barnstable's plans. His facilitative communication was mostly, if not all, snake oil. She suspected it had been the Doc who peeked in the envelope and read the results of the DNA tests. The moment was poetic, but Mazel knew that Al wasn't typing "sunsunsunsun." It was his Velcro-ed partner.

Dr. Barnstable would use facilitative communication to cloak the actual author of Al Pozzo's second book–himself and probably his father. And why not? A book by an unknown like Quentin Barnstable would garner little attention or probably not get published at all. Out there in the dark, Al's Agnostic Angels wanted to believe that the mystical man lying here in a veggie-state could write another book and illuminate their world with a thousand, thousand points of light.

"A pile of pennies for your thoughts, Momma." Bubba had returned without Mazel noticing. He handed her another Dr Pepper and leaned against the wall on the other side of Al's window.

"Just wondering why you sat out there in the snow and started eating the wedding cake. You weren't that far from the building. Why didn't you come on in?"

Bubba popped open his own Dr Pepper and moved his head forward to catch the bubbles spewing from the opening. Once the fizzing can was under control, he answered, "Maybe I was just really hungry."

Mazel had grown so used to Bubba's deflections that she almost allowed this one to pass, also. But she wanted more. "What do you think about Al being your father?"

"Okay, I guess," he answered and smiled. "You sure knew how to pick them, Momma."

With time Mazel thought she might be able to break through Bubba's surface. But for now, he was home and that was good enough.

On the other side of the room, Mazel noticed a change in the way Clovis and Windy interacted. An intimacy seemed to have developed that didn't exist earlier in the day. Of course, she could be mistaken. Clovis' hand touched Windy's shoulder and stayed there a moment. Mazel didn't feel mistaken.

"Let's get these pennies rolled," Clovis announced to the room.

Windy Day remained in her chair while Mazel and the boys sat cross-legged on the blanketed floor. "I'm just going to keep playing if you all don't mind." Nobody minded. They sat quietly counting the coins, finagling the wrappers to accept them, and then folding the ends. This is home, Mazel thought. Tonight, on the floor of Al Pozzo's room, it all came together.

"Do you take requests?" Mazel asked Windy Day.

"Yes, ma'am. Just put a roll of pennies in my tip jar."

"I'm hearing some music inside me, but it's still got a little static. Do you know any Johnny Cash?"

"Sure enough."

"Do you know 'Ring of Fire?'"

Windy picked out a few chords.

"Yeah," Mazel said, "that's right. It's coming in clearer now."

Windy said, "June actually wrote the song."

Bubba and Clovis eyed Windy with questioning looks.

"June Carter, his wife," Windy said. "Are you musical morons?"

They went back to counting pennies.

When Windy came to the chorus, she didn't have to ask for a sing-along. First Mazel, then Clovis, and finally Bubba joined in.

I fell into a burning ring of fire
I went down, down, down and the flames went higher
And it burns, burns, burns, the ring of fire
The ring of fire

"What are we going to do with all this money, Momma?" Bubba asked.

"I'm thinking there's about a hundred and fifty here," Clovis said.

"Let's start saving for a vacation. A family vacation." Mazel knew she was overstepping her bounds, but her bounds didn't bind her any longer. "And Windy here, she can come with us."

"Where to?" Bubba asked.

"I think I know," Clovis said. "You're going to Disneyland."

"Nah," Mazel said. "I'm past...we're past that. I'm thinking more like...Tahiti."

1991
Monday, September 9, 1991

Fathers are biological necessities, but social accidents.
Margaret Mead

42

I'VE GOT A NAME

Richard McDonald spun the gun in his right hand while sitting on the edge of his La-Z-Boy. As he watched the Dallas Cowboys break huddle and amble toward the line of scrimmage, the gun passed with ease from his right index finger to his left. He didn't usually twirl the Smith & Wesson Lemon Squeezer. The gun stayed in the drawer of his nightstand, loaded and ready for any middle of the night intruder. Not that one had ever shown up in forty years.

Twenty minutes ago a young woman knocked at his front door. He only let her disturb his *Monday Night Football* because she said, "I'm your daughter." Now that she was gone, Richard tried to focus on the game but couldn't quite shake off what the girl said.

She had sat on the sofa and explained that Sunny Day was her mother. Having already consumed seven or eight cans of Bud, Richard couldn't remember a Sunny Day. Then the girl said that her mother was a cheerleader at TSTA&M. He could sketch out a fuzzy memory of Sunny, the White Buffalo sweater she pulled up while walking down his hallway.

"Why do you think I'm your father?" Richard had asked. "She wasn't exactly a virgin when I met her."

"My grandma figured it out," the girl said.

"You don't look like me," he replied. "If you want money or something, I don't have any."

"I just wanted to talk to you. I thought we might–"

Richard had kept his attention split between the girl and the game. Troy Aikman completed a pass to Michael Irvin over the middle. Richard fist-pumped and yelled, "Yes!"

"You're going to sit there and ignore me?" she asked.

"You're not my kid. I couldn't make a baby."

"But you've got two sons."

Richard changed his focus from the television to the girl. At least her hair was dark like his. He noted the girl's slight resemblance to some old black-and-white photos of his mother. Her full, rounded cheeks. Her dark brown eyes.

"No, they're not," he said. "It was all a big fake. I never believed either one was mine."

"Well, I'm not a fake," the girl said.

Richard had popped another Bud and chugged half of the can. If what this girl said was true, what kind of mean-ass trick was the universe playing on him? "If you're looking for money, I haven't got any," he repeated.

"Look, I wanted you to know that I exist. I thought you might give a damn."

He didn't want to believe the girl but wondered how she got this notion in her head.

"Obviously, you don't care," she said. "I'll leave."

"No, wait," Richard had said, "wait." What if she was his? The least he could do would be to impress the girl–whether she was his kid or not. Richard thought of the one thing that he did better than most anyone else. "I want to show you something." He stumbled as he rose out of the La-Z-Boy but righted himself by grabbing onto the door jamb.

He went to the nightstand and retrieved the Lemon Squeezer. Surely the girl would be mesmerized by his gun spinning talent. The guys in town always seemed dazzled with his tricks. Hell, they might even clap or buy him a drink when he performed his over-the-shoulder-and-around-the-back twirl. Maybe by some fluke, this girl really was his daughter. He thought again of his mother's rounded cheeks.

Performing a simple twirl, he entered the living room, but the girl was no longer there. A small piece of paper rested on the La-Z-Boy. It read:

I've got a name. You never asked what it was.

Richard had crumpled the paper as he walked to the kitchen and then threw the small wad into the trash.

His focus shifted back to the game as the Cowboys defense forced Washington to attempt a long field goal. Chip Lohmiller kicked it through, and the Cowboys' chances of winning, along with Richard's chance of covering the spread, diminished greatly. That's when he moved to the edge of his chair and started twirling.

With the gun already out, he decided to get in a little practice. He stood up and moved a few steps toward the television.

Richard transferred the gun from one hand to the other several times. He increased the spinning speed, dialed it back, and then spun it faster. The Lemon Squeezer felt a little odd in his hands since he never before performed tricks with it. But he was getting used to the feel. In fact, he decided to do the over-the-shoulder-and-behind-the-back twirl. He fumbled the exchange and the gun fell to the floor.

The Cowboys were driving, down by nine. Not much time left and they needed two scores. But they weren't quite finished. He picked up the gun and began twirling again. Troy Aikman went back into the pocket as Richard's right hand traveled upward. Michael Irvin caught the pass in the end zone as the Lemon Squeezer twirled over Richard's right shoulder. Maybe the Cowboys have a chance, he thought, and he began the gun's transition from right hand to left.

But again he lost control and felt the Lemon Squeezer coming free from his finger.

Richard's left hand moved quickly behind his neck to make a last ditch effort to intercept the falling gun. His index finger missed the trigger hole, but Richard's middle finger accidentally found the opening.

His attempt to catch the gun proved successful.

The twitch of Richard's middle finger, however, proved his undoing.

His face slammed against the floor. The last thing Richard McDonald saw was the Lemon Squeezer scuttle across the wood floor and disappear under the La-Z-Boy. He heard the gun hit the baseboard, and then the announcer, Al Michaels, called the extra point kick good. But Richard knew it was all over. That would be the final score.

ABOUT THE AUTHOR

Dan Hammond Jr. is a writer living in Denton, Texas, with his wife, Sandra. His novel, DELBERT JUDD, debuted in 2014. Kirkus Reviews wrote that DELBERT JUDD is "lighthearted and funny thanks to the humor of oddball Delbert, but it also explores some substantial issues, which gives it poignancy and weight."

Born in eastern Kentucky and raised in Lexington, Hammond graduated from Transylvania University. He later earned an MSSW from the University of Texas at Arlington. In 1997, Hammond attended the Iowa Writers' Workshop under the direction of Frank Conroy.

To learn more about Dan Hammond Jr. and his writing, go to www.danhammondjr.com.